THE PARGITERS

BOOKS BY VIRGINIA WOOLF

The Voyage Out, 1915
Night and Day, 1919
Kew Gardens, 1919
Monday or Tuesday, 1921
Jacob's Room, 1922
The Common Reader: First Series, 1925
Mrs. Dalloway, 1925
To the Lighthouse, 1927
Orlando, 1928
A Room of One's Own, 1929
The Waves, 1931
Letter to a Young Poet, 1932
The Second Common Reader, 1932
Flush, 1933
The Years, 1937
Three Guineas, 1938
Roger Fry: A Biography, 1940
Between the Acts, 1941
The Death of the Moth and Other Essays, 1942
A Haunted House and Other Short Stories, 1944
The Moment and Other Essays, 1947
The Captain's Death Bed and Other Essays, 1950
A Writer's Diary, 1954
Virginia Woolf and Lytton Strachey: Letters, 1956
Granite and Rainbow, 1958
Contemporary Writers, 1965
Collected Essays (4 vols.), 1967
Mrs. Dalloway's Party, 1973
The Letters of Virginia Woolf. Vol. I: 1888–1912, 1975
Freshwater, 1976
Moments of Being, 1976
The Letters of Virginia Woolf. Vol. II: 1912–1922, 1976
The Diary of Virginia Woolf. Vol. I: 1915–1919, 1977
Books and Portraits, 1977
The Pargiters: The Novel-Essay Portion of The Years, *1977*

THE PARGITERS

by VIRGINIA WOOLF

The Novel-Essay Portion of THE YEARS

Edited, with an Introduction, by
MITCHELL A. LEASKA

A Harvest/HBJ Book
Harcourt Brace Jovanovich
New York and London

Printed in the United States of America

Library of Congress Cataloging in Publication Data

Woolf, Virginia Stephen, 1882–1941.
The Pargiters.

(A Harvest/HBJ book)
"The essays originally written for the novel-essay, The Pargiters, as well as a direct, unaltered transcription of the first holograph version of the fictional 'extracts' which would eventually become principal scenes in the 1880 section of The years."
I. Woolf, Virginia Stephen, 1882–1941. The years. II. Title.
PR6045.072P3 1978 823'.9'12 77-84901
ISBN 0-15-671380-2

First Harvest/HBJ edition 1978
A B C D E F G H I J

Contents

Acknowledgments v

Introduction vii

Explanation of Editorial Symbols and Procedures xxiii

SPEECH

Speech before the London/National Society for Women's Service, January 21 1931 xxvii

THE PARGITERS

Genealogical Tree 2

First Essay: "The Pargiters A Novel-Essay based upon a paper read to the London/National Society for Women's Service" 5

First Chapter: "Chapter Fifty-Six" 11

Second Essay 28

Second Chapter 39

Third Essay 50

Third Chapter 59

Fourth Essay 76

Fourth Chapter 85

Fifth Essay 106

Fifth Chapter 131

Sixth Essay 150

Appendix

Manuscript Notes for the Speech of January 21 1931 163

Illustrations

First page of the Novel-Essay, Holograph [1 5] 4

Ink blots between sections are reproduced from the author's own ink drawings in the manuscript.

Acknowledgments

I would like to express my gratitude to Quentin Bell and Angelica Garnett, administrators of the Author's Literary Estate, for the opportunity to edit this text; to Mrs Quentin Bell for her reading of my transcription and offering valuable corrections; to Louise DeSalvo, Anderson Fellow, New York University, and Mr Jay Redfield for the care with which they read my original typescript of the Woolf text; and to the Henry W. and Albert A. Berg Collection of English and American Literature of The New York Public Library, Astor, Lenox and Tilden Foundations, for access to the eight manuscript volumes of *The Pargiters*.

Special thanks go to David V. Erdman, who not only meticulously checked and improved the final version of my transcript but also located and filled in the quoted matter indicated by Virginia Woolf.

Lola L. Szladits, Curator of the Berg Collection, long ago recognized the importance of such an edition and suggested that I undertake the task. To her I owe my greatest debt: first, for her good faith; second, for having, herself, transcribed five of the six Essays (and the better part of the Manuscript Notes for the Speech) with the kind of accuracy that would inspire the envy and admiration of the best Virginia Woolf scholars.

M.A.L.

New York University
November 28 1975

INTRODUCTION

IF *The Pargiters, A Novel-Essay* had been written to completion as Virginia Woolf originally envisaged it in 1932, it might well have found its place today on that still narrow shelf of books on the equality of women — pressed beside Mary Wollstonecraft's *Vindication of the Rights of Women* (1792). The "Novel-Essay" would have been for Virginia Woolf a new and profoundly challenging experiment in form, calling into action both the creative and the analytical faculties almost simultaneously. More important, it would have committed her in the Essay portions to the very difficult task of adopting and sustaining a brand of rhetoric alien to her artistic temperament — the pressure of granite against rainbow — in order to impress upon her more enlightened readers, men and women alike, the fundamental and sometimes hidden injustice that still in 1932 weighed upon the lives of women.

The Speech of January 21 1931 printed below — the provenance of the "Novel-Essay" — and the Essays themselves unequivocally represent and express the view that both in the nineteenth century and in the twentieth the social arrangement of the sexes was one which effectively smothered the aspirations of women, corrupted authentic humane values, and eroded human relationships, whether close or distant. Virginia Woolf depicts a world in which the male represented power, status, and authority and in which everything he willed was potent with consequence. It was also, we are asked to see, the world in which Virginia Woolf was born and grew up.

Little wonder that one should see a small cloud of black crosses over the manuscript page as she wrote about herself as a writer, a profession which in no way intruded upon domestic peace, which required only the cheapest of materials, and which was so different from that practiced by the men who made up great armies and navies requiring great and expensive instruments of manly warfare.

But Virginia Woolf wanted us to take a closer look than this at masculine power and control; to analyze with greater precision some tacit manifestations of sexual polarization and to examine their effects upon young women in England in 1880. So we are moved into the Pargiter drawing room to find healthy young women sighing in boredom, peeping out of windows at unknown young men, fussing with tea kettles, sexually frustrated, and helplessly caged. But why? Why are these healthy young women not out free to explore, free to engage in some important work, free to earn their own livings and enjoy independence? Virginia Woolf's answer is simple: the privilege of a university education was denied them; and without that education, the professions were closed to them; and without a profession, there was no opportunity whereby a healthy young woman might earn her living and have the money and thus the independence to make choices, express vigorous opinions, contribute in significant ways to the society in which she presently found herself trapped. The only choice open to girls of the Pargiter social class — where well-to-do fathers looked after their material needs — was to become models of virtue; to repress any attraction to members of the opposite sex, until the day when a man slipped "a wedding ring on her finger, to canalize all her passion, for the rest of their married lives, solely upon him." But sexual repression to this degree, Virginia Woolf wishes us to see, runs counter to the flow of nature, causes rivalry among sisters over an available male, forces them to conceal from one another thoughts which ought to be communicated, makes them lie, affects them mentally through onslaughts of guilt, and in the end creates such distortions in their human development as to make their behavior as unnatural as their lives were manacled.

This structure of male governance had a pernicious influence not only on young women, but also on little girls — as the episode of Rose Pargiter, aged ten, eloquently details. In an ambience of sexual suppression, where virtue and chastity are synonymous, the little girl's traumatic experience of lust and perversion outside the walls of Abercorn Terrace generated a feeling of guilt so strong as to make the innocent victim powerless to express it. Hers was the kind of powerlessness characteristic of an atmosphere where matters of real human importance are either hushed up or totally suppressed; where communication is either not possible, by the rules of decorum, or dead, from atrophy. And out of that decorous silence grows an appalling confusion between what *love means* and what *sex is*, a confusion enshrined in the double standard, or the notion of conduct becoming to a lady of virtue.

Behind that muddled decorum was a silent population of men long since dead, as well as men of the present who preserved and practiced their tradition by tapping their mallets in courts of law; clutching their maces in academic procession; or waving their sceptres from high seats of authority — men demanding that the women obey, serve, soothe. Not always overtly, of course. In one of her subtlest analyses, Woolf carries us to Oxford, to Edward Pargiter's college rooms, to show us how that male-dominant tradition had instilled in young men the idea that their chief duty in life was to perpetuate the value system by which they themselves were conditioned — "the sterner and more robust virtues — fortitude, self-reliance, intrepidity, devotion to the common weal; readiness for united action and self-sacrifice" — those resilient and impulsive ties of male fellowship.

But male chauvinism can be confusing to the male himself, especially to one of Edward's age. For no matter how sensitive he might be to the subtleties of Greek syntax, he too, although we are told that he had considerably more exposure to sexuality than his sisters, was almost totally ignorant of the relationship between love and sex. Thus under the stimulus of *The Antigone* and a glass or two of port, Edward Pargiter is aroused to sexual thoughts of his cousin Kitty Malone (for whom his feelings of adoration were "largely imaginary"). But he has been trained by centuries of tradition that auto-eroticism is evil, disgusting, degrading: arousal must be "conquered," and Edward conquers it by writing a poem to Kitty, and a bad poem at that, a poem which idealizes her while it simultaneously sentimentalizes himself. The real point of Woolf's analysis, however, is that implicit in Edward's "exorcising" of his erotic impulse was a ratification of his notion of self-mastery, and hence an excessive self-approval. So that while he felt that confederate presence of self-mastery and self-approval, at the same time he felt entitled to require in his vague image of womankind, the high virtue which, if lacking, served only to reinforce his conditioned sense of dominance. By idealizing Kitty — sexually purifying her almost to an abstraction — he also exalted himself; and that self-exaltation released in him a flow of self-love mixed with self-pity — all because Edward Pargiter approved of himself for having "conquered" himself.

From Edward's rooms we are shifted to another part of Oxford to have a better look at Kitty, the daughter of the Master of one of the University's Colleges. Here Virginia Woolf begins her analysis of that wealthy and powerful city of learning which had fed the minds, and the mouths, of young men for hundreds of years. It is, we soon discover, a travesty of manhood and a mockery of humane values: a fortress against the real world outside, protective of male vanity; a citadel designed to maintain the glow and the glitter of the masculine image. It was also that city of learning which held women's minds in contempt, and forced the poor and bespectacled Lucy Craddocks — women who had sacrificed food and clothing and fire for education — to live in poverty because professorships were not open to them. It was that unlighted world of Gladstones, Bagehots, Pattisons, and Paters who clung stoutly to the belief that women must be chaste; that women could be laborers but not capitalists; that women were created by God to provide man with restful sympathy; that a woman who accidentally dropped her glove was a shameless flirt; that the cleverest woman was intellectually inferior to the lowest man.

Despite Oxford's inhospitality to women, we can still understand, through Virginia Woolf's eyes, Mrs Malone's marrying an Oxford don, not out of love, but out of the desperate need to escape the deadening monotony of life in her native Yorkshire. For in the year 1848, when she was twenty-one, all she had was an excellent training in keeping house — and nothing else: no education, no freedom of opinion, no liberty of choice. Thus to come to Oxford; to be the wife of a learned man; to run the Master's Lodge without sound, without complaint; to be methodical, unquestioning, and selfless as it behooves the wife of a learned man to be, was a very great privilege for her, even though in escaping from the primitive narrowness of the country Mrs Malone came to Oxford only to be taught the new art of genteel servility. To be the daughter of this couple, however, to have as father the great gowned and hooded Dr Malone and as mother a glorified and grateful academic charwoman, had very serious consequences for Kitty Malone in the year 1880. For she too, like so many other young women of her age, had been trained to bear the burden of her sex submissively, to pour out tea to tongue-tied undergraduates, to choke desires and smother opinions, and to neglect even her scant education in order to please the learned men making demands on her time. Moreover, conventional taboo had subdued Kitty's sexual nature to the point that her physical responses were unnaturally weakened.

At Kitty's Oxford there was, however, a class of men apart from those who, with their vestments of patriarchal pomp and circumstance, upheld the forms and consequences of male dominance. They were few in number and without much influence, it is true. Some of them were sons of poor mothers, working-class women, who labored long and hard so that their sons might be educated and life might be made just a little easier. One such man — a beacon light to Virginia Woolf — was Joseph Wright, who in time was to become Dr Joseph Wright, the great dialect scholar. And it was precisely in his attitude toward women that Dr Wright differed so significantly from Oxford dons like Woolf's character Dr Malone.

The influence of Joseph Wright's mother upon him was profound, and his respect for women had no limit. For Joseph Wright spoke not through the voice of poets who exalted women in the scriptural sense only, but through the conviction born from experience that "the world may talk of the 'weaker sex' as much as it likes, the whole idea is based upon the body and not upon the mind. . . . I have always held women to be higher than men in God's creation" (Elizabeth Mary Wright *The Life of Joseph Wright*, [London: Oxford Univ Press 1932] I 315: quoted by Woolf in the Holograph II 79). Wright went fearlessly on to blame the first Christian for the tyrannical oppression of women: "It is due to St Paul and the likes of him, and them *alone*, that woman has been such a downtrodden creature in the past. It is only the present generation of women that is beginning to realize the abject state of woman in the past."

Wright's impoverished beginnings, his immunity to the distorting influences of public schools and great English universities, and his devotion to his working-class mother, made him one of those rare men whose egalitarian views were not merely professed in the solemn finery of rhetoric, but resolutely practiced. So revolutionary were his ideas on the equality of women that he proposed to his future wife in living phrases which would make their marriage not only unique in itself, but an ideal to be followed. For her there would be no darning of socks or mopping of floors or scouring of pots. "It is my greatest ambition," he wrote to the future Mrs Wright, "that you shall *live*, not merely exist; and live too in a way that not many women have lived before, if unlimited devotion and self-sacrifice on my part can do anything towards attaining that end. . . ."

In her sixth and final essay in *The Pargiters*, Virginia Woolf had introduced her ideal model of manhood in the person of Joseph

Wright. From her marginal notes in Essays Five and Six, and from the content of these Essays, it is clear that the characters of Mr Gabbit, Sam Hughes, and Mr Brook are all disguised versions of Wright. In him she saw all the virtues and values which were either opposed by or lacking in the men who inhabited the world in which she had grown up. And one wonders how Wright would have figured in this "Novel-Essay" had Virginia Woolf continued according to plan.

But *The Pargiters, A Novel-Essay* was not written to completion as Woolf originally envisaged it. Exactly what went wrong during the novel's early months to bring the Essays to a halt must remain a matter of conjecture. But since the publication of *A Writer's Diary* in 1953, we have had the opportunity of watching at closer range the artist reflecting on her own work. From the *Diary*, November 2 1932, we learn that the book she was writing was not only to be a "Novel-Essay" but also that she was calling it *The Pargiters*. Now this was written on November 2nd 1932. If we look through all the entries of 1932, we discover another one written four months earlier, July 13 1932, in which she spoke of "sleeping over a promising novel"! Was she referring to *The Pargiters*? We cannot be sure. But what is particularly interesting in that entry is that almost directly beside "sleeping over a promising novel" we come upon what appears to be a digression — a passage about Dr and Mrs Joseph Wright: "Old Joseph Wright and old Lizzie Wright are people I respect. . . . He was a maker of dialect dictionaries: he was a workhouse boy — his mother went charring. And he married Miss Lea a Clergyman's daughter. And I've read their love letters with respect. And he said: 'Always please yourself — then one person's happy at any rate.' And she said make details part of the whole — get proportions right — contemplating marriage with Joe. Odd how rare it is to meet people who say things that we ourselves could have said. Their attitude to life much our own." And considering Virginia Woolf's fondness for Joseph Wright

— and her fondness for playing with sounds of words and with people's names — one consults a volume of his *Dictionary* to see if the word "pargiter" appears; and if so, what it means.[1] The word is not to be found, but the word "parget" is there, which according to Wright is a verb meaning "to plaster with cement or mortar, esp. to plaster the inside of a chimney with cement made of cow-dung and lime."[2]

With curiosity aroused, one turns to the *Oxford English Dictionary* and again finds no "pargiter" — but "pargeter" which means "a plasterer; a whitewasher"; and by figurative extension refers to "one who glosses and smoothes over." The question then arises: Is there any connection between "pargeter" and that "promising novel" mentioned earlier? For if there is (and there is good reason to believe so) then we are encouraged to trace the strange evolution of this "Novel-Essay," called *The Pargiters*, which Virginia Woolf began in a state of exhilaration and completed four years later — in despair.

The record of the book's growth which follows suggests that its author gradually realized that all the factual matter which would constitute the Essay portions was weighty substance that somehow collided with the artistic design she originally planned. That is to say, the truth of fact and the truth of fiction could not meet in felicitous alliance. "For though both truths are genuine, they are antagonistic; let them meet and they destroy each other . . . . Let it be fact . . . or let it be fiction; the imagination will not serve

1 In a letter of January 10 1976, Professor Quentin Bell informed me that Leonard and Virginia Woolf knew and liked a man named Pargiter, a signalman at Southease Station who stood as Labour Candidate in 1918. Credit for this discovery goes to Miss Michele Barrett of the University of Hull.

2 Vol IV, M-Q, *English Dialect Dictionary* (6 vols) ed Joseph Wright (London: Henry Frowde 1903) p 423. I want to thank Professor Jane Marcus for suggesting that I pursue the definition of "parget" to the source in Joseph Wright, and for calling attention to E. M. Wright's *Life* of her husband as the work cited and quoted in the Holograph.

under two masters simultaneously."[3] So that in one sense *The Years* as a finished product is a remarkable specimen in fiction where fact and feeling are in deadly conflict; and throughout the book's course, the recurrent question was: How was she to "cement and smooth over" those deep chasms which normally separate historic fact from immediate feeling?

Although it is difficult to pinpoint the moment when some long-buried seed suddenly germinates in a writer's mind, Virginia Woolf records that moment for us. In her Diary on Tuesday, January 20 1931, she wrote: "I have this moment, while having my bath, conceived an entire new book — a sequel to *A Room of One's Own* — about the sexual life of women: to be called Professions for Women perhaps — Lord how exciting! This sprang out of my paper to be read on Wednesday [January 21 1931] to Pippa's [Pippa Strachey's] society." What is of special interest, however, is a marginal note she made more than three years later in 1934 when she was re-reading the January 20 1931 entry: "(This ["the entire new book"] is *Here and Now,* I think . . .)." This note is important because "the entire new book" based on the Speech was not *Three Guineas,* as Leonard Woolf noted in his edition of *A Writer's Diary,* but *The Years,* whose second title (of nine altogether) was *Here and Now.*[4] It also confirms our suspicion that the "promising novel" of the July 13 1932 entry was indeed a reference to *The Pargiters,* the same entry in which Wright is given so much space. (A glance at the Sixth Essay below, devoted almost entirely to Wright, will indicate the extent to which Woolf not only respected but felt emotionally aligned to him.) And although some risk is attached to it, if we place these slim threads

3 Virginia Woolf "The New Biography" *New York Herald Tribune* October 30 1927; reprinted in *Granite and Rainbow* (London: The Hogarth Press 1958) p 154.

4 *The Pargiters, Here and Now, Music, Dawn, Sons and Daughters, Daughters and Sons, Ordinary People, The Caravan, The Years.*

of evidence side by side, it becomes possible to hazard the guess that Joseph Wright, the word "parget" from his *Dictionary*, and the novel's first title were all somehow intimately connected in Virginia Woolf's mind — and that she was apparently fully conscious of the implication of calling her fictional family by that name.

Approximately twenty months after the delivery of the Speech, the curious history of *The Years* began. On October 11 1932 Virginia Woolf, with an almost fresh manuscript volume before her, dipped her pen and wrote: "THE PARGITERS: An Essay based upon a paper read to the London / National Society for Women's Service."[5] Sometime between October 11 and November 2 1932, she returned to the title page, deleted the "An" and revised the subtitle to read "A Novel–Essay." This insertion of "A Novel–" tells us a good deal about the author's original plan. *The Pargiters* was indeed intended as a sequel to *A Room of One's Own,* but the design of the book was to be a new experiment in form. She would create an imaginary audience as she had done in the earlier book; only now, after her First Essay on the professions for women, she would narrow her range specifically to the restrictions imposed upon a woman who chooses writing as a profession. Having done that, she would provide her reader with "short extracts from a [non-existent] novel that will run into many volumes" — each "extract" being a set of ideas ranging from sex and feminism to politics and education; and this fictional illustration would be followed by an Essay explaining how the woman novelist deals with certain principal controlling ideas from factual life and transforms them into fiction. That is to say, Virginia Woolf intended to invent as she went along; and it suited her plan to present a fictional "extract"

5 The paper cited is the Speech printed below, p xxvii–xxxxiv. Between January 1931 and the middle of October 1932, *The Waves*, *A Letter to a Young Poet*, and *The Common Reader: Second Series* were published as well as about a dozen periodical and newspaper articles.

to be followed by an Essay, then a second "extract" with another Essay, and so on to the end. By December 19 1932 (according to her own calculation) she had written 60,320 words. By that day, she had written what she considered to be the first draft of "Chapter One," consisting of six Essays and five fictional "extracts" — that is, the complete first draft of what was to become the 1880 section of *The Years*.

She returned to her manuscript volume on January 31 1933, with a fresh page beginning: "*The Pargiters* (*additions to Chapter One*)." Two days later, February 2: "Today I finished — rather more completely than usual — revising the first chapter. I am leaving out the interchapters [the Essays] — compacting them in the text: and project an appendix of dates." We know from the published novel that the projected appendix of dates did not appear. And as far as the "compacting" of the interchapters is concerned, although we get a strong sense that much of the emotional content of the Essays was assimilated into the published text of *The Years*, the emotional weight was conveyed not so much in the form of didactic discourse — though some preaching does indeed cloud many of the novel's pages — as in the poetic dramatization of the characters' lives and destinies through expressive systems of interlocking symbols and complex orchestrations of interrupted metaphor.

For Virginia Woolf, the truth of fact and the truth of the imagination simply would not come together in that queer "marriage of granite and rainbow." Essentially, this means that the whole idea of the "Novel-Essay," this "novel of fact," was abandoned by February 2 1933; and from that date on, the novel form would govern the design.

But another reason for giving up the original plan suggests itself here. In her Speech, we will recall, she singled out her difficulty as a woman, writing about the minds and sexual passions of women. Because of the prudery of men, the female writer was not expected to speak out with the same candor permitted the male. Therefore if she was going to describe on paper the restrictive taboos and inhibitions to which her own generation of women were conditioned, the very act of daring to write them out would, on the contrary, disprove the existence not only of the taboos themselves but also of the inhibition in describing them. And if she did not describe those repressions with the directness they required, she would be unable to analyze and explain their debilitating effect upon the minds and bodies of women. So that as an artist, Woolf found herself trapped in both directions. And how was she to free herself? The one avenue of escape was to relieve that pressure of granite against rainbow by recasting her material and adjusting the weights of fact in such a way as to create, in its stead, that aesthetic tension which is generated from documented vision in union with poeticized truth — an artistic task carrying great risk and difficulty.

By March 1936 she was so certain that the novel was a failure that she took the unusual step of having it printed before Leonard Woolf was allowed to read it; and we know from the number of galley-proof pages (about 600) and the length of the first published edition (472 pages) how large a chunk of the original text was deleted from the finished novel. With such drastic cutting, if the novel's semantic integrity was to be preserved, Virginia Woolf was forced once more to render with the high compression of poetry many of the sections which were originally written with the broader explicitness of prose. In consequence, many parts of the novel are highly ambiguous. Throughout the published text of *The Years*, we come across splinters of memory, fragments of speech, titles of quoted passages left unnamed or forgotten, lines of poetry or remnants of nursery rhymes left dangling in mid-air, understanding between characters incomplete, and utterances missing the mark and misunderstood. In one sense, the novel eloquently communicates the *failure* of communication.

Virginia Woolf rarely, if ever, brought anything into her books as pure decoration: everything was put to some service, had to be functional in some way. So that with the disappearance of the explanatory Essays, and with the novel itself so severely cut and edited, we as readers are thrown perhaps too much upon the fertility of our own imaginations to deduce some meaning from the book's seemingly endless ambiguities. But a close reading of the holograph Essays and fictional "extracts" printed in this volume will show the degree to which Virginia Woolf, in *The Years*, did indeed succeed in conveying the lives of the Pargiters — a family who because of the sexual premises of the age and their accompanying economic circumstances were themselves pargeters, and taught their children to be. But more important, the text that follows will show the extent to which Virginia Woolf as novelist was also forced into becoming a pargeter — and ultimately one of great artistic fluency and moral courage.[6]

In this volume then, we have published — for the first time in any edition — the Essays originally written for the Novel-Essay, *The Pargiters*, as well as a direct, unaltered transcription of the first Holograph version of the fictional "extracts" which would eventually become principal scenes in the 1880 section of *The Years.*

The seven and one-quarter manuscript volumes, with their many revisions, may be considered the first complete handwritten draft of *The Years.* Of those, the entire first volume and approximately three-quarters of the second constitute the body of this text.

Fascinating as it is to study these manuscripts at first hand, one is immediately struck with a sense of chaos: the small angular and elegant hand begins clearly enough; but soon the ideas and impressions begin to surface too quickly and flood the page. As they do, the pale blue unlined sheet becomes filled with deletions, additions, substitutions, marginal notes, unfinished sentences, false starts, more deletions, more additions — and the initial sense of fascination soon

6 This aspect of the novel is fully developed elsewhere. See Mitchell A. Leaska "Virginia Woolf, the Pargeter: A Reading of *The Years*" in *Bulletin of The New York Public Library,* 80:ii (Winter 1977) 172–210.

becomes one of utter bewilderment at what appears to be overwhelming disorder. It is not disorder at all, however: it is a rich imagination joined to a lively memory, attempting — at incredible speed — to organize on paper the rush of ideas which somehow could not be held in abeyance whenever she lifted her pen to write this "novel of fact." A glance at the facsimile page will bear this out. But we must remember that this first chapter (as she considered it) of more than 60,000 words was written at irregular intervals between October 11 and December 16 — with *Flush* hanging heavily upon her mind. For this reason, *The Pargiters* volumes are among the most heavily corrected manuscripts in the entire Woolf archive.

The novel Chapters have been transcribed with all possible faithfulness to the path of Virginia Woolf's pen as it wrote and deleted and revised. But the Essays, as discursive argument not previously published, have been edited with a concern for maximum clarity while leaving among the deleted matter nothing essential to the discourse. There are instances in which three or four clauses, even whole sentences, are written, and *all* are deleted. There are others where three or four are written, and all remain untouched. In every case the alternative has been chosen which seems most consonant with the over-all direction and tone of the passage. There are other instances, indicated by the use of square brackets, in which passages either partially or totally deleted have been reconstructed and incorporated into the text. Always the purpose has been to clarify further or to strengthen the point of the argument. Even in transcribing the Essays, editorial intervention has been held rigorously to a minimum.

Making these Essays available in published form will serve some very useful purposes. In the first place, the instances in literature are indeed rare when we find a novelist of Virginia Woolf's stature presenting a fictional specimen and then immediately analyzing, explaining, and interpreting the scene for us. For through the Essays we get the chance to examine at very close range the principal motives and governing ideas which guided the novelist in the selection of her material for the fictional portions. Second, the Essays provide us now with considerably more substance for studying the method by which Virginia Woolf objectively correlated those governing ideas and motives of a scene. Rose's lying to her sister about the washing not having arrived together with her quickly covering the stain on her soiled pinafore in front of her father is an excellent case in point. For despite the surface simplicity of this small act, we see all the complex circuits of guilt, sexual confusion, the desire for approval, and the need to lie built into that simple gesture of the ten-year-old girl who — to use some shorthand — was "growing up Victorian." Third, with access now to all the original holograph material of *The Pargiters* which constitutes the 1880 section of *The Years*, we shall almost certainly recognize differences between the two texts and in consequence be able to examine more systematically the ways in which the author was forced to recast her material and to rely more upon the techniques of poetic compression, to redistribute the emotional ballast of each scene. We shall also see how at times she was forced deliberately to obscure certain parts of the section in order to communicate to her reader through implication those controlling ideas which were originally either more explicitly set down, or, if not, could be explained in the Essay which was to follow.

The decision to publish the fictional "extracts" as they presently appear — that is, as close to the holograph version as typesetting skill and editorial symbols permit — may require a word or two. First, anyone who has read *The Years* will easily identify enough of the material to make his way through these sections. These fictional "extracts" will also be of particular interest to teachers of literature (and creative writing), specialists in rhetoric, analysts of style, and even practitioners in psychology. For these portions provide a rich aesthetic resource never before available in published form — a resource susceptible to numerous kinds of analyses and capable of generating countless questions of epistemic choice. For every change Virginia

Woolf made represents her recognition that the original (or the second or third) choice of word or phrase was not adequate to capture the view of life or the feeling of living she wished to convey.

To enumerate the kinds of questions these fictional "extracts" raise would take us far afield. But the one insistent question which cannot be ignored is: Why the change? Is the third sentence better than the two previously deleted ones? Why is a particular insertion made above the line when a phrase or clause as it stands is perfectly clear? Why are surnames changed twice, even three times, in a single paragraph? Why does the angle of perspective shift four or five times within one short scene? Is the author creating with one part of her mind and at the same time editing — perhaps censoring — with another part? Invariably, such questions emerge from any "unedited" text.

A third and final word. When one reads through the holograph volumes, one senses Woolf's uppermost feeling throughout the writing: "There's no time now! That can be fixed later!" And as soon as the handwritten page is set into a printer's type, some drastic change takes place. The undotted "i", the uncrossed "t", the neglected apostrophe, the impatient deletion slashed across the page — all of these lose their immediacy. The urgency at the moment of composition has vanished. So that even the most faithful transcription from manuscript to printed text is almost inevitably a falsification, calculated — just a bit affected. That loss and that metamorphosis notwithstanding, our effort in these fictional portions has been to provide the reader with what might be looked upon as a slow-moving picture of Virginia Woolf — unobserved and uncensored — during those vibrant moments of creation.

Explanation of Editorial Symbols and Procedures

[word] = a reading editorially supplied.

[*word*] = a deletion editorially restored.

⟨word⟩ = an insertion made by Virginia Woolf.

⟨[*word*]⟩ = an insertion deleted but editorially restored.

●{passage}● = a long deletion made with diagonal strokes or with a wavy line.

[I 1] = The roman numeral refers to the volume, the arabic to the page, of the Holograph.

Inferred deletions. Virginia Woolf did not always run her deleting stroke through the whole phrase or clause which she intended to cancel, but in this transcript whenever a cancellation can be clearly inferred from the manuscript evidence and the context, as it usually can, we have treated the inferred deletions as actual ones — except when the inference can be made automatically. For example, in "being wanting to be alone" [I 83], the context makes clear that "being" was replaced in the act of composition by the longer phrase; no deletion is indicated but we infer it thus: "[*being*] wanting to be alone." Or, in a more complicated revision, Woolf wrote "if he knew what she had seen." [I 59] with no deletion or insertion mark, but "the truth." was written in the margin. We interpret thus: "if he knew [*what she had seen.*] ⟨the truth.⟩".

Format. Our bracketing is devised to present the manuscript readings in an order which is not always that of the words' spacial arrangement on the page but which should make clear what the first reading of a revised passage was, how it was revised, and what the final reading was meant to be. The reader is thereby saved from having to reconstruct the path of the author's pen from deletion to insertion, on, below, above the line, to the left or to the right margin, to the back of the previous leaf, and so on. The aim has been to incorporate all the Holograph variants into a text that can be read straight along. The reader in a hurry can skip the deleted matter (in bracketed italics) with little loss of stride. In the Essays, however, we have presented only a final reading, enriched by a select variant here and there of unique substance or character. Even in the Essays we have retained Virginia Woolf's spelling and punctuation.

The text that became The Years.– The chapters of *The Pargiters* transcribed here from the original Holograph must have gone through several stages of revision before final publication as the opening chapters, the "1880" section, of *The Years.* It was Virginia Woolf's usual practice to type in the afternoon what she had written in the morning. A few typescript pages of later chapters are extant, but none for this "1880" section. In March 1936 she began sending typed copy to her printer, who began returning galley proofs in April. Only a few fragments survive of the author's set of these galley proofs, heavily revised; there are none for this section. An unmarked set, almost complete, is in the Berg Collection; in the "1880" section these proofs differ only slightly from the final published text. A few of the final page proofs also survive, pulled in December 1936, but none for this section. For an account of the proof stages of later chapters, with sample facsimiles of the revised and unrevised galleys, see Grace Radin " 'Two enormous chunks' " *Bulletin of The New York Public Library* 80:ii (1977) 221–51.

Both volumes I and II of the Holograph begin with gaps where only the stubs (5 in vol I, 19 in vol II) remain of notebook leaves that were written on but later removed carefully by pen knife cuts along the inner marginal rule. The first leaf removed from vol I contained a centered head of three words, which is almost legible in its blotting on the back of the preceding leaf, and the marginal date "1931 / July 20th". That one preceding leaf (I 2, because the end paper containing the genealogy of the Pargiters is I 1) is the first leaf of the notebook; it bears a centered, underlined heading: "Notes for / *The Knock on the Door?* / July 20th 1931."

Since the January 21 1931 Speech concludes with expectation of a step on the stairs and since it is acknowledged as the origin of "The Pargiters" in the subtitle above the first Essay, there is a possibility that the text removed consisted of an earlier version of that Essay. Woolf did not remove the title page, "*The Knock on the Door?*", but retained it enclosed within her Novel-Essay by putting the Pargiter genealogy ahead of it on the end paper — as if, perhaps, her thought was that "The Pargiters" might be the title only of part of the work, leaving "The Knock on the Door?" as an over-all title.

Eleven of the 19 stubs at the beginning of the second volume contain what must have been marginal insertions for the writing on the leaves that were cut off; stubs numbered 1 and 9 bear the dates "5th Sept. 1932" and "Sept 17th" respectively.

SPEECH
of January 21 1931

[Speech before the London / National Society for Women's Service, January 21 1931]*

When your Secretary invited me to come here, and I so rashly agreed, she told me that your Society is concerned with the employment of women, and she suggested that I might perhaps tell you something about my own professional experiences. Well of course I am a woman; and I am employed but I wonder what professional experiences I have had?

None at any rate to compare with those of Dame Ethel Smyth. After what she has told us — after what she has not told us but we can guess for ourselves — I feel rather like an idle and frivolous pleasure boat lolloping along in the wake of an ironclad. [*She is of the race of pioneers she is one of the ice breakers, the gun runners, the window smashers. The armoured tanks, who climbed the rough ground, drew the enemies fire, and left behind her a pathway — not yet smooth and metalled road — but still a pathway for those who come after her. Thus we honour her not only as a musician — not only as a writer—and when I read what Dame Ethel Smyth writes I always feel inclined to burn my own pen and take to music—for if she can write as well as all that, why shouldn't I compose, straight off — a masterpiece — we honour her not only for being a musician & a writer, but also for being an armoured tank. I never know whether to be angry that such heroism was needed, or glad that such heroism was shown.*]**

She is of the race of pioneers, of pathmakers. She has gone before

* Text transcribed from an untitled typescript by Virginia Woolf (with current manuscript corrections) of 25 pages, in the Berg Collection. Woolf's related manuscript notes are given below in an Appendix. A much reduced version (about one third the length of the typescript) was published as "Professions for Women" in *The Death of the Moth and Other Essays* (London: The Hogarth Press 1942) p 149–54. For an enthusiastic account by a member of the audience, of Virginia Woolf's speech and of the superbly humorous speech by Ethel Smyth which preceded it, see footnote below, p xxxv.

** Cancelled in the typescript. A few cancelled trial words are not transcribed.

and felled trees and blasted rocks and built bridges and thus made a way for those who come after her. Thus we honour her not only as a musician and as a writer — and when I read her books I always feel inclined to burn my own pen and take to music — for if she can toss off a masterpiece in my art without any training why should not I toss off a symphony or two without knowing a crotchet from a quaver? — we honour her not merely as a musician and a writer, but also as a blaster of rocks and the maker of bridges. It seems sometimes a pity that a woman who only wished to write music should have been forced also to make bridges, but that was part of her job and she did it.

But in my own profession — literature — the way was cut long ago. I have no doubt that I owe a great deal to some mute and inglorious Ethel Smyth. I have no doubt that there were women two hundred years ago who [*smashed, and broke and toiled and*] drew upon themselves hostility and ridicule in order that it might not be <wicked or> ridiculous [*or impossible*] [*disgraceful*] for women <nowadays> to write books.* But when I came to hold a pen there were very few obstacles of that sort in my way. Writing was a reputable, a harmless accomplishment. The family peace was not broken by the scratching of a pen. No great demand was made upon the family purse. And pens and paper are cheap. For ten and sixpence one can buy enough paper to write — if one has a mind — all the tragedies of Shakespeare. Pianos, models, studios, north lights, masters and mistresses <Berlin, Paris, Vienna & all the rest of it> are not needed. One has only got to sit down and write. The cheapness of writing materials [*has been I believe*] <is of course> the [*chief*] reason why women have succeeded as writers before they succeeded as painters or musicians.**

* Revised in *The Death of the Moth* to read: "For the road was cut many years ago — by Fanny Burney, by Aphra Behn, by Harriet Martineau, by Jane Austen, by George Eliot — many famous women, and many more unknown and forgotten, have been before me, making the path smooth, and regulating my steps."

** For earlier variants of this paragraph see Appendix below, manuscript paragraphs 3 and 10–12.

Thus you see my story is compared with Dame Ethel's a very tame one. You have only got to figure to yourselves a girl [*sitting and writing*] <in a bed-room with a pen in her hand> a girl who had plenty of pens and paper at command. Then it occurred to her to do what again only costs a penny stamp — to [*send*] <slip> an article [*on to a newspaper*] <into a pillar-box>; and to suggest to the editor of that newspaper that she might be allowed to try her hand at reviewing a [*novel. He*] book. He replied that Mrs Humphry Ward had just written her fifty sixth masterpiece and that it would not matter a straw to her or anybody else if an uneducated and probably incompetent young woman said what she thought of it. Hence I became a reviewer. Hence, on the first day of the following month I received a cheque for one pound seven and sixpence; and it will show you how little I deserve to be called a professional woman, or a working woman — it will show you how very little I know of life and its [*struggles*] <realities> when I confess that instead of spending the money on bread and butter, [*on rent,*] on shoes and stockings [*on the needs and*] I went out — flown with glory — and bought [*merely*] a cat — a beautiful cat, a Persian cat; a cat which <in being of the male sex> soon involved me in rows with all the neighbours.*

What could be easier, simpler and in its way more delightful than to review Mrs Humphrey Wards novels and to buy Persian cats with the proceeds? But after all the story is not quite as simple as all that. There is a villain in the piece.** That villain was not, I grieve to say, our old friend [*Man*] <the other sex—> Or at least only indirectly. [*He may have had a finger in it. But*] The villain of my story was a woman, and I propose to call her, after a figure in a well known poem, the Angel in the House. You who come of a younger and happier generation may not have heard of the Angel in the house. Therefore I will describe her. [*She was the woman that men wished women*

* The sex of the cat and the allusions to Mrs Humphry Ward are omitted in *The Death of the Moth*.

** These two sentences are the result of some revision in the typescript.

to be.] She was intensely sympathetic. She was immensely charming. She was utterly unselfish. She excelled in the difficult [*scenes*] <arts> of family life. She soothed, conciliated, sacrificed herself took the hash if there was only chicken enough for one, and in short was so constituted that she never had a wish or a mind of her own but preferred to sympathise with the wishes and minds of others. Above all — I hope I need not say it — she was pure. There were a great many things that one could not say without bringing a blush to her cheek. Almost every respectable Victorian house had its angel. And when I came to write — though I was not an angel myself — I had five hundred a year and angels never have a penny — there was [*one*] <an Angel> in the house with me. The shadow of her wings fell upon the page; I heard the rustling of her skirts in the room. Now this creature — it was one of her most annoying characteristics — never had any real existence. She had — what is much more difficult to deal with — an ideal existence, a fictitious existence. She was a dream, a phantom — a kind of mirage like the pools and the palm trees which nature places in the desert to lure the caravan across. The Angel in the house was the ideal of womanhood created by the imaginations of men and women at a certain stage of their pilgrimage to lure them across a very dusty stretch <of the journey>. They agreed to accept this ideal, because for reasons I cannot now go into — they have to do with the British Empire, our colonies, Queen Victoria, Lord Tennyson, the growth of the middle class and so on — [*reality*] <a real relationship> between men and women was then unattainable. If you disbelieve me, let me quote you this scrap of dialogue between men and women in the age of Victoria. Tennyson speaks first. He <addresses his ideal of womanhood — She, he says,>*

On tiptoe seemed to touch upon a sphere
Too gross to tread, and all male minds perforce
Swayed to her from their orbits as they moved

* Typescript before insertion: "He is speaking as the man to the woman; and he says that how [*sic*] about women that she". This dialogue is omitted from *The Death of the Moth* and the whole Angel section is greatly simplified.

[*Then*] ⟨To which⟩ Christina Rossetti ⟨in duty bound⟩ replied,

Woman was made for mans delight
Charm O woman be not afraid;
His shadow by day, his moon by night
Woman was made.

⟨Then Lowell said

It is not woman leaves us to our night
but our brute earth that glories from her sun.⟩

[*And so they went on paying each other compliments, in a style which to me is really disgusting.*] ⟨Those words seem to me to imply a relationship between men and women that was both [*untrue*] false and disagreeable.⟩ At any rate when I came to write reviews the Angel in the House stole behind me and said "You have got yourself into a very queer position. You are young and unmarried. But you are writing for a paper owned by men, edited by men — *whose chief supporters are men*; you are even reviewing a book that has been written by a man — one Mr Arnold Bennett — Therefore whatever you say let it be pleasing to men. Be sympathetic; be tender; flatter; use all the arts and wiles which I Heaven help me have used till I am sick of the whole thing (The Angel did sometimes speak like this to women ⟨when she was alone⟩) but believe me it is absolutely necessary. Never disturb them with the idea that you have a mind of your own. And above all be pure." With that she made as if to guide my pen.

I now record the one act for which I take some credit — though the credit belongs rather to my income than to me — if one has five hundred a year there is no need to tell lies and it is much more amusing to tell the truth — I turned upon that Angel and caught her by the throat. I did my best to kill her. My excuse — if I were to be had up in a law court and charged with murder — would be that I acted in self defence. If I had not killed her, she would have killed me — as a writer. That woman — but she was not a woman she was an Angel — has more blood on her hands than [*Crippen or Peace* or the man who murd*] all the murderers <who have ever been hanged.> Writer after writer, painter after painter and musicians I dare say too she has strangled and killed. One is always meeting their corpses laid out in biographies. But she has a special hatred for writers and with good reason. Her province, you see, is the House. Painters and musicians — it is one of their chief assets — have very little to do with the house. When Vanessa Bell paints a picture it is as often as not a picture of red apples on a plate. Thats all right, says the Angel. It may be a pity to waste your time painting; but if you must paint [*paint apples*] < there is no harm in apples.> Ethel Smyth writes a Mass. Its a pity says the Angel, but music doesnt much matter — [*that is merely*] [*is only*] <Music> is sound after all — no nasty meaning is attached to [*music*] <it>. And so she lets them be.

But writing is a very different matter — you cannot even review a novel without expressing an opinion upon charac[ters,] morality, human relations — all matters of vital importance in the conduct of the house, and thus coming directly under the notice of its Angel. Young and ignorant and unmarried as I was, I did have to say for example that I thought that Mr Carlyle ought to have had a child and that Mrs Carlyle ought to have written a novel; I did have to say that there was a good deal <more> to be said for Fanny Brawne <as a lover than for> Keats; I did have to [say] that it did not matter a straw whether [*George Eliot were married to Mr Lewes or not*] <Mrs Lewes wore a wedding ring or not> — In short I was forced to attack many of the most sacred objects in the house, and that the Angel did not like. Therefore I did my best to kill her. Whenever I felt the shadow of her wings or the radiance of her halo upon the page I took up the inkpot and flung it at her. But though I flatter myself that I did kill her in the end, the struggle was severe; it took up much time that had better have been spent in learning Greek grammar or in roaming the world in search of adventures. Well,

* Charles Peace, notorious criminal hanged in 1879.

that is one professional experience — killing the Angel in the house.

And now when the Angel is dead, what remains? You may think that what remains is something quite simple and common enough — a young woman. [*But what is a woman?*] [*So it might appear.*] Having rid herself of falsehood, so we might put it, she has now only to be herself ⟨and write⟩. But what is 'herself'? I mean, what is a woman? I assure you, I dont know; I do not believe that you know; I do not believe that anybody can know until she has expressed herself in all the arts and professions open to human skill. [*That*] ⟨What a woman [is]⟩ is a discovery which you here are in process of making — a piece of very important knowledge which we shall owe to you. But I am limited to my own experience, which as I began by saying is narrow. All I can tell you is that I discovered when I came to write that a woman — it sounds so simple, but I should be ashamed to tell you how long it took me to realise this for myself — is not a man. Her experience is not the same. Her traditions are different. Her values, both in art and in life are [*different*] ⟨her own⟩.

[*You will I think find a perfectly simple example of this difference of values if you will look at a copy of this week's Nation. I happened yesterday to glance through the reviews in that estimable paper, not very attentively I fear. My mind was wandering; I was thinking perhaps of what I should say to you tonight; and so I thought that I had a piece of good news for you — that I* [had] *read in a review by Mr Keynes that the fellows of Clare had given in pious memory of their founder the lady of Clare six thousand pounds to a woman. "Clothed in the finest dress . . . armed with intellect and learning, adorned with curiosity and fancy" I read;* [*and asked myself*] *so Mr Keynes described her. Who is this woman I asked myself; and reading more attentively discovered that it was not a woman at all, but a book. The members of Clare college have spent six thousand pounds upon a history of their college. And that made me angry.*] *

* John Maynard Keynes's review of *Clare College, 1326–1926* edited by Mansfield D. Forbes (Cambridge University Press, 2 vols) appears in *The Nation and Athenaeum* of Saturday, January 17 1932 (vol 48 p 512–13).

To show you how this difference works out in my own profession, I will take a practical example — one is provided, as it happens, by the current number of the Nation. If you will look at that number, you will find Mr Keynes there reviews a book — a history of Clare College Cambridge. Mr Keynes begins by saying that this book cost it is rumoured six thousand pounds to produce. He goes on to say that Clare is a very ancient and famous college; he dwells upon the beauty of its buildings, the fame of its butler, and the [*beauty of its plate*] <excellent claret>. And he ends with an eloquent description of this book and all that it implies which I will read you. "Clothed in the finest dress of paper and black buckram, armed with intellect and learning, adorned with curiosity and fancy . . . there is here embodied the Sentiment of one of those of the ancient foundations of the country which have outlived the centuries with least loss of the past and least sacrifice of the present, a college. It is a gracious sight — worthy, but difficult, of imitation." That is the way that Mr Keynes reviews that book.

Had the Editor of the Nation sent it to me, I should have been compelled by that different sense of values to write in a very different strain.

O you old humbugs. I should have begun. O you who have enjoyed for all these centuries comfort and prosperity — O you who profess devotion to the lady of Clare and love for the Sentiment of colleges, would it not be better to spend your six thousand pounds not upon a book, clothed in the finest dress of paper and buckram, but upon a girl, whose dress allowance is very meagre, and who tries to do her work, as you will read if you turn the very next page in the Nation, in one cold gloomy ground floor bedroom which faces due north and is overrun with mice. (Somerville it seems is very hard up.)* A college I entirely agree with Mr Keynes is a gracious sight;

* On p 509 of the same week's *Nation*, in Vera Brittain's regular weekly column headed "A Woman's Notebook," we read that "the poverty of the women's colleges bears hardest upon those who have to live out." Of her own college experience Brittain writes: "When I lived out during my last year at Somerville, my one room was a

worthy but difficult of imitation. If the members of Clare college handed over the six thousand pounds that they have spent upon a book to Girton [*say*] some of the difficulties of imitation would be removed, and what is more I am sure that the lady of Clare would rise from her grave and say Gentlemen you have done [*me honour*] <my will>.

---

cold, gloomy, ground-floor bedroom, which faced due north and was overrun with mice, but others in the same house fared even less enviably." In the next paragraph Vera Brittain cites "Virginia Woolf's little masterpiece, 'A Room of One's Own,'" as "the classic expression" of women's need for "more space, more food, more comfort . . . more opportunities in more professions."

In the *Nation* of January 31 (p 571) Vera Brittain in her column reports as a member of the audience her enjoyment of the speeches of Ethel Smyth and Virginia Woolf. The speakers were "hilariously serious," and Brittain was delighted to hear Woolf quoting her own column from the *Nation*. As a fresh document of the occasion the whole paragraph from "A Woman's Notebook" is worth reprinting:

"Two functions on the same day last week gave additional prominence to three women who in their diverse fashions are among the greatest of this generation. From the At Home arranged on the eve of her seventy-third birthday by Mrs. Sidney Webb, where several of the older guests recalled the Fabian-Socialist group described in the final chapter of "My Apprenticeship," I went on to a delicious entertainment provided for a large audience by Dame Ethel Smyth and Mrs. Virginia Woolf. This hilariously serious party was organized, incidentally, by the Junior Council of the London Society for Women's Service, that lively body of young professional women which includes Miss Amy Johnson, and somehow captures exciting visitors who will not so much as put their distinguished noses into the offices of other associations. Dame Ethel, whose superb humour gives the lie to the common belief that all women are heavy and conscientious speakers, told us that, having expressed in her diary at the age of nine the ambition "to be made a Peeress in my own right because of music," she accepted her D.B.E. with alacrity, "especially as it was all due to an absurd row in the Woking Golf Club." I was interested, in view of what I said on this page a fortnight ago about the poverty of women, to hear both Dame Ethel and Mrs. Woolf attribute their success largely to the possession of a private income, which enabled the one to take up a non-lucrative career, and the other to flout the displeasure of authors and editors by writing honest reviews. Women, Mrs. Woolf maintained, had succeeded better in literature than in other arts because paper was cheap and pens made no noise. I am delighted to record, from the internal evidence of a quotation in her speech, that Mrs. Woolf is a reader of this Notebook."

In *Three Guineas* (1 note 18) Woolf cites the Keynes review, draws upon Brittain's account of her room, and quotes her (anonymously) on the financial plight of Somerville college (p 508–09).

That is more or less how I should be forced to write that review, if the editor had sent me the book; but I doubt that that review would be printed; < for I am a woman.> My sense of values — [*for I am not an economist — would*] differs too much I am afraid from that of a very celebrated economist. Now that difference is bound to show itself in all kinds of ways. And you are bound to find when you come to practise your innumerable professions that your difference of outlook is bringing you to loggerheads with some respected [*head*] <chiefs> of your profession. [*This sense of values is a very queer thing* —] But one of your most amusing and exciting experiences will be precisely on this account — [*when you*] <that you will have to> make your profession adapt itself to your needs, your sense of values, your common sense, your moral sense your sense of what is due to humanity and reason. [*I have no right to speak; but*] as a member of the general public, who sometimes has to employ lawyers, then architects, then builders, then doctors, stock brokers and so on — I can assure you that I think it is high time [*you got to work upon these professions and brought them rather more into line with common sense.*] <that these ancient and privileged professions came more in touch with human needs.>

Well now to go on with the tame story of my professional career. I suppose that the Persian cat which I bought out of the proceeds of my first review did not satisfy me. I grew ambitious. I desired not merely a cat but a motor car. You cannot afford a car on five hundred a year; but it is a strange fact that people will provide you with a motor car if you will tell them a story. That is one reason for writing novels. And then to imagine, <and> to create would seem to be an easier, a simpler [*and a happier*] occupation than to reason and to criticise. Ignorance [— *and I was extremely ignorant* —] does not so much matter. I could let my heroes and heroines be born when they liked in a novel; but if I said in the Times or elsewhere that Shakespeare was born in [*April*] <May> when he was born in [*May*] <April> it roused a storm of indignation in every capital in Europe.

Hence, along these natural avenues of greed and laziness I reached the next stage in my professional career — that is to say novel writing. Now your secretary asks me to tell you what experiences of a professional nature did I have as a novelist?

That is an extremely difficult question to answer. A novelist is not nearly so conscious <or so reasonable a person as a critic>. Fiction is not nearly so conscious, or so reasonable [*a practise*] <[an] art> as criticism. I do not wish you to infer from this that a novelist is in a perpetual state of inspiration. I mean rather that the novelist is in a perpetual state of lethargy. [*He wishes*] <It is his desire> to be as unconscious as possible. He wants life to proceed with the utmost quiet and regularity. He wants to see the same faces, to read the same books to do the same things day after day and month after month so that nothing may break the illusion; that nothing may disturb the flow, that nothing may interrupt the mysterious nosings about, feelings round, darts and dashes and sudden discoveries of that very shy and illusive fish the imagination.

Therefore I find it very difficult to describe to you what happens to a novelist, what are the incidents of her professional career. Outwardly I can perhaps sketch her for you. That ignorant girl who used to sit scribbling reviews and now and again getting up to shy an inkpot at an angel, now sat and dreamt. She spent her time mooning. She mooned and mooned. [*Sometimes perhaps she wrote a sentence; sometimes she looked out of the window. But what did she see? Nothing real. What did she think? I doubt that she thought at all. Did she not construct a plot? No never. What she was doing was to let her mind — if we like to grant her one — feed unfettered upon every atom and crumb of her experience; to let her imagination sweep round every angle and rock and cranny of the world as it lies in the depths of her subconsciousness.*] I figure her really <in an attitude of contemplation, like a fisherwoman,> sitting on the bank of a lake with [*a*] <her> fishing rod <held over its water.> [*Yes that is how I see her.*] She was not thinking; she was not reasoning; she was not constructing a plot; she was letting her imagination down into the depths of her consciousness while she sat above holding on by a thin <but quite necessary> thread of reason. She was letting her imagination feed unfettered upon every crumb of her experience; she was letting her imagination sweep unchecked round every rock and cranny of the world that lies submerged in our unconscious being.

Then suddenly this fisherwoman gave a cry of dismay. What had happened? The line had suddenly slackened; her imagination had floated limply and dully and lifelessly upon the surface. The reason hauled the imagination on shore and said What on earth is the matter with you? And the imagination began pulling on its stockings and replied, rather tartly and disagreeably; its all your fault. You should have given me more experience to go on. I cant do the whole work for myself.

And I — the reason — had to reply: Many forms of experience are lacking to me because I am a woman.

Well that is one experience — quite a common one if you are a woman — of the novelist's profession. But there is another. The novelist is sitting on the shores of the lake, holding the little line of reason [*between her fingers*] <in her hands when> Suddenly there is a violent jerk; she feels the line race through her fingers.

The imagination [*darts away*] has rushed away; it has taken to the depths; it has sunk — heaven knows where — into what dark pool of extraordinary experience. The reason has to cry "Stop!" The novelist has to pull on the line and haul the imagination to the surface. The imagination comes to the top in a state of fury.

Good heavens she cries — how dare you interfere with me <!> [*and pull me to the top*] <How dare you pull me out> with your wretched little fishing line" And I — that is the reason — have to reply, "My dear you were going altogether too far. Men would be shocked." Calm yourself, I say, as she sits panting on the bank — panting with rage and disappointment. We have only got to wait fifty years or so. In fifty years I shall be able to use all this very queer knowledge that you are ready to bring me. But not now. You see I go on, trying to calm her, I cannot make use of what you tell me — about womens bodies for instance — their passions — and so on, because the conventions are still very strong. If I were to overcome the conventions I should need the courage of a hero, and I am not a hero.

I doubt that a writer can be a hero. I doubt that a hero can be a writer. And then I point out to her <that the moment I become heroic,> I become shrill and hard and positive — in short I become [*a preacher*] <more like a critic —> and that I say, is extremely unpleasant for you, poor imagination. And I go on to tell her that even men, who can let their imaginations go much further than women can, because the convention allows men to be much more open in what they say than women — even men I tell her, have to say Stop.* Thackeray for instance. And in our time, though things are better, still there are conventions, even for men; and if a man like Lawrence, I tell her, runs against convention he injures his imagination terribly. She becomes shrivelled and distorted; and you would not like to become shrivelled and distorted would you? I say. It is your nature to understand and to create.

Very well says the imagination, dressing herself up again in her petticoat and skirts, we will wait. We will wait another fifty years. But it seems to me a pity.

This then is another incident, and quite a common incident in the career of a woman novelist. She has to say I will wait. I will

* Crossed out trials of this passage read:
"And then I point out to her that even men, who can let their imaginations go much further than I can, because the convention is much less because you see, the moment I become heroic, the moment I [*make that great effort which is required to overcome opposition,*] <dart my imagination against an obstacle> [*I become — at least I think this is so — so conscious of my own heroism, and of opposition, that I wake up; and then I cannot write,*] <;[*it shrinks up and hardens and becomes and I become a preacher not a writer*]> <that my imagination shrivels up and hardens and I cease to be a writer: I become a preacher.> Why even men, I say, who can let their imaginations go much further <before they say stop,> because the convention allows them to."

wait until men have become so civilised that they are not shocked when a woman speaks the truth about her body. The future of fiction depends very much upon what extent men can be educated to stand free speech in women. But whether men can be [*educated*] civilised, what capacities lie dormant in them, how far their condition is the result of reeducation or of nature, whether given a better environment the results might be such that women too can be artists lies on the lap of the Gods, no not upon the laps of the Gods, but upon your laps, upon the laps of professional women.

Here then I am really [*at*] come to an end of my professional experiences — I have told you how I tried to murder the Angel in the House — [*how I tried to on the other hand to resuscitate, encourage and revive the imagination within*] <I have recorded the [*rage of the imagination when she is not*] little dialogue between the reason and the imagination, which some times breaks [*our man**] the peace of our solitary hours of contemplation.> That these are very tame experiences I know. But as I explained to you, I have had [*two great advantages*] two peculiarities which made it unnecessary for me to go through many of the experiences which fall to the lot of you who are pioneers — I had five hundred a year of my own, and my profession is the one profession which, owing to the cheapness of writing paper, and the fact that pens scarcely make any noise, women have practised for many years with some success. When people said to me What is the use of your trying to write? <I could say, truthfully, I write, not for use, but for pleasure. When they said, Women cannot write, I downed them> with the sacred name of Sappho — a very difficult writer whom few people have read.

But for you it is very different. You who are now for the first time practising as barristers, architects, decorators, solicitors, — you have no Sappho, no Jane Austen to fall back upon. <You must be the Sappho and the Jane Austen of your profession.> Therefore you will

* our manners?

meet with much more ridicule than ever fell to my lot. And then, you have, I imagine, to make your livings — which I never did. And therefore you will meet with an opposition much sterner than any I [*could*] had to face, because [*you are competing with men,*] you are trying to make [*them*] <men> pay you for work which [*no woman has ever done before*] <they have hitherto done themselves>. Now I cannot delude myself into thinking that you have an easy task before you. You are bound I am afraid to meet with a great deal of derision and opposition. You will want all your strength and courage. And for this reason it is of the highest importance that you should not add to your burdens a very heavy and unnecessary burden, the burden of bitterness. If you are always comparing your lot with the lot of men, if you are always thinking how much easier it is for them to earn a living than for you — you will have an enemy within who is always sapping your strength and poisoning your happiness. Here I would beg of you, speaking from the [*very comfortable*] <easy armchair> position of a woman who need not earn her living, <but> who <can spend her time imagining how> other people earn theirs — speaking as a novelist, I would ask you to use a novelist's prerogative — to use your imaginations and to try [*that*] <imagination> as a specific against bitterness. Imagine what it is like to be a man. Put yourselves into his shoes for a moment. Now directly that you try to put yourselves into the shoes of a man, I think you will find that <those shoes> change <their size: they become very large.> A delicious sense of [*size*] <weight> and importance pervades you. You feel that you are a very respectable and responsible human [*being. You have a house and servants.*] on [*your*] <whose> shoulders rests the burden of providing for that house and servants.* [*Now you who are for the first time in history, earning your own livings in so many different professions have put this man into*] <This large and important and responsible person is being put by you into> a very difficult position. Let us imagine how it appears to him. He has been

* For the brief manuscript draft of this passage, see the Appendix below.

out all day in the city earning his living, and he comes home at night expecting repose and comfort to find that his servants — the women servants — have taken possession of the house. He goes into the library — an august apartment which he is accustomed to have all to himself — and finds the kitchen maid curled up in the arm chair reading Plato. He goes into the kitchen and there is the cook engaged in writing a Mass in B flat. He goes into the billiard room and finds the parlourmaid knocking up a fine break at the table. He goes into the bed room and there is the housemaid working out a mathematical problem. What is he to do? He has been accustomed for centuries to have that sumptuous mansion all to himself, to be master in his own house. Well of course his first instinct is to dismiss the whole crew. But he reflects that then he would have to do the work of the house himself, and he has not been trained to do it. — Nature has denied him certain <quite essential> gifts. He therefore says that these women servants may practise their silly little amusements in their spare time, but that if he finds them neglecting the sacred duties which nature has imposed upon them he will do something very dreadful indeed. But what can he do? [*His perplexity*] It is difficult to say. It is extremely amusing to see. He can stand upon his dignity. He can appeal to precedent. He can say that nature intended servants to be servants, and that there is no getting over nature. He can make the most cutting and disagreeable remarks about housemaids playing the piano and scullerymaids reading Plato; he can turn them out of the library, lock the billiard room door, and put the key of the cellar in his pocket — because after all he pays the rent and the house is his property. But there is a spirit in the house <not by any means an Angel> — a very queer spirit — I don't know how to define it — it is the sort of spirit that is in Dame Ethel Smyth — you have only got to look at her and you will feel it for yourselves — and this spirit [*is not a thing that*] <of adventure and daring> is impossible to lock up — or to lock out. Hence the man came home one day to find that although the servants had managed to keep the house going all the time — and that is really one of the most [blank space] they had yet contrived, by practising their silly little accomplishments, to have saved enough money to hire rooms of their own. Therefore they need not go on living in his house any more. That did place the man in a very awkward predicament. His deepest instincts were outraged — and his most cherished traditions were flouted. [*And then think of his surprise.*] He had thought that nature had meant women to be wives, mothers, housemaids, parlourmaids and cooks. Suddenly he discovers [*by reading*] ⟨that nature — but he did not call it nature — he called it sin — had made them also⟩ doctors, civil servants, meteorologists, dental surgeons, librarians, solicitors' clerks, agricultural workers, analytical chemists, investigators of industrial psychology, barristers at law, makers of scientific models, accountants, hospital dieticians, political organisers, store keepers, artists, horticultural instructors, publicity managers, architects, insurance representatives, dealers in antiques, bankers, actuaries, managers of house property, court dress makers, aero engineers, history instructors, company directors, organisers of peace crusades, newspaper representatives, technical officers in the royal airships works, — and so on.*

[*Naturally he swore They are mutinous base, ungrateful hussies. They are taking the bread out of my mouth and making it quite unnecessary that I should support them. I am the bread winner; how am I going to support a wife and family, if my wife and family can support themselves? No, I will make it as hard as possible for my wife and family to support themselves because* [*I then I hope they will give up doing it, and they will let me support them and it*] *for reasons which I need not go into but they have to do with the most profound instincts of my nature it is much pleasanter to support a wife and family, than to allow a wife and family to support themselves.* [*Therefore Imagine I*]]

* The list differs in the manuscript draft; see Appendix.

That is the sort of position that you have put this man into, and it is an extremely difficult one. Remember what a tremendous tradition of mastery man has behind him — consider what prestige and power he has enjoyed. And reflect, as I think in all honesty you can, that there are men [*who are generous, humane, and men who do believe*] who have triumphed over all the difficulties of their very lopsided education, of their very specialised and arduous careers, men of [*generous and wide humanity,*] <civilisation, not only of education,> men with whom a woman can live in perfect freedom, without any fear. <Men too can be manipulated.>

Do not therefore be angry; be patient; be amused; It is a situation of extraordinary interest and amazing possibilities both for the present and for the future. You have [*already a room*] earned your room; you have paid the rent for it. It is a little bare at present I agree. I suspect that the sofa turns into a bed; and the wash stand is covered with a check cloth by day to look as much like a table as possible. You picked up the carpet at the Caledonian market for half a crown or so on condition that you carried it home under your arm. <And I convict you of eating poached eggs instead of mutton chops — because poached eggs are cheaper.> But these things are your own — you have bought them with your own money. There, in the privacy of your own room, you can sit and write or paint, [*or compose music, or design buil*] <design houses — aeroplanes — or whatever it is. There you must [*earn your livings, because you have the rent to pay;*]> do nothing but [*look out of the window, if it pleases you*] <work, because you have your livings to earn.> That is perhaps enough at the moment. But, then as Dame Ethel asks, what will be the next step? There will have to be one. And I predict that the next step will be a step upon the stair. You will hear somebody coming. You will open the door. And then — this at least is my guess — there will take place between you and some one else the most interesting, exciting, and important conversation that has ever been heard. But do not be alarmed; I am not going to talk about that now. My time is up.

THE PARGITERS

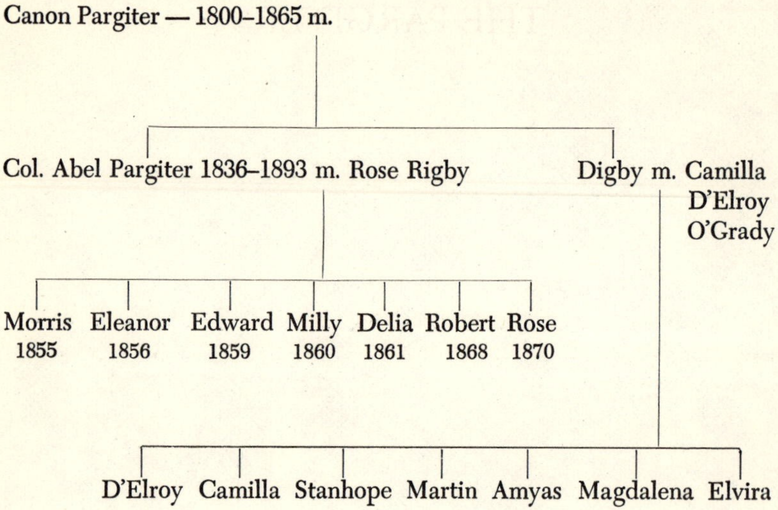

[*Genealogical tree* (11)]

[14] *11th October 1932*

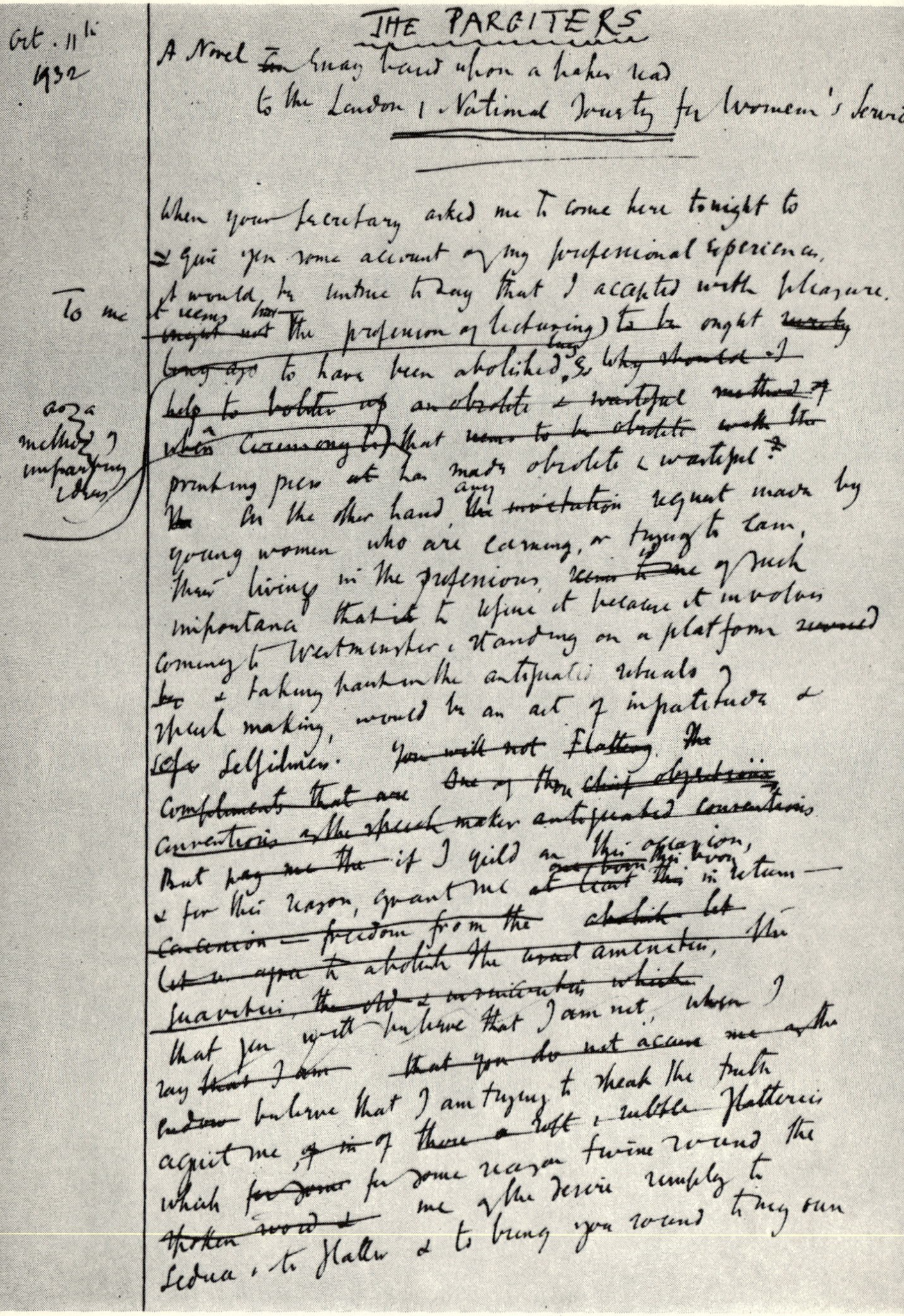
Oct. 11th 1932

THE PARGITERS

A Novel ~~An~~ Essay based upon a paper read to the London & National Society for Women's Service

When your secretary asked me to come here tonight to ~~&~~ give you some account of my professional experiences, it would be untrue to say that I accepted with pleasure. To me it seems ~~too~~ ~~ought not~~ the profession of lecturing ~~to be~~ ought ~~surely~~ ~~long ago~~ long ago to have been abolished. So why ~~should I~~ ~~help to bolster up~~ an obsolete & wasteful ~~method of~~ ~~whose~~ a ceremony [as a method of imparting ideas] that ~~seems to be obsolete~~ ~~with the~~ printing press ~~at~~ has made obsolete & wasteful? ~~The~~ On the other hand, ~~the~~ any ~~invitation~~ request made by young women who are earning, or trying to earn, their living in the professions, ~~seems to~~ ~~be~~ of such importance that ~~it~~ to refuse it because it involves coming to Westminster & standing on a platform ~~and~~ ~~by~~ & taking part in the antiquated rituals of speech making, would be an act of ingratitude & ~~selfi~~ selfishness. ~~You will not~~ ~~Flattery~~ ~~The~~ ~~Compliments that are~~ ~~One of those~~ ~~chief objections~~ ~~conventions of the speech maker~~ ~~antiquated conventions~~ But ~~pay me the~~ if I yield on this occasion, & for this reason, grant me ~~at least~~ ~~one boon~~ this boon in return — ~~convention~~ — freedom from the ~~abolish~~ ~~let~~ ~~let us agree to~~ abolish the usual amenities, ~~the~~ suavities, ~~the old & inveterate~~ ~~which~~ that you will believe that I am not, when I say ~~that I am~~ ~~that you do not accuse me of the~~ ~~endeav~~ believe that I am trying to speak the truth acquit me, ~~of in~~ of ~~those a soft~~ & subtle flatteries which ~~for some~~ for some reason twine round the ~~spoken~~ ~~word &~~ me of the desire simply to seduce, to flatter & to bring you round to my own

First page of the Novel-Essay, Holograph [15]

[15] # THE PARGITERS

A Novel-Essay based upon a paper read to the London / National Society for Women's Service.*

[FIRST ESSAY]

Oct. 11th 1932 †

When your Secretary asked me to come here tonight to give you some account of my professional experiences, it would be untrue to say that I accepted with pleasure. To me it seems that the profession of lecturing ought to have been abolished long ago. [*Why should I help to bolster up a method of imparting ideas that the printing press has made obsolete and wasteful?*] On the other hand, any request made by young women who are earning, or trying to earn, their livings in the professions is of such importance that to refuse it because it involves coming to Westminster and standing on a platform and taking part in the anticipated rituals of speech making, would be an act of ingratitude and selfishness. But if I yield on this occasion, and for this reason, grant me this boon in return — believe that I am trying to speak the truth, acquit me of the desire simply to seduce and to flatter and to bring you round to my own [1 6] way of thinking by means of flattery and seduction.

The phrase that I have just used, for example — that I am grateful to you for earning your livings, that I respect you, that if I could help you, I would — is not flattery; it is strictly true. No other audience would have overcome my belief that speech making is an effervescence of foam — intoxicating to vanity, obstructive of truth — as deleterious to the health of the mind as cheap and nasty champagne to the health of the body. Had the House over the way asked me to

* First written "An Essay".

† Virginia Woolf usually entered the date as she began each chapter or essay.

address them on the Ottawa Conference [or] Tariff Reform; had the majestic houses of Oxford and Cambridge asked me to lecture on the Victorian Novelists — both invitations are not only imaginary, but beyond the bounds of imagination — I need hardly say that to refuse would have been easy.

But your society has, for me, an importance which Westminster and the great universities lack; you, who are trying to earn your livings in the professions, are making an experiment; are attempting what has never been attempted before. You call out, as the old and established societies at Westminster and Oxford and Cambridge cannot call all those sympathies which, in literature, are stimulated by the explorers who set out in crazy cockle shells to discover new lands, and found new civilisations. And your enterprise is not "in literature"; it is in being — a difference that makes it less easy to describe with the fluency of a flowing pen; but far more interesting. [1 7] When I turn to your request, to tell you something about my professional experiences, I am faced with the fact that, in one sense, there is less to tell about the profession of writing than about any other. It has not the material difficulties in [*the sense*] that many professions are difficult. Ten shillings will buy enough paper to contain all the tragedies of Shakespeare. One fountain pen is said to last a life time. A gallon of ink will write a dozen novels and would have served even Anthony Trollope for ten years. The cost of a writer's materials is negligible compared with the pianos, the paints, the scientific instruments, the battleships, and the guns that are needed in other professions. If you asked a musician or a painter or a scientist or a soldier to give you his professional experiences, you might justly expect, even if the lecturer were a man, to hear an exciting story of hardships overcome and difficulties surmounted. Not only are the materials of a writer's profession easy to obtain, but the profession itself is one of those home industries which can be carried on without any derangement of family life. [1 8] Hence the fact that this is, with one exception, the first of all professions practised by women.

But the profession of a writer which can be practised so cheaply, so domestically, [*in a bed sitting room, or at a desk in a public library*] is lacking those exciting incidents which are likely to occur if you adopt a profession which requires an expensive apparatus or specialised instruction. Your request that I should describe the profession of writing has [*made that abundantly*] clear. [1 9] Hence, I am going to deal not with my profession in particular, although I hope to say something also about that, but with professions in general — the professions that you are not practising, and that you are practising, and that you might practise. (This, I am aware, is to enlarge the scope of my paper very considerably — perhaps very foolishly. But the subject is one of such importance that I have brought myself to believe that even so ill-informed and imperfect a sketch as I can make may give you something to re-write and think over and bring to much better proportions and deeper meaning among yourselves, than it is possible for me to achieve alone.)

But how can I possibly say anything of interest to you about the professions that you are practising and that I am not practising? How can I say anything that you do not know a thousand times better than I do about medicine and law and architecture and engineering and politics and banking and the civil service — to name a few of the professions in which, as I see from your report, you are now engaged? That is an objection that has already occurred to me. It has great [1 10] weight. But perhaps an outsider — and it is part of a writer's profession to be an outsider — can see aspects of things that are not visible from the inside. I have already given you proof of this. I have spoken of gratitude and respect. I said that you call out those sympathies which are excited by the explorers who set out in crazy cockle shells to discover new lands and to found new civilisations. And as I spoke the words, I saw come over your faces [*that*] rather strained look of polite acquiescence with which we receive amiable commonplaces of benevolent well-wishers. And I understood it to mean, "Heavens, how little she knows what it means

— to earn one's living in a profession!" Some of you, as I spoke, saw in a flash the crowded noisy office in which you have spent this particular day. You have been working there from half past nine to six, with an hour off for luncheon. You will be working with a fortnight's holiday in the summer and the usual Bank holidays, from January to January. The crazy cockle shell may stand for the motor omnibus which brings you from Clarence Road, S.W.19 to Whitehall; but "discovering new lands and founding new civilisations" seems to you a highly metaphorical way of [*describing*] the three-roomed flat above the grocer's shop in Clarence Road S.W.19, which is your lodging.

It is true, of course, that it is pleasant to have a room of one's own. But when you have to pay the rent — out of a salary which is round about three hundred pounds — [I 11] and when you thought of the hours spent in hard and sometimes harassing work, and of the rooms in which you live, and of the effort that is required to pay the rent of those rooms, you concluded that to talk of discovering new lands and founding new civilisations was merely a speaker's way of being polite. On the contrary, it was a writer's way of showing you, who are inside, what is visible to some one who is outside. And I hope that in the course of this paper, I shall bring you to understand why it is true to me; even if you find much to add, much to correct, before you are satisfied that it is in any way true for you.

[I 12] Both my aims in this paper — I wish to discuss professions in general and to justify my statement that, in trying to earn your living professionally, you are doing work of enormous importance — require some few pages of historical preface. This is obvious because we cannot understand the present if we isolate it from the past. If we want to understand what it is that you are doing now, I must ask you to forget that we are in this room, this night. We must forget that we are, for the moment, ourselves. We must become the people that we were two or three generations ago. Let us be our great grandmothers. But as this being somebody else is not part of your profession — it would [be] a serious drawback in some of them, I imagine — and as it is a very large part of a writer's profession, I am going to take the liberty of effecting this transformation for you. [ɪ 13] I am going to read you chapters from an unpublished novel which I am in process of writing, called "The Pargiters."

As it happens, [the novel] lends itself to our purpose, because it tries to give a faithful and detailed account of a family called Pargiter, from the year 1800 to the year 2032. Thus, if I select the Chapter which deals with the Pargiters in the year 1880, I ought to be able to show you what you were like fifty years ago: to provide that perspective which is so important for the understanding of the present. If you object that fiction is not history, I reply that though it would be far easier to write history — "In the year 1842 Lord John Russell brought in the Second Reform Bill" and so on — that method of telling the truth seems to me so elementary, and so clumsy, that I prefer, where truth is important, to write fiction. This novel, "The Pargiters," moreover is not a novel of vision, but a novel of fact. It is based upon some scores — I might boldly say thousands — of old memoirs. There is scarcely a statement in it that cannot be [*traced to some biography, or*] verified, if anybody should wish so to misuse their time. I hope that I am not making an empty boast if I say that there is not a statement in it that cannot be verified.

[ɪ 15] As I am only able to give you short extracts from a novel that will run into many volumes, I must explain that the family of Pargiter is one of those typical English families whose members are to be found in the Army, the Navy, and the Church; the Bar; the Stock Exchange; the Civil Services; the House of Commons; who never rise very high or sink very low, although some Pargiters have married the daughters of Earls, and others have kept small tobacconist's shops in the suburbs of London. My intention, that is to say, is to represent English life at its most normal, most typical, and most representative.

The Chapter that I am about to read is taken from volume five and describes a scene in the life of the Abel Pargiters — Captain Abel Pargiter, R.N. (1826–1890), the father, being the third in descent from John Pargiter (1730–1785), the Yorkshire cotton spinner and banker, with whom the book begins. Captain Abel, now aged, is father of three sons, Thomas, Henry, and Sinclair; and of four daughters, Milly, Eleanor, Mary and Rose.* Mrs. Pargiter, the mother (née Rose Dalton of Stockton-on-Tees), is now a confirmed invalid — and has indeed not many months to live. The Pargiters inhabit number fifty-six Abercorn Terrace, one of [those] large old fashioned houses with flights of steps in front and long gardens behind which are still to be found between Ladbroke Grove and Bayswater. It is the 16th of November 1880, about five o'clock in the afternoon; and the Pargiters are at tea.

* On the facing page [I 14] are written the ages of the sons (20, 16, 12) and the daughters (21, 17, 15, 10). Their names are written in the top left margin of I 16: "Milly Eleanor Mary Rose: Thomas Henry & [*Sinclair:*] <Robert>."

[1 16]

CHAPTER FIFTY-SIX*

"I wish the kettle would boil" said Milly

"Why cant one make tea without boiling water?" asked her [*sist*] Eleanor. "I dont think anyone wd. know" [*Wilkins*] The door opened & [*Wilkins*] Susan brought in a covered dish of hot cakes< . > [*which she*]

"I'll boil the kettle in the kitchen if you like, Miss" she said.

Oh no thank you, Susan" said [*Milly*] <Milly> "It'll boil in time.

When the maid had shut the door she took a hair pin from her head & [*tried by*] <began to> fray[*ing*] the wick of the [*kettle, to*] <lamp> so [*that it might*] so as to increase the flame. The [*kettle of beaten brass,*] [*"Its the most incompetent*] <I hate that> kettle [*that ever was*]" said Mary; "[*why dont*] why [*not boil it downstairs*] Cant we buy a new one?

"[*Papa*] <But [*Eleanor*] Mary> gave it to Mama on their wedding tour" said Milly. "[*It comes*] [*They bought it in Bourges. "And*] [*They'd never let us*] He would[*n't like us to*] never let us use another."

"[*It is very*] <Besides you couldn't> have an ordinary kettle in [*a*] the drawing room. How late everybody is!" she continued. You'd better put the scones to keep hot by the fire.

"[*Eleanor*] [*Its*] Milly[*'s day at in the Grove" said Wilk*] wont be in much before six said Mary. "Its her day in the Grove."

The sisters sat <in silence> looking at the kettle. They were [*girls*] typical Pargiters. [*Th*] Without being exactly pretty, each [*was*] <had the> clear skin[*ned,*] & the dark eyes of the family; & [*the b*] each [*was endowed with*] a [*beau*] the thick & abundant hair; but whereas Milly's hair was dark, Mary's had the red tinge which had come in with the Daltons.

"Do learn to shut the door *quietly* Rose" said Milly [1 17] as her

* The chapter number is clearly fictitious. The text corresponds to that on p 8 of the Hogarth Press edition of *The Years* (Fifth Impression, 1975).

little sister rushed in. "And I think Nurse might have seen [*had*] that you had on a clean pinafore . . .

"It hasn't come back from the wash" said Rose.

"[*Thats*] <[*Heres*]> Bobby" said Mary, looking [*over her shoulder as the gate*] through the side window from which one could see the front steps. [*No*] In another moment [*the door*] there was the sound of a satchel flung down on the hall table, & Bobby Pargiter came in, smoothing his hair.

[*Run up & change your sho*] [*boo*] [*What about*] <Go &> wash[*ing*] your hands" said his sister severely. "You've plenty of time. The kettle isn't boiling yet."

"Blast the kettle" said Bobby, looking resentfully at it.

"Mama wouldn't like you to use language like that" said [*Elea*] Milly.

"The tray, Miss," said Parkins, opening the door.

Now who's going to take up Mama's tea?" said Milly. Not you, Rose — its too heavy. Let Bobby carry it; & you can go with him. But [*come down*] dont [*be long*] <stay>. The kettle [*is*] <will soon> —" She again applied her hair pin to the wick. . . . . .

(I skip the next few pages which describe how at last the kettle boiled; <[*about 5.30*]> [*& all the Pargiters child*] [*family sat down to tea.*] Mary, Milly Rose & Bobby [*all*] sat down to tea; & then, at about five thirty five in came Captain Pargiter, their father)

"Oh Papa!" said Milly, & Bobby who had been sitting in his father's arm chair scrambled out. The Captain [*was glowing*] sat <himself> down [*with that m*] [*single motion, as of one*] with that single movement that characterises elderly gentlemen of naval upbringing who now weigh well over twelve stone. Abel Pargiter was aging before his time. He <had [*kn*]> was a disappointed man, & the change from an active life at sea to the sedentary occupation of a retired naval officer was telling upon his spirits. He tended to brood over the past.

"Mama [*quite comfor*] <all> right?" he said, as his daughter handed him the [*specially large*] breakfast cup of old china — it had been his father's ⟨out of⟩ which he [1 18] always drank his afternoon tea. [*But it was*] rather for the form of the thing than for any [*pleasure*] ⟨liking⟩ he had for tea. The little veins about his nose indicated that he had quite lately taken one glass of sherry at the Club. [*He was a*] ⟨A⟩ fine judge of sherry, ⟨he restricted himself to one glass⟩ [*& like*] most fine judges of [*wine*] ⟨sherry⟩, despised tea. [*"Where's Eleanor?"*] And [*where is everybody?" he asked*] ⟨[*where have*]⟩ what[*s*] [*everybody*] ⟨have you all been⟩ up to? he asked; looking about him [*with the*] [*in that shrewd authoritative manner which*] ⟨with⟩ small shrewd authoritative eyes [*which his*] children [*admired,*] ⟨both⟩ respected & feared. One might take in Mama; but it was no use [*telling*] ⟨trying that on⟩ Papa [*a lie. And*] It was his habit to require a full account of his children's conduct. "Eleanor had her music lesson; & I went to Whiteleys —" Milly began, [*almost*] as if she were a child reciting a lesson. "Spending ⟨more⟩ money?" said her father sharply but not unkindly; "No Papa; I told you; they sent the wrong sheets. I took back the twill sheets, & I got unbleached linen instead. They are sending them. . .

And [*what about*] you Bobby?" said her father. "Bottom of the class as usual?" "Top!" said Bobby, [*who*] bursting out with the information which he had with the greatest difficulty restrained. "[*Well done, old chap*] ⟨Congratul⟩" said his father, extracting a handful of silver from his trouser pocket.

His children watched him with a curious mixture of feelings as he proceeded to select the [*sixpence which*] promised coin. Abel Pargiter had lost three fingers ⟨of the right hand⟩ in that affray off [*Cor with*] off the Coromandel Coast which had had (this has been described in volume three)* such momentous results. The muscles [*of the*] ⟨had⟩ shrunk; & his right hand resembled nothing so much as the [*claw*] shrivelled claw of an aged bird — [*a strange*] an appearance [*that contrasted*] strangely ⟨out of keeping⟩ with the ro-

* This sustains the pretense that we are in the 56th chapter.

bust & well developed appearance of his other limbs. Rose always looked at her father's right hand with a mixture of repulsion & awe. It frightened her. [*It was so horrid to look at. And yet, since*] Yet she could not keep her eyes off it. Her nurse had told her that her father had lost his fingers "fighting savages" and she connected it with the dagger that was fastened [1 19] [to] the wall above the dining room mantelpiece. [*She had a vision* [of] *her father, fighting for*] [*She worshipped her*] father for his courage; & yet [*she*] the sight of the shrivelled hand made her feel rather sick. <As> Captain Pargiter never alluded to the injury; & [*it would have been*] & always used his right hand, as if it were [*comp*] complete, [*by way of*] <partly in order to> disciplining the muscles, his children [*were*] <[*which*] were> unable to help him, & the selection of a particular new sixpence from a shoal of other coins was a matter of time & difficulty. "And Eleanor?" he asked, as he presented the sixpence to his son. [*She*] "Its her afternoon in the Grove' said Milly; but no sooner were the words spoken than the door opened & •{Eleanor & Harry came in together — They had indeed met in the street. While Harry explained to her father the reason why he had come home an hour earlier than usual — <[*old*]> Mr Parker [*had come into the office unexpectedly, &, saying that <as> everything had been*] & had said that as [*there was a*] it was impossible to post the China orders that night, it was useless for him to stay on — he might have to work overtime tomorrow — Eleanor took off her gloves, raised her veil, & gratefully accepted [*the*] <her [*half share of the*]> muffin which her sister had [*p*] reserved for her}• <She raised her veil, took off her gloves, & gratefully accepted the last tea cake which her sister had reserved for her.> She looked tired. She had been collecting rents for a philanthropic society in <among the poor of> Lissom Grove, & she had it [*rather*] on her conscience that she had hurried away [*w*] without actually inspecting [*the dropsi*] Mrs. Levy's dropsy. On the other hand she had seen [*old*] the running sore in Mrs. Pecks poisoned leg.

"Now Papa tell us what [*you've been up to*] [*doing*] <about your adventures>" said [*Mary*] Delia rather pertly. [*She was her father's favourite daughter &*] <She> [*could say*] <said> things to him that none of the others dared to. But [*it*] <her remark> was an unfortunate [one.]

"There[*'s not much doing for*] <arent many adventures for> me nowadays" said Abel Pargiter. "Not much doing for a [I 21] retired old fogy, on half pay"

[*His d*] [*Eleanor was really too tired to*] His daughters [*were*] [*racked their brains*] did their best to think of something to distract their father from his [*gri*] grievance. <But> As if he realised that he [had] been a little surly — Delia <also> was his favourite daughter — he [*pulled a letter from his pocket & said*] added "I [*met*] <ran into> old Blake at the Club[*. They want us*] by the way. [*Young Blake is*] Told me Roger is home again. [*They want us to come &*] [*Want me to*] Asked me to bring one of you to dinner. [*Think he said Thursday next*] — They'll write." Eleanor from her low chair by her sisters side [*could see*] saw a curious look cross Milly's face. Instinctively, she glanced at Delia. She knew [*instan*] as if the<y> [*words*] had spoken, what was passing through their minds. "[*Which of us is it to be?*] I want to go to dinner with the Blakes. [*I want to meet Roger.*] <Only one of us is asked.> Which of us is it to be?" [*From the*] Neither spoke, but from the hardness of Delia's lips & the tremor with which Milly moved a tea cup, unnecessarily, she was aware [*that the sisters would*] [*of the jealousy which was*] that each was acutely jealous of the other. They [*scarcely*] <It is true that neither of them> knew Roger Blake <save as the son of their parents old friends,> but he was a young man & in their circle young men were rare. But her father had finished his tea. <He set down his cup he told Bobby that it was high time he started his prep he wiped his moustache.>* He wiped his moustache with his bandanna handker-

* This insertion is written on I 20.

chief; & <he> rose [*"Well, girls <he said> I must be off to my den,*] [*he said."I'm off to my den. And . . . I suppose Mama would*] "Let me know when your mother's ready to see me" he said. "I'm off to my den" He stood for a moment, erect among them, a splendid figure of a man, still, & then, pinching his little daughter by the ear, & strode off to his own room. They all relaxed immediately. Eleanor poured herself out another cup of tea. <[*stretched her hand to the tea pot.*]> •{ [*But in a moment*] <as she did so> Captain Pargiter [*was back*] <returned>; Eleanor paused as if she had been caught in [*an*] some guilty act: [*ind*] [*She*] There was a look on their father's face that [*they all knew*] [*always alarmed them*] made them all feel guilty.

"Has anyone [*remembered to*] written to Harry this week?" [I 22] [*he demanded. The sisters looked at each other guiltily. Remember, one of you, to write to Harry* [*tod*] *tonight. He'll*] [*he said." She hoped that Milly would go to the Blakes*] }• It seemed to her that Milly [*was*] had the right to go to the Blakes party: Milly was the elder: but Delia was her father's favourite. Delia had the stronger will of the two. "Delia is a selfish little pig" Eleanor [*thought as she ref*] was thinking, when Rose, standing erect, in a way that was [*str*] oddly like her fathers, brushed the crumbs from her frock & [*said*] <demanded> "May I go to Lamleys?" Lamleys was the toy shop [*at the end of the*] [*of the*] in Abbotsford Road. <[*But*]> "Its much too late" said Eleanor <wait till tomorrow.> •{But Rose said that [*it*] <the shop> was open [*on Friday*] till seven. It was not quite half past six. "Well you can go if Uncle Edward had}•

Rose's face puckered. Owing to the fact that Nurse had [*had*] stayed so long [*in*] gossiping [*with*] at [*Bramleys. <Hardysings>*] <Hendersens> they had [*had to come the short way home that afternoon*] not been able to go round by Lamleys [*as Nurse*] had promised. [*&*] But Lamleys did not shut till seven. There was still time to buy the [*red*] squirt upon which she had set her heart. [*"Ask Bobby to go with you there" said Eleanor. It was impossible to wait till tomorrow.*] She must have the squirt that night in her bath. Uncle

Edward had given her a shilling.

"Well then, ask Bobby to go with you" said Eleanor realising [*that to wait, for a child of ten,*] how much the little girl cared. "But Bobby wont. [*Bo*] He's doing his lessons" said Rose. [*"Then ask Nurse" said Eleanor. All right. I'll ask Nurse" said Rose, moving towards the door. "You're on no account to go*] "Oh yes he will if you ask him nicely" said Eleanor. And if he wont, ask Nurse" Rose moved towards the door. "Anyhow you're not to go alone" said Eleanor, commandingly, as the door shut, [*because*] for though Abbotsford Place is only five minutes from Abercorn Terrace, [*it was*] it was not safe for a little girl of ten to go alone.

•{And now the sisters settled down in the lamplight [1 23] to enjoy perhaps the nicest moments in the day <Buses rumbled by. Hansom cabs jingled. The>. . . . But [*it was*] <they> were soon interrupted. As the clock struck seven, [*a*] the unmistakable sound of Morris's latch key — no two people [*open*] <use> a [*front door*] <latch key> in [*the same way*] — was heard at the door; & the girls all slightly re-arranged their postures as their brother came in. Morris Pargiter was [*perhaps*] the [*cleverest*] of the Pargiters. Rather to his father's dislike he had [*gone to the*] <adopted the> Bar <rather than the Church or the Navy for his profe> [*But already, though he was only twenty five,*] he [*was*] [*been*] had [*attracted favourable attention; & was*] had [*today received a brief marked twenty-five guineas. He was in high spirits.*] [*Very bus*] [*He told his sisters with*] & there was a}•

And now the three sisters were left alone, round the tea table. Eleanor put down her cup & leant back in her chair. How large the drawing room looked; how luxurious it seemed after [*Canning Street*] Lissom Grove! It was so nice <too> looking through at the trees in the back garden. The buds were just beginning. Of course the spring light did show up the shabbiness of the chair covers — But she was aware of some tension in the atmosphere. It was [*that*] <the> question of the dinner party at the Blakes. She did wish people wouldn't say "Bring one of your daughters." She wished they would say [*which daughter of them they wanted.*] bring Eleanor or Milly or Delia; as the case might be. "Well" said Delia abruptly, "I shall . . ." She got up as if she were going [*off*] somewhere. She stopped. It was not worth while [*beginning to practise*] getting out her fiddle. Besides, she disliked practising [*before*] <with> her sisters in [*the*] [*they*] the room. [*They*] [*Only yesterday she had*] [*Milly had*] [*they said, "One couldn't*] One had to [*go over*] <repeat> the same phrase <over> again & <over> again: <One could not learn it unless one did. Bobby called it 'the tune the old cow died of!'> Besides it was already half past six — There was only an hour before the dressing bell rang. She strolled to the window that looked out on <to> the street. [*There was nobody passing*] <Dark was falling>. The houses opposite were [*all exactly like*] had all the same little front gardens, the same steps the same pillars the same [*few*] bow windows. But they were growing dim. The lamps were being lit. Here came a hansom <jingling past> . . . was it going to stop? [*No, it*] [1 24] [*It was too late for callers.*] She had a momentary thrill. [*No it went on.*] No it went on. It stopped [*three doors down across the road*] <at the house next door>. "Somebody is calling on the Constables —" she said. [*M*] Milly came & stood beside her sister & they watched a young man in a top hat get out & stretch his hand up to pay the driver. "[*You mustn't*] <Dont> be caught looking —" said [*Elen*] Eleanor. For a moment the two girls stood at the window as the hansom jingled away. [*Abercorn*] The crocus's were out in the front garden. The almond trees & the privets were tipped with green< . >[*buds.*] A sudden gust of wind tore down the street blowing an old piece of paper in which meat had been wrapped along the pavement. Above the [*houses*] <roofs> was one of those red, quickly changing London sunsets which, [*reflected in the*] [*make*] [*cull out gold panels*] make the bedroom windows [*shine*] burn [*red &*] gold. There was a wildness in the spring evening which made it hard for the girls to settle [*to anything*] <down to any occupation>. [*Unlike Eleanor*]

They had had no exercise — except a short walk to Whiteleys & back <unlike Eleanor>.

"Oh my God!" said Delia suddenly, coming back into the drawing room. Eleanor, who was beginning to check the figures in her rent book, looked up startled <but not surprised>. Delia was the discontented one of the family. "Well —" she said putting her finger on the figure she had just reached <I really do believe, if you were> — Why dont you ask Papa to let you go to College?"

"[*Ask*] Papa . . . <with all Bobbys bills to pay>! ask Papa" Delia said derisively. And I dont want to go to *College.* I want to go [*abroad*] <Germany> to learn music —" Eleanor wrote £1.18.6 [*It in*] at the bottom of the column. <Germany—> that was hopeless of course. The door opened & Crosby came in. One by one she put all the cups, the plates, the knives & jam pots & the dishes of cake & bread & butter on a tray. She then stood the door open & put the tray on the hall table outside. She then came back [*& drew the curtains. Each*] [*The rings slid with a peculiar click*] [*with the large*] [*the lamps*] <carrying two lamps>. She then went to the windows & drew the curtains. [*The heavy curtains of* [1 25] *ruby plush*] <They> swung with a [*pec*] familiar click along the brass [*rod; & soon fell in massive folds,*] & soon the windows [*were covered with the massive folds*] were obscured by [*su*] sculptured folds of claret coloured plush. [*In*] A deep [*hush*] <silence> seemed to fall upon the room. <A paper boy cried in the next street.> The two lamps [*did little to*] made yellow pools of light upon the two drawing room tables. & [*Ele*] [*Delia took the poker & began to break up the coal.*] Eleanor, drawing [*herself*] her chair under [*the*] one of them finished her calculations.

"I [*must go*] <m going to> sit with Mama" she said.

"Look here [*Nell*] Eleanor, said Milly, "[*I'll do that*] You've been out all the afternoon. [*Sit & twiddle your thumbs. You deserve a rest. Besi*] I'll [*sit with*] <go up to nurse> her now. Or Papa said he would."

<"But> Papa fidgets her so" said Eleanor. [*"And she's*] [*"She*] <She

will> [*He gets so annoyed with her He doesnt mean to. And*] [*She's seen you already. You've been in & out all day. I could*] [*She will tell him all her*] I'll go."

Delia however, rose, &, saying, [*I never do anything for anybody*] <No; I'm the victim:> "Its my turn — I [*had*] cut my [*morning*] visit [*owing to*] [*sigh*] [*old*] after lunch," went off to <sit with her> mother.

"She did get two hours practising this afternoon" said Milly, [*as if to exculpate herself.*] [*justify the relief with which*] & [*the*] [*with this excuse, &*] as if to exculpate herself. The sisters had very little chance of [*private*] talking <alone> together, & [*this*] the opportunity which [*Delia*] had given them was not to be [*rejected*] refused.

"She's not a bad sort, really, Delia" said Milly.

What about Mama today? said Eleanor.

Oh its the night nurse now, said Milly. Mama [*is actually convinced*] <swears> [*that she*] <saw her> steal[*s*] the sugar. She says she can see her shadow on the wall. I told Dr. [blank space] I [*offered to have the*] suggested moving the screen — [1 26] Nurse was quite nice about it. People get these fancies <when theyre ill>, she said. And it may go on for months & months & months said Eleanor.

[*But*] <And> sometimes she seems quite herself" said Milly. She was telling me today about [*her childhood. You know, the old stories*] when they were children — you know, the old stories. [*But*]

•{"If only one could keep her off the present" said Eleanor. [*You cant take her in a*] <Its one everlasting worry.> [*We must see <do something> about*] these shadows. [*We might rig something up."*] But one begins to know those old stories by heart — [*how*] Did Dr. Champin come? Nothi

"[*How Uncle John*] How Uncle John —

[*"I daresay Harry will write tonight she likes that."*] The sisters were interrupted by the sound of a latch key in the front door.

"[*Morris" said*] [*Oh thats*] <Now theres> Morris!" said Milly irritably. "One never has a moment to oneself in this house." She was slightly jealous of her sisters affection for Morris. When he came in, she would get up< . > [*& go.*] She would go off & see whether she could get a hot bath. She passed Morris as he came in; & he took her seat by the fire.}●

Morris Pargiter the*

Thats what worries her"

They were silent for a moment, looking at the fire.

"I was thinking that the poor enjoy their lives more than we do" said Eleanor [*suddenly.*] at [*length.*] <last>

●{ [*"The Levys, Old Mrs. Levy? said Milly.*] [*Your old friend, Mrs. Levy?*] <Oh [*do tell me about the Levys*]>" [*said*] Milly,—

Eleanor's [*friendship*] relations with this old Jewess, [*& the*] [*whose sayings were*] amused her [I 27] [*sisters*] —— How [*was your old Jewess*] <were the Jews> today?" said Milly.

[*"The Levys?" said Milly rather absent mindedly*] [*Old Mrs*] <the> Levy" said Milly absent mindedly <while thinking of> [*Eleanor*] [*The slum in*] [*'Is she alive still?*]}● [*I love hearing*] <do tell me> about the Levys" she added <brightly>. [*It was true.*] Eleanor's relations with 'the poor' were [*part of*] [*one of the*] amused her family. The Levys & the Gages & the Zwarts — George, [*Rislin*] who had [*only*] six toes on each foot — Mabel, & her tubercular glands — [*played*] their sayings & doings were [*often*] discussed by the Pargiters: as if they were in a book; [*but Eleanor was the only one who ever saw them;*] [*though*] [*but, as Morris complained, one was*] & it was a family joke that it was unsafe to leave a pair of old trousers in one's cupboard <press>; Eleanor gave them to [*the Ge*] <Bert> Zwinglers. [*Morris maintained that*] [*t*] <T>he whole of Lisson Grove was dressed in his old trousers.

●{ [*"They enjoy life more than we do"*] said Eleanor

"She [*hadn't paid*] <[*had*]got> her rent for a wonder" said Eleanor.}●

* Here, in space left for several lines, is written in pencil: "I was thinking that the poor enjoy their lives more than we do —".

How they manage it, heaven only knows." She saw the [*little pile of*] coins that Mrs Levy had piled up — six shillings & sixpence — [*in the corner*] on the mantelpiece under the clock. Lily had helped her this week. [*Lily<'s> came in while I was there.*] <Lily acts> [*very smart nowadays. What an*] She came in while I was there. I suppose its being Jews. [*Shes rather striking in a way — fat*] [*sham pearls sham emeralds*] — they <do> love finery [*so*]. [*She did look too extraordinary — like a sort of gipsy*] <that necklace — & an ostrich feather>—Emeralds as big as hen's eggs—[*I rather think she*] <Im not sure she dont> paint[*s*], <too.> [*She's an awfully good sort though*] You cant get away under an hour when they start talking. All about loathesome diseases? said Milly. Oh [*everything*] <a good deal that> comes in," said Eleanor. "Everything's discussed [*quite openly. Mrs Levy's funeral for instance.*] Imagine discussing how one was going to be buried — <when one's still alive."> She made Lily show me the nightgown. They've got it all [*ready*] put away. And she's going [128] to have a proper grave, all to herself. [*Isaac has*] promised her that. And "some little token" for them thats been good to me" — [*I wish I could remembers her words*]! — (I'm afraid [*on the other hand*] <I'm to have the> & <As> them "thats ridden in the coaches [*& seen me*] (I wish I cd remember her words) when I was a widder [*woman*] <a> wrangling & <a> mangling ([*her hands*] <are like great white roots)> with six little children & [*the father*] sitting [*idle*] <a husband [*arching up in*] <green in> his grave> — <& I've seen them> [*them thats passed by*] riding in their coaches —' (thats the rich brother, who made a fortune out of pills) . . . But what [*to*] is to be, has to be. [*I envies nobody. I grudges nothing.*] I dont ask your charity I said." •{(—— [*They are,*] of course, <theyre> extraordinarily good to each other — [*the poor.*] While I was there at least three neighbors looked in. [*I wish I could remember her words.*] }•

[*Is Lily what you might call — I mean is she*]

Eleanor broke off. "I cant [*get*] <remember> the words [*right*] <right>. [*Its rather like the Bible.*] And then Lily [*says*] <spoke

[*to me*]> quite [*openly,*] <briskly,&> Ma cant last much longer. [*It's*] [*Her hearts nothing but wind & water. Lily makes button holes.*] The little picture of the woman in Canning Street Lissom Grove hung for a moment before the sisters. Then [*Eleanor said*] Milly said, They looked at it with a curious mixture of feelings. Then "Suppose [*we were*] [*one*] <you> could [*be*] <do> what [*one*] <you> liked, — [*I know what I should do" said Eleanor.*] What would you be? "I shouldnt live like this, said Eleanor, looking round the room — •{& glancing, quickly, at the oil portrait of her mother — when she was young, that hung over the [*fireplace,*] mantelpiece.}•

"[*I think*] I should take a room, somewhere [*in quite*] <but in> a poor neighborhood: & [*& then*] I [*should get to know the people*]; & [*then*] I['d] pull down all these awful [*little*] slums & — well, start things fresh, [*in a better system.*] — if I had the money"

"I suppose most [*sisters*] <people> make plans" said [*Elean*] Milly. And then they marry. [*D'you*] suppose we shall marry! Eleanor leant back in her chair & looked at the portrait of her mother as a young woman that hung over the mantelpiece. She was all in white: she held a posy: it was a silly simpering picture. Her mother [I 29] had never been beautiful, but she had had a [*nice*] <quiet>, [*sensible kindly*] <kind> face, until [*illness —*] her illness [— *Brights disease* <*had*>] overcame her, which the artist had smoothed * & refined into insipidity.

'What is to be, has to be' she said, quoting Mrs Levy. [*She was thinking of the Blakes party. She would never speak openly, even*] It was curious [*that though the sisters were*] how much reticence <for all this> existed between the sisters. Eleanor knew that Milly was 'attracted' by Roger Blake: [*She knew that she*] But she could not [*say to her straight out "Go*] discuss it with her. [*She could not*] She did not even know [*how far*] <what> Milly, who was nineteen, knew about marriage. [*There were things about*] Lisson Grove

* There is a caret here, but nothing is indicated for insertion.

[*that*] <had taught> Eleanor [*never told her family*] <a great deal about marriage:> [*Mrs. Levy had*] [*She*] <but she> [*could never forget*] <discuss it with her family> . . .

"Oh there's Morris!" exclaimed Milly irritably. We never get a moment alone in this house." She jumped up as her brother came in. It was not merely that she liked talking to her sister. [*She*] Without admitting it she was jealous of their [*relationship*] affection. Eleanor, Morris, had always been devoted to each other. "I shall try & [*seize a hot*] <make an atem> <get into the> bath" [*she*] Milly said, passing him in the door. [*There was always*] "Getting into the bath" was a feat that required [*some skill*] <[*both*]> an unusual combination of [*skill,*] force, skill, & luck. <For a> There was only one bathroom at 56 Abercorn Terrace; [*The*] [*There might be*] somebody else [*in the bath. She*] was likely to be there. [*They might have taken all the hot water. As can be*] <[*First*]> Since the supply <of hot water> depended, to some extent, upon the [*good*] temper of the cook, & this, with nurses in the house, <who> requir[*ing*] to have their meals served separately on trays, •{ [*varied from day to day,*] fluctuated, [*violent un*] from day to day, [*Getting*] it was [*more their*] essential to get into the bath first<.> [, *& this*] [*Few people succeeded; feeling ran high; the*] needless to say, feeling ran high; the [*water*] }• Therefore it was essential, not merely to get into the bath, but to get into the bath first. [*Needless to say, this was a*] That this was difficult [I 30] [*that it roused the passions; that*]

Moreover 'the children', had a first claim; & thus, though Milly [*started upstairs*] started upstairs, she did not [*think of*] [*get her sponge, or*] begin to undress <rush in brush in hand> [*before*] <until> she had [*delivered*] rattled <at> the bath room door; found it locked; & [*commanded*] told her brother [*that he*] to jump out at once. [*The glass*] <?steaming> pane of frosted glass [*was*] in the bathroom door was steaming. The water had been hot; but would it be hot by the time she got there? [*Would Bobby*] One could only fling on a dressing gown & hope for the best.

Morris Pargiter came in & sat down [*by his sister*] ⟨in Milly's chair⟩. He was the eldest of the Pargiters; ●{ [*he was at the Bar; & ha had*] & was at the Bar. [*⟨But⟩ No brief had yet come his way, & as he had*] [*as yet no briefs had come his way, & as he had*] [*as yet no briefs had come his way, & the*] [*But as no briefs had*] [*This was*] by his own choice, & ⟨rather⟩ against his father's [*will*].}● — Rather against his father's will he [*was read*] [had] gone to the Bar — ⟨&⟩ [*He*] was ⟨now⟩ devilling for [*Mr.*] Mr. Sanders Curry KC: [*but*] [*He looked*] [*But*] No briefs had yet come his way. Would he ever be able to support himself? [*Would he*] Had he [*done*] been a fool to refuse Uncle [*Joseph's*] ⟨Sam's⟩ offer of a post in the family business? [*But he detested business, & he loved the law.*] These thoughts worried him⟨.⟩ [*& made him look a*] He looked a little jaded already — he was no longer [*the*] ⟨a⟩ boy [*that Eleanor had*] with a boy's [*careless high spirits*] ⟨careless⟩ self-confidence. ⟨But⟩ Eleanor was convinced that he would succeed — ⟨she was sure he was a born lawyer — ⟩ [*She*] had pleaded for him with her father. ⟨Anyhow he [*too*] loathed the business & loved the bar.⟩ [*Of course he would mature*] [*She had*] Morris [*could never*] [*did not get on with his father.*] [*Eleanor had*] [*could*] [*was never at ease*] ⟨did not get on⟩ with his father.

It [*was Eleanor who had bearded the Captain & at last won the day, & forced him, at last to agree.*] [*So that*] ⟨So she⟩ knew therefore [*Eleanor*] they were [*conspirators*] ⟨in league together⟩, as they had always been[,] [*against the others: only*] ⟨as children⟩ When Morris went to school Eleanor took his old monkey to bed with her. So now they sat over the fire, & Morris [space] [1 31] how he had been hanging about in Court most of the day. [*He was watching a case*] ⟨today⟩ [*The*] Evans case was still going on.

"About the Right of way?" said Eleanor. [*Which*] ⟨Who⟩ is going to win?" But Morris, though the Evans Case raised some very interesting points, did not want to [*talk about*] ⟨discuss⟩ [*law cases*] law with his sister. [*Dear old Eleanor got*] He [*had tried*] to explain;

but "The female" as he put it, "hasn't got a legal mind." [*She didn't see the point*] [*Eleanor muddled things up when* [*sh*] *he tried to explain. She didn't listen.*] He had tried to explain cases to Eleanor; but she muddled things up. — <so he evaded the Evans Case;> [*Perhaps*] she did not attend to what he said. So they talked <generally> about people; about [*what he had*] where he had lunched; about [*Curry's temper*] <[*San*] old Sanders & his lease>; about [*Jigsen*] the clerks; about. . . . [*prospects in general*] <& how Mama was>. •{Lord, theres the dressing bell, said Eleanor, picking up her gloves. "No chance of a bath[, *I suppose? said Morris*]."}• — You dont think I've been an awful fool about the Bar, do you Eleanor" [*he*] said[,] Morris [*stretching himself out*] <at last> — "I [*mean — Papa has an awful lot of expenses.*] with all this illness, & Harry at Oxford, & Bobby [*going to pay fcr.*] <to be paid for:> Papa must find [*things*] it a<n> [*bit of a*] <awful> strain: "I dont see [*when*] <how> I'm <ever> going to be able to support you."

[*My dear Morris, said Eleanor, I*]

[*"My dear Morris" said Eleanor,*] "Oh you'll be Lord Chancellor one of these days["] No doubt about it" said Eleanor; — feeling perfect confidence [*that*] <in> her brother though, even as she spoke, she [*suspected*] <knew> that she had once more forgotten whether he was [*the*] Common Law [*side*] or Chancery: [*how*] whether she ought not to have said Lord Chief Justice, instead of Lord Chancellor. •{ [*She never bothered him to tell her*] <He was giving up telling her> about [*his cases*] now;}• [*but*] <because> she often wished that she had been better educated. [*Morris was giving up talking to her about his cases.*] [*They*] <she feared> the law was so very difficult to follow. [*Morris was giving up talking to her about his cases.*] And so Morris was giving up telling her about his cases; [132] & she kept back a good deal about the Levys. [*It was a great pity*] Morris called them 'the poor' too. <More a pity, for> They had been such friends when they were children — they had shared everything — she could remember bringing him back a piece of toffee in a pocket handkerchief.

"Lord thats the dressing bell" said Morris, getting up. "I suppose there's no chance of a bath."

[I 34*]

[SECOND ESSAY]

October 23rd [1932]

This then is what happened at 56 Abercorn Terrace on March 16th 1880 — a long time ago, you will say — over fifty years ago. That is more than fifty years ago; and, as you will see from this sketch, things have changed very greatly. Those young women, Milly, Delia, and Eleanor rouse pity and contempt in you. I have only been able to give an outline of them. They are young and healthy, and they have nothing to do but change the sheets at Whiteleys and peep behind the blinds at young men going to call next door.

Why, you may ask, did they not go to College? But, if you think for a moment, you will remember that the women's colleges were only just in existence; there was a great prejudice moreover against them. Walter Bagehot, for instance, when he was asked to help in founding Girton, replied [sentence unfinished].† Captain Pargiter was not an intellectual man like Bagehot [*; but he respected them*] but he would have agreed with him that a girl's place was the home. Even if Delia, who was his favourite, had gone to him in his study and helped him with his stamps and somehow wheedled him into giving his consent, still there would have been the money [*difficulty*]. With three sons to educate, Captain Pargiter might reasonably have said, "My dear, I would if I could — but just look at these bills!" Delia [I 35] was not one of those forcible characters who get their own way at the expense of other people's feelings. She would have

* Manuscript note on facing page (I 33): "What is impractical, because the Novel of fact depends for its [*solid*] value upon a great many facts — [*War & Peace is a very long*] Think how long War & Peace is — & never an image in the whole book — images belong to the Novel of Vision — as you will see, if you will help me cultivate your imagination." Compare "November 5th" below (I 41).

† See below, footnote reference to Bagehot (I 41).

been more interesting ⟨if⟩ she [had] been able to say, "If you cut down Harry's allowance, if you gave up sending Bobby to Eton, but send him to a cheaper school, which is just as good, there would be enough for me to go to College — or to Germany — where I shall be taught music properly." But neither Harry nor Bobby would have liked her; and Delia was one of those people who like being liked. That was one of the reasons, then, why the Pargiter sisters stayed at home in 1880, and had violin lessons from Signor Morelli, a sad little man with great pouches under his eyes, who lived in Maida Vale and supported his old mother, not, as he had once hoped, by his glorious operas — they were never played — but by teaching young ladies their violin. How he hated teaching young ladies the violin. It was sheer waste of time. "They don't practise — they take up a violin, and they put it down," he said, in Italian, to his old mother, as they twisted the maccaroni round their forks, after these dreadful lessons. The Signora was an excellent cook. "How is it you women can be so musical; and yet, why is it that no woman has ever been a great composer?" Giuseppe would ask when the Signora had played him into a good temper after the meal. She played admirably.

Perhaps Delia was right; perhaps one must go to Germany and be taught, if one wants to write music seriously. [136] Even painting *which seems so simple an art, needs a room with a north light and models. Milly had a turn for painting. But though it would have been possible for her to go to the Slade (the Slade was opened to women in 18—), painting at the Slade meant painting from the nude. Without going so far as his father (Canon Pargiter, 1800–1865) who positively forbade his daughter, Caroline, from painting, because it was unthinkable that a girl ⟨an English lady⟩ should see a naked

*A cancelled passage here reads: "Perhaps the practice of any art requires, at least during adolescence, a good deal of hard work, & a room of one's own — a quiet room, if you are a musician; a room with a northern light if you are a painter. Milly Pargiter, whom you are rather inclined to despise, for all her interest in the young man next door, and her rather irritating habit of bringing the conversation round, indirectly, to the subject of marriage, was very fond of painting."

man, Captain Pargiter did not like the idea. So that Milly joined a sketching club which went for expeditions in the summer — and painted flowers in her bedroom. Her most successful sketch — of a cottage in Surrey — was hung in the dining room over the mantelpiece under the dagger.

But we do not want to spend too much time over these details. In reading a novel, if it is a novel of any value, we must now and again shut one eye to the detail, and try to realise the structure; that is, the conviction which, though never explicitly stated, is yet always there, in a novel of any merit, controlling the apparently inevitable [I 37] succession. It is the same, with obvious differences, in life.

Now of the scenes. In considering the life of the Pargiters, it is well from time to time to ask ourselves, What convictions lay beneath them? If we shut our eyes to the detail — how Crosby came in with the tea cake; how Eleanor took off her gloves and blew into her fingers; and so on — we shall find certain principles underlying that particular scene and controlling it, so that it [is] not a succession of unrelated events. Nor are those principles so very deeply hidden — one is money; the other is love. The Pargiters were well off, compared with many people. Captain Pargiter had inherited some fifteen hundred a year from his father, the Canon. His wife, Rose Dalton, had brought him eight or nine hundred more, and he had his pension as a retired Navy officer. Therefore, the money principle did not interfere violently when they had tea — servants waited on them; there was cake and tea cake and bread and butter; the Captain could quite afford to indulge his hobby for collecting stamps; and the sons were given educations which must have cost from start to finish round about three thousand pounds each. Mary Kingsley, who was brought up in much the same way, says that her brother's education cost £2000; but counting school and college fees at £300 a year, and reckoning that the Pargiters went to school when they were eleven, and stayed at college till they were 21, that makes a sum of £3000 for each boy; nine thousand for the three of them.

The girls, of course, cost less; but it is difficult to say exactly what the cost of their education was. "I don't know," Mary Kingsley wrote, "if I ever revealed to you the fact that being allowed to learn German was *all* the paid-for education I ever had." [I 38] But the Pargiters had violin lessons and sketching lessons; and though they never went to school or had a governess, they attended classes at Bedford College. Thus their education may well have cost Captain Pargiter fifty pounds a year each; or two hundred a year for the four of them. But then there were allowances. Morris had to have an allowance while he was devilling for Sanders Curry, Q.C. It may have been round about a hundred and fifty a year. And the girls had to have pin money for clothes and purses. Perhaps they had thirty or forty pounds a year. Thus, although they lived very comfortably in Abercorn Terrace, money was an active agent in their lives and asserted itself; money made itself felt. It was a nuisance, for example, having only one bathroom. Morris could not possibly afford to go to Italy for the long vacation. The girls had to spend an absurd amount of time, if they were to dress decently — and their father liked them to — going to sales, picking up cheap lengths; visiting Miss Edwards, the small dressmaker, who could cut out quite well, but one had to stand over her.

Thus the money principle did have its effect upon the Pargiter children; and even more, of course, upon Captain Pargiter himself. The money belonged entirely to him. He was, as it happened, a good man of business; and amused himself a good deal of the time, now that he was retired, in following the money market and consulting his brokers. But the fact that the money was entirely his, [I 39] that none of his sons and daughters could take up a profession or marry without asking his consent, had its effect on him — gave him a position of great power and responsibility. And though he was a just man, and held his money in trust for his children, it was inevitable that there should be occasional discontent when he refused some request, and [there was] the temptation to get round him; and that being accustomed to command as he was, he should not only enjoy the exercise of power, but tend, as time went on, to be a little secretive about the exact amount of his income. His children never knew exactly how rich or poor he was. His income varied with his mood.

Love was, of course, the other power that lay beneath the surface of the Pargiter family and helped to control their lives. But a glance at the tea party scene is enough to show that love is not one simple emotion; nor do we always recognise [it] when we see it. Several kinds of love existed at 56 Abercorn Terrace on the evening of March 17th 1880. Captain Pargiter loved his children. But his love for them was different, naturally, from their love for him. His love had a mixture of pride and protection; he looked forward to the time when, grown old himself, his sons would be distinguished men — he was proud of being a Pargiter — and his daughters, married, all save one perhaps who would live with him, brought their babies to blow open his old gold watch, and hunt for half crowns hidden behind ornaments, or buried in other out-of-the-way spots. He loved games with his children. That again was a strong element in the love his children had for him. They always remembered his games, when he was home on leave, [or] at one of those seaside [140] houses with large gardens that Mama would take in a hurry when she knew there was a chance of his being with them. Mama was rather worried and bothered, and nagged about their clothes; but Papa never bothered. He took them sailing and fishing, threw them into the sea; made them run races; taught them how to rig boats, how to build wigwams. Even now, they loved him because of the games he had played in the summer holidays years ago. Then Delia loved Eleanor in one way — frankly, rather casually; and Milly loved her in another — obsequiously, rather dependently. And Bobby, who was twelve, had a deep but completely concealed passion for Miss Miriam Parish. She was a friend of Eleanor's, and rather plain, and rather quiet. But Bobby thought her so intoxicatingly lovely that when she came to tea, to talk about Lisson Grove and the Levys, he would secrete himself in the hall, and get possession of her umbrella, or of her mackintosh — she almost always left something, if only a string bag, in the hall — so that when she came out, and looked for it, he would step forward in a casual way, carrying the umbrella and say, "Is this what you're looking for?" and then she had to thank him.

Eleanor again loved Morris, more perhaps than she loved anybody; and differently. He was her elder brother; the grown man looked up to, the Lord Chancellor, or Lord Chief Justice whom she [*respected*] literally, devotedly; but he was also the little boy who used to come to her and say that everybody liked Ned better than they liked him; and how he hated Papa; and how beastly the chaps were at school — except the Parrys. And then he [I 41] would tell her all about Hugh and Dick until Eleanor felt convinced that they were practically the same as Wellington and Nelson — those young little boys who were now something in Lloyds.

November 5th [1932]

This scene in the Pargiter drawing room, on the 16th [of] March 1880, depends, of course, for its effectiveness largely upon the degree of truth — truth of fact, as distinct from truth of vision — which it contains. Hence perhaps it may be advisable to dwell for a moment — not too much upon the jingling of hansom bells, and the shaded lamps which were as familiar in 1880, as the hoot of cars and the clarity of electric light are to us, but upon the more important differences which such a scene, though at such a place only some fifty years ago, reveals. That three healthy girls should be sitting round a tea table with nothing better to do than to change the sheets at Whiteleys and peep behind the blinds at young men who happen to be calling next door may seem incredible. And yet the facts drawn from life seem to support that picture. There were colleges for women in existence — Girton was opened in 1873 — and Eleanor, Milly, and Delia might therefore have gone either to Girton or to Newnham or to Somerville. But there was a certain prejudice against women's colleges. [Blank space],* Bagehot wrote, for example — which might well have deterred girls themselves from going, and have influenced a man like Colonel Pargiter, though he was no more intellectual than [1 42] any officers of respectable attainments usually are. Why then did they not play games, if it was on a fine spring day? But in 1880 women played very few games. "I should have been of little use in games, but we had no games," writes a distinguished lady who was at school in the eighties. True, there was, it appears, and had been for some time, what was called "Physical Education." But this meant "dancing and the study of deportment (i.e. of graceful manner and the proper way to behave in society)." Exercise at school was "limited to walking round the garden wearing a black board." The black board was "a wooden bar about 2 feet 6 inches long. . ." and you walked round the garden with the black board placed across the shoulder blades, "and held in the hands, palms forward at the level of the shoulders" — a game that was salutary, one might suppose, rather than enjoyable.

Delia and Milly might have taken music and their painting seriously. On the other hand, perhaps. . . . Delia had 2 [lessons], and the comment of that sad little man used to be, as he ate his evening meal with his old mother in Maida Vale, "Bah—" (he spoke in Italian) "What is the use of my giving lessons."

Morris again loved Eleanor, perhaps more deeply than he loved anyone. But his love for her was both dependent — he needed her sympathy in many ways — and he was her champion. He would always defend her; which led him, of course, to look upon John Lowry,

* Woolf apparently left the blank space for a quotation from Walter Bagehot, one with a deterrent effect on women's ambition to go to college. In *Three Guineas*, chapter 1 note 23, she gives an extract "from a letter from Walter Bagehot to Emily Davies, who had asked his help in founding Girton," which begins: "I assure you I am not an enemy of women. I am very favourable to their employment as *labourers* or in other *menial* capacity. I have, however, doubts as to the likelihood of their succeeding in business as capitalists. I am sure the nerves of most women would break down under the anxiety, and that most of them are utterly destitute of the disciplined reticence necessary to every sort of co-operation."

when he came to visit them of a Sunday, rather [143] with an hostility, a jealousy, which he had never felt when they were boys. So, too, Milly's love for Morris was always diminished and checked by her jealousy of Eleanor's peculiar affection for him. It was with some bitterness that she went off to try and get into the bath that evening leaving Morris, as she knew he would, to settle into her armchair and talk to Eleanor. They both wished her to leave them alone.

(But besides these kinds of love, each of which is susceptible of infinite analysis, there [was] another kind of love.) Also there was Rose's love for her father — a love so implicit and awe-stricken — she thought of her father as of a god who was infallible and omnipotent, that her love was more like that of a savage for the God of Sun and Thunder — and perhaps anthropologists would do well to study children's passions when they want to understand the primitive emotions — than it was like Morris's feeling for his sister, or the Colonel's for his wife.

But besides these kinds of love, each, of course, susceptible of infinitely further analysis, another kind of love was present that evening in the Pargiters' drawing room: a different kind of love. It was not for a sister or for a son; it was not for any person in particular: it was the feeling that came to Delia and Milly when the Colonel told them of the Burke's dinner party, and mentioned Hugh. They felt something of the same emotion again when they peeped behind the curtain and saw the young man in a top hat get out of the hansom cab two doors down the street. [144] The emotion was so generalised that the object of it [was] scarcely wanted. The thought or the presence of someone of the other sex had the power to quicken in each of them a sense of something outside herself, that was unknown, exciting, and that stimulated in her the consciousness of her [*own*] body. It also roused a certain hostility: Delia felt that Milly, Milly that Delia, was a rival who would intercept this excitement, this stimulus; and the thoughts of each sister at once went to her personal appearance, and to her clothes. Delia remembered with a start of joy that Miss

Edwards had just sent back her pink silk evening dress: she was glad that in the quarterly conclave about clothes, Milly had plumped for a new cloak, and had decided to wear her old evening dress another season. And both, as they stood at the window, had seen a woman pass, pushing a perambulator. The sight of the baby had stirred in each quite a different emotion. Milly had felt a curious, though quite unanalysed, desire to look at the baby, to hold it, to feel its body, to press her lips to the nape of its neck; whereas Delia had felt, also without being fully conscious of it, a vague uneasiness, as if some emotion were expected of her which, for some reason, some vaguely discreditable reason, she did not feel; and then, instead of following the perambulator, as her sister did, with her eyes, she turned and came back abruptly into the room, to exclaim a moment later, "O my God," as the thought struck her that she would never be allowed to go to Germany and study music.

[1 45] There were all these kinds of love then, openly or secretly, in existence, in the Pargiter drawing room on the evening of March 16th 1880; and, since the drawing room of 56 Abercorn Terrace was, after all, only a small space artificially partitioned off from the rest of London, it is probable that the same forces existed presumably outside; and must also be taken into account by anyone who should wish to estimate the forces at work in the Pargiter family on that particular evening. When Eleanor, for example, warned her sister, "Don't be caught looking," she was at once alluding [to the] fact that a young man was on the pavement two doors down; and that he was, because of his sex, exciting a certain interest in her sisters; and she was assuming, as one assumes a fact well known to *every one*, that the girls must hide their interest in the young man.

Nothing perhaps influenced the lives of the Pargiters in March 1880 more powerfully and more completely than the principle of that love which — to distinguish it from the different loves of the drawing room — may be called street love, common love, love in general. This love affected the lives of the girls far more strongly than it affected the lives of their brothers. Eleanor and Milly and Delia could not possibly go for a walk alone — save in the streets round about Abercorn Terrace, and then only between the hours of eight-thirty and sunset. An exception might be made in favour of Eleanor, when she went to Lisson [1 46] Grove; but even she, whose mission was charitable, was expected either to take a cab, or to get one of the girls at the Settlement to see her into the omnibus, if she went to a meeting or concert after dark. For any of them to walk in the West End even by day was out of the question. Bond Street was as impassable, save with their mother, as any swamp alive with crocodiles. The Burlington Arcade was nothing but a fever-stricken den as far as they were concerned. To be seen alone in Piccadilly was equivalent to walking up Abercorn Terrace in a dressing gown carrying a bath sponge. A large radius of the West End indeed was closed to them, whether by day or by night, unless they went with a brother or their mother; and even the hansom cab, in which they were forced to make their transit of the dangerous area, had to have both flaps of its door shut.

The Pargiters, of course, though some of their cousins had married earls, and some were little shopkeepers up in Yorkshire, occupied a middle station, and were free to walk about Abercorn Terrace alone; whereas some of their distant relations were in the dismal predicament described by a Lady Lovelace "as being unable to leave the house on a summer day. How many a long dull summer afternoon have I passed immured indoors because there was no room for me in the family carriage and no lady's maid who had time to walk out with me. We lived," Lady Lovelace continues, "near St. James's Street and all the clubs, so that for my sisters and me to go out alone into the streets would have been to defy the social taboo in its severest form." But there were, as she remembers, "quiet squares [1 47] and terraces in the outlying districts where young girls could at least go about in pairs." Happily for the Pargiters, Abercorn Terrace came under this heading, and they could walk there alone — at any rate between the hours of nine-thirty and sunset.

Still, the influence of this street or common love was felt at every turn — it affected their liberty; it affected their purses; and since their mother was an invalid, it greatly diminished their chances of meeting friends, since it was impossible to go to a party without a chaperon. And though friends were very kind, it was impossible always to make sure that an elderly lady would be able to go with them to a dance. Inevitably, too, the prevalence of this form of love, and the necessity of escaping it, affected them mentally, as well as physically. They did sometimes walk down Bond Street alone; they had peeped into the Burlington Arcade; and they had lied to both their parents quite often about it. More profoundly, they lied to each other, to themselves. Both Delia and Milly blushed with a peculiar shame when Eleanor said "Don't be caught looking" — they wanted to look at the young man; they knew it was wrong to look; they did look; they were caught looking; they disliked being caught; they were ashamed, indignant, confused — all in one — and the feeling, since it was never exposed, save by a blush, or a giggle, wriggled deep down into their minds, and sometimes woke them in the middle of the night with curious sensations, unpleasant dreams, that seemed all to come from this one fact — that Abercorn Terrace was besieged on all sides by what may be called street love, common love, and general love: a love that seemed different from the other loves inside the drawing room.

[1 48] But so complex and important an emotion can scarcely be analysed effectively. Perhaps a quotation from the novel may help to bring the scene into a better perspective. Rose, it may be remembered, the little girl of ten, had asked Eleanor if she might go round to Lamleys and buy a toy after tea. Eleanor had said she might go if she could get Bobby to go with her. "You're not to go alone," she had warned her, as the child left the room.

[SECOND CHAPTER]

Rose shut the drawing room door behind her, & went slowly upstairs. She considered the matter, as she went. [*Nurse would have got out her sewing in the day nursery;*] She was set upon getting the fleet of ducks & swans to swim in her bath tonight. That was of prime importance. They might be sold if she waited till tomorrow — anyhow she could not possibly wait — She wanted them now, this instant. She had a battleship & a three masted clipper: she must have the ducks & the swans to float with them. Nurse always allowed her five minutes play in the bath every night, while she folded up the clothes. And then Rose swirled the water about in great waves. [*She*] The vision of the swans & ducks riding up & down among the ships was overwhelmingly attractive. She [*opened the*] went into the day nursery first. Nurse was sitting under a green shaded lamp, buzzing round the wheel of the sewing machine. Mrs. C. was in the basket chair by the fire place. Mrs. C. (her real name was unknown; but she was a nurses great friend, & used to come from Shepherds Bush [1 49] about twice a week, with the washing or something;) & [*then*] Mrs. C. was still sipping her tea. It was quite useless to ask Nurse to come out again to Lamley's. She would [*take*] ⟨nip⟩ a [*pin out of her mouth*] ⟨piece of cotton between her front teeth⟩ & say she had "a bone in her leg." [*Rose therefore said she was just going to get her "Run*] ⟨As it was Nurse looked up & said, Now Rosie, go [*&*]⟩ along & fetch your sewing [" *Nurse remarked;* "] You'll never be done ⟨in time⟩ for [*Mamas*] ⟨Papa's⟩ birthday at this rate." Rose was embroidering a [*long*] boot bag for Papa's birthday. She was embroidering a design drawn by Milly of wild roses in red and green cotton. She pretended that she had left her workbox downstairs ⟨left the nursery⟩. Next she went to the school room, on the landing below & very cautiously opened the door. Bobby considered that he had a right to the school room between tea & dinner — indeed, he was seeking to establish a right to keep all his cabinets there — his egg cabinet, & his butterfly & moth cabinets; <& was secretly determined to claim it for his own room. [*thu*]> — [*but getting*] the room was [*not*] nominally still a common sitting room for them all, — [*it required &*] Thus Rose entered apologetically, for since she was the youngest, she was supposed to keep to the day nursery, especially [*now*] after tea when Bobby had his prep. to do.

Bobby was sitting at a bare kitchen table under a lamp that had no shade at all, because it was always being broken. [*He*] The table was littered with exercise papers; [*&*] there was one great book open in front of him, and there was a little book [*on*] in front of him; & there was a little book [*on*] in front of it; & Bobby was covering the page of the little book with his right hand: & was murmuring something in [*an*] <a singsong> undertone. In fact he was learning some [*Greek*] lines [*by heart*] [*of Latin*] <in Greek by heart> [*Rose interrupted him. He fixed hi*] He looked strained & flushed. Rose interrupted him.

"Blast you, Rose!" he exclaimed, thumping his fist on the table. "Get [*out of here*] along with you — [*What d'you want here*] I dont want you here." Rose hesitated for a moment, holding the door in her hand.

'I suppose . . ." she began.

[150] "Cut along, or I'll shy something at you" said Bobby crumpling up a ball of paper in his hand. Rose remembered Eleanors instruction to 'ask him nicely' to go with her. But though [*at other times*] sometimes Bobby & she were the best of friends, — he had given her a sea-urchins egg two nights ago as a reward for not making a fuss when he broke the blade of her pen knife — [*& they had several*] tonight, she saw, he was in one of his rages. She had known that it was hopeless to ask him when he was doing his prep. because now that he was what she called "a proper schoolboy" he was apt to sneer at her & treat her as if she were a baby, especially when she interrupted his work.

Second Chapter

So, holding the door open for a moment, & looking round her, as if to assert that though Bobby claimed the [*room*] school room for himself, she was not going to give up her claim without a fight for it — [*she slowly*] she was not a baby any longer to be kept with nurse in the nursery — she departed. Her mind was made up. She would go to Lamleys alone. As she crept very stealthily upstairs again to the night nursery where her clothes were kept a sense of adventure filled her. She began instinctively to make this into [*a game. She*] one of those games that she & Bobby used to play, [*in*] about Red Indians. Only, as this was [*a*] real in a sense that the Red Indian game was not real she was more excited & [*kept half her attention upon*] [*not*] more on the alert. [*With extreme*] Very quietly she [*slipped on her*] ⟨took her⟩ coat & hat[; *but decided that, as she must make*] from the wardrobe, & carrying them on her arm, so that if she met anyone on the stairs she could invent some excuse — she did not know ⟨exactly⟩ what — she slipped down stairs, past [*each lighted room*] the nursery, past the [*sh*] schoolroom past her mothers room where the table with jugs & cups stood outside the door, & so down into the hall. [1 51] Crosby was in the hall, clearing away the tea things. Rose paused [*on*] at the top of the stairs & watched her. Now, Crosby had shut the drawing room door. She would take the tray down into the basement. She would wait there for a minute & then return with the lamps. Rose stepped silently in her house shoes, carrying her coat & hat into the hall, turned the latch of the front door, with extreme gentleness, ⟨[*shut*]⟩ ⟨closed it with scarcely a click behind her⟩ & ran down the steps into the street. She [*crouched*] ⟨ran crouching⟩ rather low ⟨[*un*] close to the wall⟩ until she had gained the corner⟨.⟩ [*where the big tree in the Stapleton's garden*] [*She was safe from*] Nobody could see her from the drawing room window now. She stood erect & put on her hat & coat. [*It was growing dark;*] She told herself that she was making preparations for her raid into the enemy's country: [*not that she believed*] for [*the feeling of*] she was half playing the Red

Indian game all the time. [*She also*] [*And*] But as she was alone, & as this was a real adventure, she added <as she slipped on her coat,> that she, the daughter of Colonel Pargiter of Pargiters Horse, was riding by night on a deadly mission through [*the*] hostile territory. She clenched her purse with the half crown in it making believe that she carried there the secret message which she had to deliver to the English who were besieged in a fortress. Her head was full of her father's old stories of the Indian Mutiny. Somehow she felt that though he would be very angry if he caught her disobeying Eleanor, he would also be very proud if he knew that she was defying all the spies who were in ambush in order to deliver his message< . > [*to the*] [*She*] Her horse, she decided would be shot dead under her just as she reached Lamleys shop[*, which was the fortress*]. [*The*] Lamleys was the fortress full of starving English.

It was growing dark. The street lamps had just been lit — the lamplighter was going along [1 52] the other side of the road, shoving his long stick up the little trap door in the gas lamps. [*A wavering net*] The trees in the front gardens made a wavering network of shadow[*s*] on the pavement, which stretched quite straight, all the way down Melrose Avenue; & then, there was the crossing; & Lamleys was the corner shop in the little island of shops [*that*] opposite. Rose had only to reach that point & she was safe. And as she ran down [*B*] Melrose Avenue [*the*] her anxiety to see if Lamleys was open almost made her forget that she was riding on a forlorn cause, until, [*suddenly, just by the*] as she ran past the pillar box under the gas lamp [*a*] the figure of a man suddenly emerged. "The enemy—the enemy!" Rose cried to herself, once more playing the game. [*He*] <The man> seemed to hesitate; as if he were doubting whether to cross the road or not, but as Rose ran past him, he stopped and looked at her. Clenching her hand, as if to pull the trigger of her revolver, she looked him full in the face. Bang! she said to herself. What a horrible face! For a moment she was frightened, genuinely; — she became herself, a little girl of ten, who had disobeyed her sister & run away from home, leaving them all safe[*ly*] there ⟨in the nursery⟩. [*He*] ⟨The man⟩ smiled ⟨very queerly⟩ at her. She dashed straight across the crossing; & there was Lamleys shop, still open — & Mrs Lamley, arranging a pile of newspapers on the counter, as if [*they were*] she were tidying the shop before shutting the shutters.

She was a great friend of Rose's, & had once given her a tea set, because it was cracked, & it was no good to them — on which condition only, her father had allowed her to keep it. Now she looked so homely & comfortable that Rose for a moment forgot to look for the box of [*s*] ducks & swans. Then she asked, rather breathlessly, for [*a*] the swans that had been in the window yesterday. They were still there. Mrs. Lamley [153] waddled round behind the counter & reached it down from the window.

"Isn't [*this*] ⟨it⟩ rather late for you to be out ⟨all⟩ alone, Miss Rosie?" she asked as she tied it up in whitey brown paper; and then she took the half crown, & gave her three coppers back in change, & went on sorting out the newspapers; [*looking over her spectacles,*] [*a*]⟨A⟩s Rose left the shop, ⟨she looked over her spectacles⟩ as if she guessed that Rose had only her house shoes on, & was disobeying somebody: but it was no business of hers. "Good night my dear" she said, ⟨& turned to her newspapers again,⟩ & Rose started back, having delivered her message to the besieged English, & having cut off the head of the chief rebel, which she carried under her arm as a trophy. When she reached the pillar box there was the man again. He was leaning against it, as if he were ill, Rose thought, filled with the same terror again; [*but*] he was lit up by the lamp. There was nobody else anywhere in sight. As she ran past him, he gibbered some nonsense at her, sucking his lips in & out; & began to undo his clothes . . .

Rose [*fle*] fled ⟨past him⟩. She thought he was pursuing her. She did not dare look round. She reached the turning into Abercorn Terrace & gained her own door step & stopped, under the laburnum tree, inside the garden gate, so frightened that she could hardly breathe. Then the thought struck her that he might be coming, padding softly behind. She ran up the steps She opened the front door, clumsily; she shut it with a nervous jerk. It did not matter who discovered her. But luck was on her side. Her sisters were talking over the drawing room fire; Crosby was in the kitchen; her father was in his study at the end of the passage. She gained the night nursery, [*put the*] put away her clothes, replaced the key in Nurses purse; & went back to the day nursery.

"Well Rosie you have been a time—" said Nurse, [154] who was still buzzing round the sewing machine. "I couldn't find my work box said Rose. "There it is, under the [*under the*] cushion." She went & got out her boot bag & her cotton. "Well you've <just> time to finish that flower before your bath" said Nurse, looking at the design; & then she went on talking to Mrs. C. about what she [*had*] would have said, if it had been her place: "but you never know. And its better to say nothing, [*when*] she's one of the funny sort" said Mrs. C." And they continued to discuss [*a*] the situation which had arisen [*when*] owing to the <sudden> death of Mrs. [*Peabody South*] Lightbody, in hospital; leaving her furniture to one set of relations & her money to Mrs. Crisp [*who lodged with her — it was*] [*& her own daughter had not attended the funeral.*] but there was quite a sum of money in the savings bank. Rose sat stitching at her flower with her head bent down, & Nurse & Mrs. C. went on talking as [*usual*] usual about all those mysterious people, the Springs & [*the*] Lightbodys & the Filtnesses, who played so large a part in Rose's life, because, being the only child in the nursery she spent an amphibious life part with the grown ups in the drawing room, & part in the kitchen where [*the*] Mrs C. & the Lightbodys & the Filtnesses were often to be found, [*in*] [*talking round the kitchen table;*] talking [*in the*] by the kitchen range; while the kettles & the saucepans simmered. [*Mr Filtness the bootmaker*] <the bootmaker> was her favourite. [*He would take her but*] She wished [*he*] <that Mr Filtness> would not take her on his knee, because he smelt rather horrid; but he had made <her> a pair of real leather boots for her doll. But they would go on talking about Mrs. Lightbodys last illness tonight. Rose wished they would stop. She was frightened; she did not like thinking of the old woman [155] lying dead in the hospital.

Then she had her bath. Nurse never asked her where she got the ducks & swans from. She made them swim with the battleship & the clipper But it was not quite so good a game as [*usua*] she had expected. Then she had her supper & went to bed. Nurse would come to bed about half past ten. Rose fell asleep; & then she woke up with a start. It seemed to her that she had been asleep for hours. The room was absolutely dark. Then she saw quite close to her, as if it were hung up on a string, [*the*] <a> grey leering face [*of the man by the pillar box*]. <She shut her eyes & it went; she opened them & there it was again.> It was only [*hi*] <a> face: but it was all spotted: & [*His*] the spots moved; & [*his*] <the> lips were sucked in & out, [*as if*] like the lips on an India rubber doll. She knew that it was a kind of dream — this grey face, hung up in the dark; but she suddenly felt that the man by the pillar box had got into the house. He was padding up the stairs. Now he was in the room. [*She leapt out of*] She cried Nurse! Nurse! But no one answered her. She was <quite> alone. She leapt out of bed — & tried to find the door. But she ran straight into the chest of drawers. [*Which way was the door? She had lost all sense*] The [*nursery*] room seemed quite altered. At last she found the door & fled into the day nursery opposite Nurse & Mrs C. were sitting at the nursery table eating their supper. A bright fire was burning & the lamp was blazing between them. <They had glasses of beer beside them & were eating cold beef.> they looked up in astonishment. Nurse was very cross. [*Wh*]

Whatever are you up to Rosie?" she said very sharply. "Go along & get back into bed. You'll be catching your death of cold with bare feet." She [*got*] put down her knife & fork & got up.

I had a bad dream" Rose said.

[156] "Thats what comes of having that rich cake for tea" said

Nurse. She was looking for [*a candle*] the bedroom candlestick. "Now you come along, & dont be silly" she said, lighting the candle, & taking Rose by the hand she led her back into the night nursery. She tucked her up kindly enough, & kissed her, & told her to go to sleep again & dream of fairies

But when are you coming to bed Nurse?" said Rose clutching hold of her hand.

"Oh I shant be long now," said Nurse. "As soon as I've had my [*bit of*] supper . . ."

But you wont be very long? said Rose, still holding her.

Now you just drop off to sleep," said Nurse, detaching herself; [*The*] a gossip with Mrs. C. was one of the treats of the week. Every other night she had to sit in the nursery alone, & tonight there was [*a*] plenty to talk about, what with the [*fun*] funeral, & the wreaths & what was the truth about Mrs. Lightbodys savings in the Post Office.

"Might I have the candle <left>?" Rose asked, as Nurse took it up & was about to go.

"Whatever d'you want the candle for Rosie?" said Nurse. You're never afraid of the dark are you? — you, such a brave girl — what would Papa say, if he knew you were afraid of the dark [*at your age*]? Now [*turn*] [*cuddle up, & turn your*] [*dont lie*] turn over & cuddle up. Dont lie on your back. Thats what gives you bad dreams." She was now by the door, holding the candle, so that there were great dark shadows in the room. Next moment she was gone. Rose could hear the clatter of knives & forks in the day nursery quite clearly. She could hear the voices talking. That was some comfort. As long as Nurse & Mrs C. [157] were there, she told herself, the man could not get into the room. She shut her eyes tightly. Her [*fa*] mother had once told her to count sheep, if she could not get to sleep. You thought of a flock of sheep penned up in a field. Then you made one sheep leap over a stile, & then another: & as they jumped you counted them. Rose counted [*twenty*] <ten> sheep. Then she opened her eyes. There was the bubbling grey face again. How horrible it was! She shut her eyes & determined that she would count twenty sheep before she would let herself look again. But the sixth sheep would not jump. It stood perfectly still[.] < and turned its horrid grey face towards her;> And the face turned into the mans [*face. There he*] <& suddenly the sheep> was standing by the pillar box. She sat up right in bed. She was terrified. It was no good. If you shut your eyes he was there: & if you opened them he was there. And there was dead silence in the day nursery. Nurse had gone down with Mrs C. to the kitchen. [*They*] <She> might stay there for hours talking with Mrs. Filtness. It was [*dea*] dead dark. She had no candle or matches.

"I am riding [*through*] the . . ." she [*tried to invent a game.*] told herself; trying to invent a game. "Riding [*alone*] —." [*But no;*] It was no good. She [*lay th*] sat there, clenching her wrists round her knees. She thought she heard the man in the passage. He was [*coming*] snuffing at the door. The door opened. A beam of light fell on the brass rail of the bedstead. It was Eleanor, come [*to as usual*] up as usual. Rose at once buried herself in the bed clothes & lay with her face to the wall. Eleanor came in, with her candle, stopped for a second at the end of the bed, & said, very gently, in case Rose were asleep, but she looked as if she had somehow tied herself up in her [*pa*] <[*bed clo*]> blankets, "Asleep Rose?"

"Not quite" said Rose, pretending to yawn. Well then let me straighten out all this mess" said Eleanor, putting down the candle & trying to [*fold*] straighten the bed clothes. [158] Rose looked rather flushed & her eyes were bright. Yet she was generally sound asleep when Eleanor looked in. She was a sturdy little girl; [*with*] she grew enormously[.] & ate enormously; & was a worse tomboy than Bobby — in fact Eleanor thought it would be a good thing when Bobby went to his boarding school, & left Rose to settle down [*in*] to her business.

"What's been keeping you awake?" Eleanor asked "You look quite flushed. Have you been dreaming?"

Rose could not possibly tell Eleanor what she had seen. It was not only that she had been very naughty, running out alone. It was that she was terrified, not only terrified: somehow, it was horrid, nasty, what she had seen: she could not tell any one: not even Eleanor. He had undressed . . .

Oh Eleanor she said, I'm so terrified': [*& burst into tears.*] She did not burst into tears. She gave a queer nervous shudder.

Eleanor cd. not imagine what had happened. [*Some fight with Bobby?*] Had Bobby been teasing her? He was getting very rough in his ways. Had he been up to mischief again & sworn Rose not to tell? Had they been in one of their raids into the back garden next door! [*Has Bobby been*] ⟨And broken Miss Pym's conservatory again?⟩ "You haven't been shooting [*at Miss*] cats again with Bobby have you?" she asked. "Its so unkind. Cats feel just as much as we do." But it was not that, she could see. Rose was grasping her hand & staring straight ahead of her. "But I cant tell Eleanor" she was saying to herself. Only at all costs Eleanor must be made to stay until Nurse came to bed.

[*Was it a*] ⟨Did you have a bad⟩ dream then? Eleanor asked.

I thought I saw a man in the room" Rose said at last, with great difficulty. "A robber."

A robber? here? said Eleanor. "But Rose dear, how could a robber get into your nursery? We're all sitting down stairs in the drawing room. [159] Theres Papa, & theres Morris. [*You know*] They'd never let a robber get into this house.

Rose thought of her father's sword over the dining room mantelpiece.

Papa would kill him she said. And yet [*if Papa knew what she had seen,*] [*she could never tell Papa what she had seen — never*;] she felt he would [*think her*] be very angry with her if he knew [*what she had seen.*] ⟨the truth.⟩ So would Eleanor. So she asked Eleanor to tell her what they were all doing in the drawing room. Were they playing a game — had they none of them gone to bed yet? It must be ever so late —

"Its only just half past ten" said Eleanor, ⟨looking at her watch⟩ & at that moment Nurse came in with another candle, & said rather guiltily that she had only run down stairs to wash the supper things; & Rosie seemed upset tonight.

"Did [*she*] ⟨you let her⟩ eat a great deal of that rich cake at tea, Miss?" she asked, trying to put the blame on Eleanor.

Did you eat rich cake at tea? Eleanor asked. I came in so late" she said to Nurse.

Now Nurse is coming to bed, so you[*ll*] wont be frightened any-more, will you?" she asked. & she [*smoothed out*] spread the quilt over Roses bed & kissed her, & took her candle & said, 'Good night' Nurse

Good night Miss Eleanor" said Nurse; & she slipped the links out of her cuffs, & put them in the pin tray [*on the*] by the looking glass on the chest of drawers.

[160] [THIRD ESSAY]

11 November [1932]

That scene, of course, is a very imperfect illustration of one of the many aspects of love — of street love, common love, of the kind of passion which pressing on the walls of Abercorn Terrace made it impossible for the Pargiter girls to walk in the West End alone, or to go out after dark unless they had a maid or a brother with them. The actual fact — that children of Rose's age are frequently assaulted, and sometimes far more brutally than she was — is familiar to any one who reads the Police Court news; so that, even today, a mother in the poorer parts of London will make an effort that her small daughter shall not run round to the grocer's shop after dark without a little brother or sister to go with her. But though the fact of Rose's adventure is easily verified, to give a faithful account of its effect upon her mind is by no means easy. Her first instinct, when Eleanor came in, was to turn away and hide herself. She felt that what had happened was not merely "naughty" but somehow wrong. But in what sense did she feel it to be wrong? The grey face that hung on a string in front of her eyes somehow suggested to her a range of emotion in herself of which she was instinctively afraid; as if, without being told a word about it, she knew that she was able to feel what it was wrong to feel. [*For also by instinct, she knew that her father would be angry — yet not angry in the way that disobedience angered him — if he knew what she had seen.*] So that she did not mind banging the front door when she came in — she did not mind being found out in her disobedience — what she could not say to her sister, even, was that she had seen a sight that puzzled [161] her, and shocked her, and suggested that there were things brooding round her, unspoken of, which roused curiosity and physical fear.

At ten years old, tomboy though she was, she was beginning to feel the desire, which was much more highly developed in her sisters, for the approval of the other sex. When her father had said "grubby little monster" and pointed to the stain on her pinafore, she at once covered it with her hand; although when Milly noticed it, she did not care in the least, and said what was a lie, for Mrs C. had brought the washing, that her clean pinafore had not come back from the wash.

This instinct to turn away and hide the true nature of the experience, either because it is too complex to explain or because of the sense of guilt that seems to adhere to it and to make concealment necessary, has, of course, prevented both the novelist from dealing with it in fiction — it would be impossible to find any mention of such feelings in the novels that were being written by Trollope, Mrs Gaskell, Mrs Oliphant, George Meredith, during the eighties; and if the novelists ignore it, this is largely because the biographers and autobiographers also ignore it, and thus reduce the material which the novelist has to work upon to a minimum. In addition, there is, as the three dots used after the sentence, "He unbuttoned his clothes . . ." testify, a convention, supported by law, which forbids, whether rightly or wrongly, any plain description of the sight that Rose, in common with many other little girls, saw under the lamp post by the pillar box in the dusk of that March evening. All the novelist can do, therefore, in order to illustrate this aspect of sexual life, is to state some of the facts; but not all; and then to imagine the impression on the nerves, on the brain; on the whole being, of a shock which the child instinctively conceals, as Rose did; [1 62] and is also too ignorant, too childish, too frightened, to describe or explain even to herself, as again Rose was.

Rose, next day, of course, began to observe Bobby more closely. She began to hunt about in the little book case in her father's study for some of his old books about the treatment of Tropical Diseases, because they had certain pictures.

But those are mere incidents. The principle itself — that love of this kind raged everywhere outside the drawing room — is of far greater importance, in considering the lives of the Pargiters: not only did it restrict their lives, and to some extent poison their minds — lies of all sorts undoubtedly have a crippling and distorting effect, and none the less if the liar feels that his lie is justified — but it also helped to bolster up, to harden, and substantiate a conception of the utmost importance about conduct, not only in the minds of the Pargiter sisters, but in the minds of their brothers.

Love, then, whether of the drawing room or of the street variety, affected the lives of the Pargiter sisters profoundly, not merely because it restricted them to certain quarters of London, and was perpetually impeding their freedom of movement, but also because it affected their minds — telling lies undoubtedly affects the mind and distorts the relationship between the liar and the lied to, even if the lie is justified; [*each of them required an attitude, according to her temperament, a conception of the right attitude to adopt toward sex and the wrong attitude toward love, which was not natural but highly artificial*].* It was impossible for the most daring of them — Delia — to disregard the convention, for example, that a [163] Colonel's daughter shall not walk down Burlington Arcade at midday. And yet they all felt that the convention was wrong. Delia indeed bought a thick veil and disregarded it. And yet they were all completely uncertain as to what conduct was right; and they all had dangling before them, as they grew older, the conviction that some convention was absolutely necessary for them, and not for their brothers; since plainly it was unthinkable for a middle- or upper middle-class woman to have a relation with a man which might lead to her bearing an illegitimate child — a disgrace which a woman could scarcely survive, socially, or practically either; for the whole cost of the child's upbringing (in 1880) would fall solely upon her; and she was disabled by law from earning enough money to provide for herself, let alone for another human being.

* A slightly corrected holograph deletion.

The question of chastity was therefore complicated in the extreme, since it was influenced by so many feelings that could not be discussed and by so many facts that might be resented but could not possibly be altered. Had not the demand for the vote, which might ultimately lead to some right to earn one's living, been again dismissed in the House of Commons? Mr Gladstone, in 1870, had based his refusal upon his conviction that [sentence unfinished]. Undoubtedly chastity for women was an extremely complicated question in the year 1880.

Bobby's case was, of course, much simpler than Rose's. He loved Miriam Parish, genuinely; he saw something in that pale gentle face that nobody else had ever seen; to Morris she was so unattractive and so dull and so prim that he used to dash out of the drawing room by the second door as she came in by the first. Eleanor indeed [I 64] had to manoeuvre so that Miriam only came when Morris was out. Nobody guessed what Bobby felt for her, or could imagine that to him she was somehow not only beautiful, but everything that was exciting, inspiring, and so "decent". Like Rose, Bobby lacked all analytic power — that when, once, she dropped her handkerchief, and had to sniffle all through the last part of her visit in consequence, being too shy to ask Eleanor for the loan of one, and Bobby, stooping under the table as if to tie up his shoe, had snatched it up — when he was alone with the pocket handkerchief, he had only to put it to his nose and the scent of Miriam, and the courage and beauty and adventure and all that she stood for, filled him almost intolerably.

But the emotion was far simpler than what Rose had felt about the man under the lamp because, going to school every day as he did, and mixing with much older boys, he already knew a great deal more about all forms of love than Rose did. He went by bus or he walked by himself to St. James's every day. No woman ever assaulted him; but once when he was coming home late on a winter's night with Robson, a laughing, tired black and red girl had shouted at them both "some filth", as Robson put it. And Robson told him that she was a prostitute. Robson had waved her off with a certain pride. But there was nothing frightening to Bobby in her jeers and laughter. He had walked on calmly, by Robson's side, secure, and rather scornful, and at the same time a little proud that Robson who was seventeen, and big for his age, should have taken part in such a grown-up adventure, and still more proud of the fact that Robson should, by using the word "prostitute", initiate Bobby into what Bobby dimly felt was a great fellowship — the [1 65] fellowship of men together — a fellowship which, he began to feel, yielded a great many rights and privileges, and required even of himself, at the age of twelve, certain loyalties and assertions; for example, it was essential to make it plain that the school room was his room; especially when his school friends came back to tea. It was essential that Rose should be kept out of it, when Parker and Sanderson came back on Saturday afternoon; although, privately, he still liked playing games with Rose, and it was much better fun to have her there to show things, like his engine, and his fireworks to, than to shut her out and play by himself. He had devised a system therefore by which she was his assistant, or sometimes merely the audience. He would write out leaflets in red ink announcing "Grand Firework Display tonight, Ladies and Gentlemen cordially invited" and lay it on the nursery table. Then, dressed in his red dressing gown, he was the Professor, or the Conjuror, and Rose, seated at the far side of the table, was the audience in the stalls. If the audience tried to grab the things herself, there was a general scrimmage, and Nurse knocked on the nursery floor above with a poker.

After the adventure in the street, Rose changed slightly but decidedly in her feeling for Bobby. Again it is difficult to say how far this change was the result of the shock; how far she felt some fear or dislike for her brother because of his sex; or how far she felt and resented the change that was making him, as she put it, into "a proper schoolboy". She was shut out of the school room whenever Sanderson and Parker came there; she was not allowed to take any part in their games, after tea in the garden; except to field sometimes; [1 66]

and on one occasion she had caught a ball so smartly, jumping up into the air and catching it in one hand, her left, that Parker had told Bobby afterwards that Rose was a jolly good catch — a compliment that made her blush with pride; and yet she felt that Bobby was always much rougher with her when his friends were there. He once turned her out of the school room and locked the door behind him; whereupon she locked herself into the bathroom, and sobbed. But, after the first spasm of weeping was over, she held what she called, in her private language, a "Grand Council of War". That is to say, she determined that after this, Bobby was in the enemy's camp, and she would do everything she could to thwart him and spite him. She then washed her face and combed her hair, and when Bobby came into the nursery later, and wanted to make it up, she sent him to Coventry — she went on pretending to read a book. Until Bobby, exasperated by her silence, called her every abusive name he could think of; and then announced that he would ask her three times to come. If she did not answer the third, he would go alone. She did not answer; and he went alone; and as, soon afterwards he was sent to Rugby, that quarrel was never entirely made up. "Adrian was new at Mr. West's school at Bournemouth" writes Mrs. Ruth Jackson of a similar case. "Quote."* [1 67] But though Bobby Pargiter lived a far freer life than Rose, in that he was allowed to make the journey to St. James's and back every day by himself, and was initiated, not only by Robson but by other boys, into a knowledge of sex which at twelve surpassed not only Rose's but Milly's and Delia's, there sprang, partly from this freedom which was so oddly combined with secrecy — he could no more have mentioned the word "prostitute" to Rose than she could have mentioned the man under the gas lamp to him — a mass of feelings, of reserves, of licenses, and of controls which made his life at school so difficult, strange, and so unnatural that Rose had no just cause for her bitter anger, for her floods of tears

* The work from which Virginia Woolf intended to quote here has not been located.

in the bathroom. Had she known what her brother was going through at school, she would very likely have decided, when she called her Grand Council, that instead of being henceforth members of opposite camps, they ought, on the contrary, to combine togther in blood brotherhood. Before Bobby went to school, this was symbolised by tying red thread round their wrists. Only, as she could not possibly tell Bobby about the man, and Bobby not possibly tell her about Robson, there was nothing for it but an enmity which lasted until a very queer scene [*between them*] after their father's death, in the school room, fifteen years later.

Meanwhile Bobby was sent off to Mr. Hurst's at Folkestone to be prepared for the Army. And at this point, in order to illustrate more fully, though from rather a different angle and age, the problems that made Bobby so [1 68] difficult at home, it may be well to give a scene from the life of Edward Pargiter, at Oxford.

Edward Digby Pargiter was the second son of Colonel Pargiter. He was much the cleverest of the Pargiters, and had done so well at Winchester that he had got a scholarship at one of the great Oxford Colleges, and was now expected to take a first in Greats, after which his tutor thought that he had an excellent, but by no means a certain, chance of a Fellowship. But as the [tutor] pointed out to the Colonel, [there were] premature symptoms of pride as he stood, very upright, in front of the fire, in the tutor's room, [and] a fellowship is a very real test of a man's merit. It by no means followed that if Edward got a first, he would also get a fellowship. Edward was by no means sure of his first, even. But Edward was a very clever lad. But he must take things rather more to heart. Some of his Greek verses were very rough still. Still he had the root of the matter in him. And the Colonel, grasping Mr. [*P*] ['s] hand almost too hard, swung off down the narrow staircase into the quadrangle determined to give Edward a good luncheon, and then, when they were both warmed with wine, to tell him what the tutor had said about brushing up his Greek verse. As the Colonel had long ceased to decipher even the pages of his Greek testament, he could scarcely advise in any detail; but he promised Edward twenty-five pounds if he got his first; and one hundred for his fellowship. Canon Pargiter, the Colonel's father, had been a Fellow of All Souls. And after lunch, Edward took the Colonel to All Souls and they looked up the rooms that the Canon had had, when he was an undergraduate [1 69] about 1820. The Colonel went straight in and disturbed the present occupant who was toasting muffins: "My father had these rooms, Sir," the Colonel said by way of apology. The young man smiled at Edward, and said, "Don't mention it" to the Colonel. And the Colonel, wringing him too [hard] by the hand, in an excess of emotion towards all young men who might be friends of his son, turned round on his heel, and marched off to the Hotel, and so back to London, where he could not resist dropping a casual hint to his brother officers at the Club that his boy was said to have quite a good chance of &c. &c.; and that night for the first time for many years, the Colonel opened his Greek testament, and shut it, concluding that he must really rub up his Greek.

*Note p. 76 **

Discussing the matter one day, not with her sisters but with a girl she had met at a party, Nora Graham, the daughter of that eccentric man, Theodore Graham, the mill owner, who went so far — he was a very rich man — as to allow Nora the same allowance that he gave his sons — three hundred pounds a year — it seemed incredible that any woman should have three hundred a year of her own — Nora had told Delia that nothing could be done about it — about chastity, that is — until women had votes. Delia, with her Pargiter caution and exactness, had asked why; [and] had been invited to join a queer little society that met in the Gray's Inn Road; had gone out of curiosity and sheer despair of being able to learn music; had not been able to

* What follows is an addition which, presumably, Woolf intended to incorporate somewhere in the subsequent revision. The page reference has not been traced.

go again, because of her mother's illness, but had begun to read papers like *Punch* and *The Times* with an eye to what they said about women's rights. *Punch* was full of jokes about strong-minded women: [170] of pictures of little delicate women in bonnets and crinolines trying to cut off legs and appealing to strong men in whiskers — "Oh Surgeon, do help me! My wrist is *so* tired!" — to illustrate what would happen if one trusted one's body to a woman doctor. And Nora, who was always dashing about the country, and suggesting ways in which, even if Delia must stay at home, she could help "The Cause" — that sort of language seemed to Delia rather silly — inveigled her once into reading the debates in the House of Commons when some bill came up, as usual, and was rejected, as usual. Delia plodded through the arguments, one day when she was sitting with her mother. And she noted Mr Gladstone's argument when he gave his reasons for opposing women's right to vote because he feared to [overweight the Bill.]* "Old humbug," said Delia.

* The phrase "overweight the Bill," comes from Ray Strachey *"The Cause" A Short History of the Women's Movement in Great Britain* (London 1928) p 277. In the Reform Bill as introduced in 1883 by Gladstone as Prime Minister there was no mention of women. "In vain did the suffragists . . . appeal to the definite and categorical election promises. The Prime Minister had said that women would overweight the Bill, so overboard they must go." See *Three Guineas* chapter 3 note 16.

[171] [THIRD CHAPTER]

17th Nov [1932]

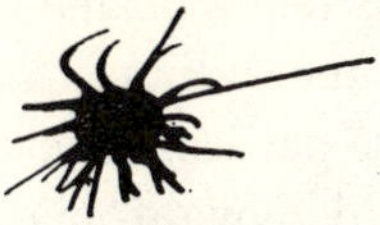

Edward Pargiter had come in from Hall, had made [*himself a cup of*] coffee in [*a*] rather a complicated coffee making machine & was allowing himself precisely twenty minutes in which to smoke a cigarette & to drink a cup of coffee before he began what the Colonel called "brushing up" his Greek [*verses*]. There was only one fortnight before the examination. A great deal depended upon his success — his whole life indeed[. *For if*] depended indirectly, upon [*his getting a first*] ⟨his success⟩; for if he got a [*first*] first, [*he was*] it would mean that he had a good chance of a Fellowship, & if he got a Fellowship then he would stay at Oxford for ever. Nothing in the whole world seemed to him so desirable. He [*lo*] lay back in his chair & looked round his room as he sipped his coffee. It was a lovely ⟨early⟩ Eighteenth Century room, [*on the seco*] [*with*] on the second floor with cream coloured panels that made any other decoration unnecessary. [*But there*] His one bookcase, [*however,*] between the fireplace & the window, was [*fu*] tidily arranged with rows of old books, — Pope, Dryden, Addison, Johnson & so on, which he had bought almost as much for the subdued ripple of brown & gold that their backs made as for their contents. His [*work*] ⟨text⟩ books, his note books, his [*lec*] [*sha*] [*ugly*] shabby dictionaries [*& textbooks*] were concealed behind a curtain on the lower shelves, & in the little dining room which, also panelled, opened out of the sitting room. He was lucky. In his last year he had been given a set of rooms, looking over the quadrangle. [*From where he sat he could see*] The rooms were absolutely quiet. From where he sat, puffing at his cigarette, he could see nothing but green branches, ⟨crossing the window, palely, truly green,⟩ for it was early in May; &, as the light was fading, the green was at its most evanescent, & here & there, almost like a [*silver*]

<golden> [172] fruit glowed [*an*] <one> lamp, then another, as other undergraduates & fellows came back to their rooms & lit their lamps in readiness for the evening. A certain hush always brooded over the College at this particular moment, & of all the moments of the day it was, Edward thought, one of the pleasantest. (Even if he did not get his Fellowship he would have learnt more at Oxford, received more.) [*For a few minutes one*] Even now when he was working eight or nine hours a day — he looked at the clock he still had seventeen minutes before he need begin again — it was [*a*] better than any life he [*ha*] could <possibly> imagine. This last year had been the best of all. He had hated his first term. He had known nobody. His [*friends*] school friends had gone to Cambridge, or to other Colleges. And at first there had seemed to be none of that feeling of fellowship that had made the last [*year*] terms of his life at Morley so [*tremendously*] important, so exciting, [*so full of*] <Edward was a considerable athlete> He looked at the silver cups on his mantelpiece — there were fifteen & each represented [*some mom*] not only the moments triumph, but — oh all sorts of things: He could still hear the cheers & the catcalls — he could still remember, how by degrees the spirit of the place had permeated him, how by degrees he had come to feel that he was winning his cup not for himself, but for his house, nor for his house, but for the school. And then the Headmaster, rising to the occasion as that man, however formidable [*& h*] he might be on ordinary occasions always did, had [*preache*] said one night what Edward [*ha*] felt to be the summing up of the whole spirit of Morley — how they belonged to a great & famous fellowship, how even the most thoughtless ([*there were*] nobody dared giggle) even the most thoughtless, could not leave Morley without feeling that our character as members of a society or fellowship is something different from our individual character when we are living apart or in solitude." Before he left [173] Morley Edward — he was called Nigs [*by his sisters*] in his family & the nickname had stuck to him, or been freshly discovered at Oxford — Edward

had felt that he had fully understood what the words meant. Prizes & cups were only the outer symbol of something much more important. It was the spirit behind these ⟨silver⟩ cups & [*bound*] these volumes bound in blue morocco that counted "As we sit here side by side" — some of us for the last time too; [*that had leas*] that evening had been one of the bitterest of Edwards life "our spirit moves as it were all together, in something like a rhythmic harmony — . . . ⟨for the time at any rate, if not for all time, our life is a different thing."⟩ And [*from*] this spirit, Edward had come to understand, was not simply the spirit of a handful of men & boys at Morley in the year 1878–79. It was the same spirit that had animated the Jew, the Greek & the Roman. "No other influences," the doctor said, [*in his*] pealing & [*reverbeat*] reverberating, his voice [*went*] broke upon the pillars of the school chapel, assumed the voice of the names carved upon marble tablets — the names of the old boys who had fought in war after war, [*who had*] for five hundred years; [*who had*] with [*Blake*] Marlborough, with [*W*] Nelson, with Wellington; whose bones lay unburied in [*the*] India; who had [*won co*] [*this*] saved Europe again & again; & dying, asked only their names might be written up in the old school — "No other influence" the doctor said, "has produced so great a growth of the sterner & more robust virtues — fortitude, self-reliance, intrepidity; devotion to the common weal: readiness for united action & self-sacrifice." [*It re*] The value of school life was. . that it preserves & calls forth these same elements of character & recreates the old classic type". . . . But at Oxford, at first, [*this fellowship had seemed*] there had seemed to be none of this fellowship, this unity, this sense of working together towards an ideal. It was not till his second year that the full beauty of Oxford [I 74] had dawned upon him; & he had made friends, friends among all sets, & ridden, & argued, & danced, & picked blue bells in Bagley wood, & boated, & eaten & drunk, night after night, with friends, & laughed at the dean, & mocked the old fogies; & seen [*fa*] such famous men — Ruskin once, once Gladstone, & Cardinal

Manning; & then wild thoughts came to Edward, in the [*lonely*] ancient chapel, of being [*himself worthy to have his name too in*] that his name too would be reverenced, as he now reverenced the names of those great men who[*se*] had been here before him. The light was fading; a bird chirped some where in the meadows; he must light his lamp too; [*sport*]* & settle[*d*] down to Sophocles once more, for his whole life depended on [*his success*] ⟨it⟩. [*Oxford depended on it. He might*] [*If he got a*] He would live for ever at Oxford — [*if he*] but only if he got his Fellowship. [*The*] He had precisely five minutes left, & his cigarette & his coffee were both coming to an end. He had done everything his tutor advised. He had worked, steadily regularly, but not too hard. He had taken the right amount of air & exercise. He had seen the right amount of his friends — these things were calculated to a nicety by his coach, who, after thirty years could train a man's mind [*almost*] precisely as the other sort of coach could train a man's body. Edward — Nigs, his sisters called him — had obeyed his coach almost to the letter. And now, the coach had said, dont overdo it in the last lap. Read [*the*] [*a*] the plays I have marked through, & take more time off — He had even advised three days complete holiday before the examination. Edward was looking a little fagged. And Edward knew that though to take time off would need more discipline than to go on mugging away up to the last moment, •{still, just as in a race, one [175] must keep a sprint for the finish, so now it would be well to slacken, to read rapidly over some of the plays again, & then to go away, for three days complete idleness, riding or boating up the river with James.}•

Edward suddenly felt, as he set the lamp with the green shade down on the table, [*&*] that he could not work seriously tonight. [*His brain was*] Without feeling ill in any way, his brain was no longer fresh, fertile, & vigorous. [*He had been using it with*] [*pressing it too regularly & too*] [*using it too regularly, now on this subject, now on that.*] He felt, as he had felt [*after a running*] at the end

* I.e., sport the oak, outer door of a college room.

of the summers term [*that he*] after all the [*running &*] matches had been played that he had not an ounce of energy left. He wanted merely to lounge in a punt & eat [*o*] strawberries. Well, Harbottle probably was wise. It would be best to relax now, & [*to*] merely to run through [*a little*] something that he knew almost by heart. He [*shut his*] drew his armchair under the light & took up his Sophocles — He would run through the Antigone.

Of all his subjects he had learnt at Oxford—& he had [*been*] in one way or another he had learnt something of philosophy, [*of*] mathematics, [*of*] science, [*of*] <&> history, [*of*] none gave him anything like the same pleasure as Greek. If he won his fellowship, he would devote himself entirely to Greek. He had the makings of a real scholar in him, his tutor had once said. A real scholar—a scholar like Bentley or Munro was to Edward, the highest type of mind [*that*] conceivable. That he should be a scholar like that was out of the question. He never [*dre*] dreamt of comparing himself with men of that calibre. But he could understand what scholarship meant. He had [*read*] learnt Greek [*since he was*] for more than ten years. Not a day had passed without his reading Greek. [*He had*] He had given up more hours to Greek than to any other subject. He had written many more Greek verses than English. He had [*perhaps*] read more Greek than any other language, save his own. [176] He could scarcely read French. He could read no German[*. He could read no*] <or> Italian, [*no*] <or> Spanish; [*&*] & though he had read a certain number of English Classics, he had certainly never read Hamlet or Paradise Lost with a tenth of the care that he had read the Antigone or the Iliad. Hence, when he opened the Antigone he could read it not only without opening a dictionary; [*he could read it with* [*com*] *instant understanding not only of every word but of fa*] he knew every word, but he also knew [*what all that*] [*the metre of*] a mass of other facts — [*who had used the*] [*who*] who had used the word besides Sophocles, & where; & how Sophocles himself had used the same word with a different meaning elsewhere; & he knew exactly when the metre in the Choruses changed, & [*what*] <why> it changed; & besides this he knew where the play was acted, & how; & also [*what generations*] the different opinions of different scholars about it in different ages. [*Besides t*] The actual text therefore presented no difficulties to him, though each time he read it, he questioned certain readings, & pencilled comments & queries of his own on the blank page which was bound in with the text. But tonight he read, as far as he could, for the mere pleasure of the [*so*] poetry — for the sound, for the meaning, for the astonishing subtlety of [*the*] <a> [*subdued yet*] style, which seemed to him the most wonderful in all the Greek dramatists. He loved to feel his mind as he read, closing firmly round the phrase & taking its imprint more exactly more clearly with each reading. [*The words were almost*] Greek words had — he [*could*] would argue this for hours with Peel, who preferred Latin — an indescribable [*hardness &*] combination of hardness & velocity as though — but Edward always checked himself when he felt the temptation to illustrate sensual feelings in images. Scholarship must be exact above all things. [*In his opinion one of the*] His whole training [*was in*] made him question any looseness or vagueness of

[177] And one had only to look at him, [*or in*] as he read, & at his furniture & [*surroundings.*] <his person> to see that [*this spartan habit*] exactness & precision [, *this distrust of any clouding*] were naturally akin to him. Edward, like all the Pargiters, was physically well made. He was just under six foot, & [*he w*] [*if at*] [*too thin at the moment*], though too thin at the moment, he was admirably proportioned. But <whereas his sisters & Morris were rather heavy & unmoulded in feature> he <Edward> had [, *what his sisters & Morris lacked,*] a clearly cut, well modelled head. •{A [*critic might complain*] that the eyes were a little small & a little too close together. But they were of the purest blue.}• His nose was straight, & the nostrils were finely cut, [*His lips were*] & beautifully modelled chin. Indeed his head [*was*] with its <cropped> crest of <hair brushed up> [*fair hair*] was much like the head of a Greek boy on a frieze; though a

critic might complain that the eyes were too small, too near together, & that the whole face lacked width, plasticity, suggestion. [*It was*] [*He*] It was a [*carved marble*] head, [*rather than a painting by*] carved in marble, rather than a face looming up in flesh colour from a canvas. Eleanor [*&*] had nicknamed him Nigs when he was a little boy; for the word, through its associations with ⟨the⟩ niggley & niggardly [*& the*] expressed a vague feeling she had that he was not generous & charming & unsuccessful like her dear old Morris. [*Perhaps there was some truth in her*] Nigs will make his fortune," Eleanor used to say, disparagingly [*"Nigs will*] when Edward came home with another cup, or another volume bound in blue Morocco⟨.⟩ [*to stand*] And the nickname, [*whatever*] [*must have had more*] though [*from her affection for Morris she exaggerated*] Eleanor, out of her love for Morris, who never got a prize, exaggerated its unpleasant associations, must have had some fitness, for it stuck to Edward at school, & was his name now at Oxford. On the other hand, [*so*] [*to*] Nigs, on the lips of one or two of his Oxford friends, [*stood for something*] was [*the*] a friends [*way*] [178] way of belittling [*a romantic, daring, adventurous boy*] ⟨someone⟩ whom they feel to be more beautiful, more romantic, more perfectly balanced between the life of the body & of the mind than other people.

Nigs [*sat absorbed in the Antigone of Sophocles*] opened his Sophocles at the Antigone & began to read. [*The usual sense of*] He read for some time; [*with the ⟨in an⟩ absorbed*] as usual the sense of his own efficiency in recording exactly [*the*] the precise impress of those perpetually changing words delighted him. As usual, there was more in [*Sopho*] the Antigone this time than there had been last time. And yet, after reading for thirty five minutes, he found that some wheel or spring in the excessively complex machine [*which*] of his mind was flagging & fumbling. ⟨perhaps he was more tired than he knew. He slackened He thought of Kitty Malone.⟩ [*He was blurring the*] He had to read [*a*] ten lines [*again to*] twice over — a sure sign that his attention was not at its best. He laid the book on his knee & looked up. After all, he remembered, he had taken no exercise for some weeks — or only a [*w*] brisk walk [*for one <of two> hours & a half from between*] from two to four. [*And*] He had knocked off his tennis & his fives & his [*boating*] rowing & his swimming. Physically he was rather off colour, [*<therefore> He bethought hi*] [*therefore, & no doubt*] which no doubt affected his brain; [*the*] his best work was always done, he suspected, when his body & his mind had reached some sort of equilibrium, though it was difficult to [*say exactly what*] <determine exactly> the best relation between the two — [*one might easily*] [*after a long days running or rowing one was sometimes*] violent exercise often left one so sleepy that there was nothing for it but bed. [*He*] There was another method of course, of stimulating the brain — [*a glass*] to drink a glass or two of wine, [*or*] — &, as it happened, his father the Colonel, had sent him two dozen of very excellent port 'by way of a stirrup cup" — for the Colonel [*took this*] was almost as set upon [179] Edward's success as Edward was himself; & the Colonel, [*had*] whose experience of examinations was <as> primitive as his knowledge of Greek, had always insisted that his men must have their rum before they went into battle. [*That was what gave their*] <You dont drive a bayonet into a chap in cold blood.> It was just that extra tot that did the trick. So, two dozen of port chosen by the Colonel himself — & the Colonel was a judge of wine whatever might be said of his Greek — was in Edward['s] cupboard. He poured himself out a glass, & [*sp*] sipped it, as his father sipped it, slowly, contemplatively, holding the glass to the light, as he had seen his father do so often, as if [*the*] part of the pleasure of drinking came through the eyes. And indeed there was beauty in the brownish yellow liquid — the colour seemed to be another version of the taste. Edward [*then*] sipped & [*be*] then [*began to read*] when the soft yet burning liquid had had time to expand itself in his veins he turned again to the Antigone. Yes, a sip of good wine undoubtedly quickened the brain. And he went on sipping & reading & reading & sipping, until the glass was almost empty. [*And*] Then he lay back on his cushions again & whether it was the wine or the Greek, or both in harmony, he felt [*so*] a mysterious mixture of power & pleasure & rest & content, which he enjoyed to the full, feeling certain that he was bound to succeed — whatever he did; the Fellowship was undoubtedly his, he felt; & [*he*] [*then,*] going over again the stanzas that he had been reading [*the*] where Antigone & Ismene talk together; another sense began to assert itself — a sense that was quite familiar to Edward; that was sometimes a perfect plague; a sense that was almost entirely physical; that was worrying, bothering, because, almost instantly, Edward's mind came into conflict with it & said "I will not let myself feel this — this is degrading — this is bestial — [*this is*] I [*will*] must fight this . . . I am not going to be beaten this time" And he looked instinctively at [*the*] [180] the [*portrait of a*] photograph of a fine austere face — [*hangin*] which stood on the mantelpiece. Old Bealby had conquered. Old Bealby had always taught them [*to*] how to conquer. Exercise was one way. That was at the back of his passion for sports — partly. That was why he had been so keen in the Home cup — partly. That was why Edward himself had always broken up those sinister little groups of boys lounging about at the edge of the playing fields. He had been a martinet <when he was a prefect> — So, too, with himself. He was going to conquer himself too. He forced himself to turn the pages & to read the Chorus [*which*] in which [*the*] Antigone & Ismene have no part. [*He was serv*] His brain [*was*] answered the demand made on it; the [*vision*] desire which the vision of the two girls had prompted, passed; & he had the reward which comes so aptly after much exertion of thinking of Antigone & Ismene [*with*] <in> another [*kind*] way — [*they so*] the thought of the two sisters, the one so fierce & daring, the other so simple, so [*charming*] <clinging>, coalesced to form an ideal of womanhood which moved Edward not to desire them, but to desire to produce something, to be something which their spirit, the spirit of all that was holy, & pure, & lovely & at the same time. Just & magnificent & serene & high — for if Ismene was sympathetic, Antigone was tremendous, would bless & sanction & reward.

"Oh Kitty — Kitty" he whispered; & his eyes, though they were too small, & set too near together, had an expression which his sister[*s*] had never seen in them, or she might have modified her opinion of Nigs. For a moment a look of extraordinary beauty filled them; the lines of the face softened; the narrow lips relaxed. He was thinking of Kitty Malone; he had passed by a natural transition from the abstract reverence for womanhood that the thought of Antigone & Ismene inspired to a [*a*] thought that was less abstract, but was still [181] lustrous with something of the same wonder & awe — ●{ [*the*] for he had been in love, all this time, ever since he had seen her act in the pageant, with his cousin Kitty Malone.}● He had been in love with his cousin Kitty Malone ever since he had seen her act last summer in a pageant.

<Edward writes a poem in a Greek hand, very Greek>*

It was impossible to go on reading the Antigone. He [*replaced his*] <shut the> book methodically [*in the shelf*] <& put it on the table>. Then he [*paused*] <rose> & went to the window, & [*looked out into the*] stood for a moment looking out into the garden. It was [*now*] almost dark now, [*There was*] the may tree was only a white spot there in the corner; — The [*trees*] [*grass looked so go grown*] turf beneath the window [*was*] looked [*half transparent*] unnatural, like water. And all round <lay> the lines of the college buildings, here broken with [*an*] a bright light, where the curtain was not drawn, here with a dull yellow or red transparency where the [*lamp*] curtains were drawn [*lay*] <bent behind> enclosing the garden with [*their lo their*] a <dark> mass [*that of*] [*that*] <here steepled often> with their chimneys & towers. The silence was [*the*] <that> curious<ly> [*silence of*] [*vocal*] <uneven> silence of a place which

* Marginal note in pencil.

is humming with life — <inhabited by innumerable people.> [*Sometimes a*] there was the tinkle of a piano, [*the sho*] a sudden burst of laughter. Then a door slammed. And then there was complete silence, [*as*] in which [*a*] one heard nothing but a bird chirping, as if it had woken, [*&*] frightened, & fallen asleep.

[*Edward* [*wen*] *breathed deeply*,] Standing at the open window Edward <took a deep> breath[*ed deeply*] — it was impossible for him to say how [*deep*] this [*v*] sight of the sleeping garden moved him, stirred him — And Kitty was not far away — perhaps she too was standing at the window of the Masters Lodge looking at their may trees, at their turf. For she was the daughter of the Master of St Katharines. From Edwards window one could just see the [*spire*] turret of St Katharines Chapel. He [*went back into his room, &*] tried to see the lines of St Katharines, but it was too dark now. He turned back into the room, & obeying an instinct which sometimes possessed him, he took a sheet of paper, & heading it "Persephone", began to write a poem, [*to his cousin.*] a love poem, a poem addressed [I 82] to his cousin. Quite by accident he had discovered that Katherine P. Malone stood for Katharine Persephone Malone. Since he had just been reading [*McAulays*] Greek, the Greek language, the Greek metres were in his mind; & the first lines of his poem [*were, to*] would have seemed, to a critic, more like Greek than English. There was a tightness, a constraint about them, though the feeling they expressed — a young man's love for a girl [*ha*] was [*genu*] [*deep*] genuine, & Edward [*Pargiter was*] was feeling[, *only what*] what was, after all, a very natural feeling — that Kitty was a lovely & mysterious [*& unknown*] being, of the opposite sex, [*alm*] whose hand he had [*taken*] held once or twice, whom he had danced with once or twice, who had somehow come to embody all that was beautiful, worshipful & desirable in life — It was for her now, more than for himself more than for his father, that he desired success. If he could go to [*his*] his Uncle Paul & say "I am worthy of your daughter . . ." [*So he*] <He> wrote on, in his little scholars hand, [*that*] with its [*neat*] Greek Es, until, as always happened, he pushed the paper away in disgust. He was not a poet. He could only imitate other poets. He was a good enough critic to know that he was only making a translation of Theocritus. It was better to read Theocritus in the original. [*Its*] [*The*] With a violence which showed how much genuine feeling had gone into his verses, how acutely his own lack of creative power distressed him, he crumpled the paper into a ball & shied it into the waste paper basket. To make the annihilation of this inadequate & [*silly*] affected verse more complete he retrieved it, & tore the paper into minute scraps, some of which he scattered among the coals, so that even Mrs Pugh whose curiosity about his private life was insatiable should be unable to gratify it when she came to do his room by reading his mutilated stanzas 'To Persephone.'

No sooner had he done this, than there was a thump on his door. It was sported. His friends [I 83] were by way of respecting his privacy; [*now that*] & many of them were in the same unenviable predicament. But Gibbs — it was probably Gibbs — thought it all [*a*] damned nonsense — mugging away over books; ⟨writing imitation Theocritus;⟩ & at the moment Edward was inclined to agree with him. It was damned nonsense, anyhow tonight; & so he opened the door; & there sure enough was Gibbs, a [*vast f*] huge young man, a rowing blue; whose bulk made Edward appear almost slight & small by comparison.

Gibbs came in not without some trepidation. He could not resist thumping on Edwards door; [*but he had a*] as he [*past*] ⟨passed⟩, not so much from a wish to interrupt, as from a desire to inform Edward that he was a damned fool [*to*]. And yet, he respected Edward from the depths of his heart for being a damned fool; ⟨he would have liked to be a poet himself;⟩ & would have gone like a lamb if Edward [*had*] showed the least sign of [*being*] wanting to be alone. However, there was a bottle on the table, & a glass. Things weren't as bad as they might have been: Edward was getting another glass from the dining room.

Edward poured himself out another glass of the Colonels port too. ⟨Nigs (Gibbs used the term affectionately) was a sport⟩ And again he held it up to the light just as his father did. He doubted if Gibbs knew what very excellent port this was — Gibbs was the son of a rich manufacturer, & the Gibbs had not reached the stage which the Pargiters had reached ⟨[*in*]⟩ almost a century ago of knowing one wine from another. Gibbs swilled his beer down; [*after a*] & used his knife & fork with a flourish which slightly offended Edward, who was naturally fastidious in such matters. But they had many more important things in common — rowing; football in particular. Gibbs was ⟨himself⟩ in the college eight, & fives[*; & hunting*]. Of course only 'a young elephant' as Gibbs used to say regretfully, could carry Gibbs; but his father provided young elephants; they had a house in the shires; & [I 84] Edward & Gibbs both shared that love of hunting which shows itself not merely in hunting with the Pytchley or the Badmytn, but in following any local pack, on any old hack, & in discussing, hour after hour, this run & that,* [*in knowing*] [*so that*] in quoting [blank space] Gibbs had Jorrocks by heart. Gibbs had been pressed into the college boat rather against his will. [*His whole heart*] He had no intention of becoming a blue. That meant too much sweating & training — [*& then one*] [*What he*] The talk soon got upon [*th*] his favourite topic — there were only two or three months now of this infernal ⟨summer⟩ heat. Then cubbing would begin And then—just as he was about to broach a scheme by which Edward should come & stay with them; & [*be h*] & see some sport ⟨by April Gibbs would promise him a decent hack with a dash of first rate sp[irit?]⟩... The door opened, & in drifted, so [*sli*] silently that neither Gibbs or Edward perceived him, [*the*] a very different figure, Jevons, Jasper Jevons a smallish pale young man, whose physique obviously unfitted him for any game or any sport.

* A marginal insertion here begins "horns, hounds, huntsmen, farmers" and continues with five undeciphered words.

Yet he moved beautifully. His hands, as he silently took the [*bi*] bottle of port, & raised it to the light to see if there were any left, [*were mad*] were so well shaped that Gibbs hands looked like slabs of raw meat beside them. The bottle was almost empty — Edward whose face showed some dismay at the sudden apparition of Jevons, protested that there was any amount more in the next room. Jevons said that he did not really want any. Edward said that anyhow they did; & disappeared leaving Gibbs & Jevons alone together.

Gibbs at once shut up completely. Jevons, on whom the burden of conversation fell since he had interrupted, [*a*] tried in vain to think of something to say. They had been talking of horses when he came in — he had [*just*] caught something about a handy hack. [*They were*] Edward was going to stay with Gibbs in the Long — he had gathered that also, & [*the*] it annoyed him [*How*] could Edward endure to stay with a brute like Gibbs? And, though he contrived to make some harmless [*remark about the*] enquiry about [185] hunting — when did it begin, or something [*very like*] inoffensive like that, Gibbs knew perfectly well that to Jevons he was simply a brute; & the old desire came [*over*] <to> him [*which*] somehow to make Jevons suffer for his insolence. But how? The usual forms of bullying which he had found effective with dirty little smugs [*at school were*] like Jevons at his public school were ruled out <at Oxford> — at any rate in Edwards rooms. So he sat fumbling with his pipe, & his glass; & both of them wished to God that Nigs would return.

When Edward came back with the second bottle he sat on a stool between his two friends with a feeling that he was keeping the peace between [*too*] two angry dogs. These encounters were always liable to happen in his rooms. He [*knew*] had friends in such different sets. And awkward as it was, when Jevons met Gibbs, difficult as it was to find some common topic of conversation, still the sense that he, Edward, was the link between them, that he could talk horses with Gibbs & [*classics wi*] literature with Jevons, & that as he sat between them <on his stool drinking his port> each was wishing the other at Jericho so that he might have Edward alone flattered the vanity which Eleanor said was [*so like*] <typically> Nigs. <(She had caught him once arranging his crest at a glass)> His face had a complacency certainly which was disagreeable; but then his face was extremely good looking. With an adroitness that showed that the [*situation*] present situation often occurred, he introduced a subject about which they could all talk — college gossip: stories about the Master; about the Mistress; about the Dons. There was a pause. Now of course Gibbs might go; or Jevons might go. But they sat on. Then, with an irritation which he scarcely disguised, Jevons stretched out his hand & took up the Antigone.

What Greek?" he said & began to read where he had opened.

Gibbs felt this as a direct insult. This dirty little swine came in; spoilt their talk; & then proceeded [186] to give himself airs at Gibbs's expense. He was a clumsy brute he knew; but still he knew the sort of thing that [*made*] Jevons minded. And he continued, as if there had been no interruption, to describe the hack that [*Edw*] he was going to get for Edward when Edward came to stay with them. Edward rather relished the situation himself. There was Jevons pretending to read the Antigone while he was really listening to every word they said & writhing with jealousy. He could not resist playing up to Gibbs. Yes — the last fortnight in September — he thought he could manage that. [*The*] [*His people in Scotland. Have the run of the place*] — [*his fam*] [*people in Scotland —*] [*only the*] [*no clothes — the*] <—Thank the Lord,> Gibbs went on — he would be alone — nobody knocking about — no clothes — nothing to bother one — & it was true that Edward knew [*that with every*] as every minute passed, that his <inescapable> scene with Jevons [*afterwards*] <was mounting in rage & hate.> would become more embittered. They had had at least a dozen scenes this term already over Gibbs; if it wasn't Gibbs it was Strauss — "Your little Jew friend." Jevons was becoming more & more exacting, Edward thought as he sipped his port. It might be well to have [*the scene*] a row & have done with it — as Jevons had threatened only last week. Only — the truth was that Edward could hardly afford to quarrel with Jevons; he soon got bored with Gibbs; & as for Strauss, that clever [*that*] little Jew was not clever in the way that Jevons was clever. No, Jevons was really much more his sort if only — he frowned, thinking of the extraordinary complications of college life — how impossible this sort of thing made it to settle down & get on with one's work — How could one work when one was always having scenes? — Anyhow, Gibbs never made difficulties of that kind. Gibbs would go off to his farmer's daughter in Exmoor; & leave Edward in peace to read his book; whereas Jevons — then Edward thought of Kitty. He [*got up*] drank off the last drop of his port & got up & stretched himself. It was [*halfpast*] almost twelve. Gibbs & Jevons both looked at him. "I'm off" he said. "Dont you hurry. The [187] wines in there" — he nodded at the other room "& there's whisky & soda." He began unfastening his waistcoat. He was going to bed whatever they said. And neither of them said anything. No, he was not going to be left alone with either of them. He walked into his bedroom & shut the door. Let them fight it out together if they liked. His own fight was postponed for the moment. He [*slid the*] [*cauti*] turned the key in the door. He put his money [*on*] in two heaps of silver & copper on either side of the looking glass as he always did, & [*gave*] ⟨gave⟩ one glance at his own rather flushed face, brushed the crest over his brow in the way which irritated Eleanor. The door slammed. Were they both gone? He was not sure. He waited, listening intently. ⟨Then he [*slid*] turned the key in the door⟩ [*Yes*] "Good night" said a muffled sinister voice, quite near him. That was Jevons — & Jevons [*was*] brewing up for a ⟨fine⟩ row. [*But*] And then Jevons went too. Edward stood for a moment at his bedroom window looking out into the garden. The may tree was invisible now — the pink splash was gone — the lamp had been put out. Still a piano tinkled; still there was a sound of distant laughter; & then again, profound quiet, & [*the cry*] a little chirp from some sleeping bird. Edward [*opened a thick*] undressed completely & then stopped, before he got into bed, & opened a book. It was a thick repulsive looking book, — the complete works perhaps of Lord Byron in double columns. He did not read it. He took out an envelope pressed between the pages. He extracted a photograph. Yes, that was Kitty Malone; Kitty, the loveliest, the purest, the most exalted of women. He looked at her for a minute, then replaced it in the complete works of Lord Byron. Nobody must know that he adored Kitty Malone.

[189] [FOURTH ESSAY]

November 23rd [1932]

That scene, though it may possibly throw some light upon the problems that worried Edward's younger brother Bobby when he first went to a public school and therefore indirectly explain his sister Rose's anger in the bathroom, and her consequent refusal to go "beetling" with Bobby in the Round Pond, is inevitably imperfect, not merely because certain necessary omissions and evasions have cramped the writer's pen. It is also imperfect because nobody who was not first at Rexby or St. James's and then at Benedict's in the summer of 1880 could possibly understand the force of the traditions and influences which had been working upon Edward ever since he was a boy of ten. Rexby, like St. James's, like Eton and Harrow or Winchester and Westminster, like so many of our great public schools, was a very old foundation. For almost five hundred years, English boys had been taught there; and since it was very closely connected with Oxford and Cambridge, had gone straight from Rexby, as Edward Pargiter had done, to one or other of the Universities; there again to become a member of a College.

In the history of the world, another four or five hundred years is no doubt less than a fraction of a second of time; but in the history of England, five hundred years is a very considerable period. The difference between 1530 and 1930 seems to us, at any rate, unmeasurable; when we reflect that during all that time Benedict's had been a college; that young men had sat, more or less, where Edward was sitting in May 1880; had been hearing lectures in the lecture room, and saying prayers in the [190] Chapel, and eating dinner in the hall; it is obvious that a variety, a complexity, an intricacy of tradition and theory and ceremony had accumulated, whose force, exerted as it was during the impressionable years that lie between ten and twenty, cannot be exaggerated and cannot be understood or described except by somebody who has actually experienced [it] himself. Happily, the habit of autobiography has become much commoner of late years; so that it is possible, even for an outsider, to make some rough estimate of the sort of influence which public schools and universities exercise upon young men. But even now, a great many inaccuracies are bound to occur, even in matters of fact. It is quite possible, for instance, that Edward would not have been reading *The Antigone*, but Thucydides and Cicero; it is also possible that the garden would not have had a may tree; and it is certain that to write "quadrangle" in a description of a Cambridge college would be as fatal a mistake as to talk of a court in writing of an Oxford college.

But granting that these are mistakes which can be corrected, and are not, perhaps, of critical importance, there remains the question of tradition, of influence; of all that is implied in the words of Edward's headmaster. To understand what Dr. Bealby meant when he preached the words that came to Edward's mind — indeed had become part of his creed, and were to influence him all his life — about belonging to a great and famous fellowship, about "being moved, as it were, all together, in something like a rhythmic harmony," about receiving and handing on an influence which derived from Jew, Greek, and Roman, an influence which made for "the sterner and more robust virtues — fortitude, self-reliance, intrepidity, devotion to the common weal; readiness for united action and self-sacrifice" — to understand what effect such teaching had had upon [I 91] Edward Pargiter and thousands upon thousands of other young men, so that as they sat in their rooms at Oxford and Cambridge, they felt themselves, as Edward felt himself, dedicated to carry on the tradition, with whatever expansions and modifications the University might suggest, to give the full effect of all this, and of infinitely more than all this, upon the whole mind and nature of an intelligent and vigorous young man, would be entirely impossible for anyone who had not spent ten years first at Rexby and then at Benedict's.

A highly educated foreigner, visiting Oxford in 1880, failed completely to understand what the life of an Oxford undergraduate meant. A working man would be equally at a loss. No doubt descriptions of young men like Edward occur in the works of the women novelists of the eighties. But, quite apart from the reserve which would have been imposed upon her, not only from ignorance but from modesty and convention, she would have been almost as ignorant as a working man of the tradition upon which the words of Dr. Humphrey or Dr. Arnold or Dr. Percival, or any of the headmasters of Eton, Harrow, Westminster and Winchester were based. The ignorance of a middle-class woman in the eighties was not necessarily as profound as the ignorance of a miner or a plate layer. It was possible by 1880 that a middle-class woman had been educated under Miss Beale at Cheltenham. But a glance at Miss Beale's life is enough to prove that the aims which inspired the founders of that famous Ladies' College were radically different from any that could have been in the minds of those ancient worthies who were responsible for the founding of Eton and Harrow and Winchester and Westminster. One brief quotation is enough to prove this: "The founders of this college and day school for girls* [were anxious to make it clear that their aim was to develop in the pupils character and fitness for the duties of later life. Hence the first report states that it was intended to afford, on reasonable terms, an education based upon religious principles which, preserving the modesty and gentleness of the female character, should so far cultivate (a girl's) intellectual powers as to fit her for the discharge of those responsible duties which devolve upon her as a wife, mother, mistress and friend, the natural companion and helpmeet of man."] [1 92] That being so,

* There is a marginal note here which reads: "87". Woolf has begun a quotation from Elizabeth Raikes *Dorothea Beale of Cheltenham* (London: Constable 1908) p 87. The remainder of the passage is supplied from that book.

the whole tradition and influence of Cheltenham were completely at variance with the tradition and influence of Eton and Oxford. For example, "The establishment of scholarships did not fit into Miss Beale's educational schemes. She was not wholly opposed to them. [One, in 1870, was accepted for the College, when Colonel Pearce bestowed a gift of £1000 to found the Pearce Scholarship for the daughter of an army officer, and Miss Beale in the last year of her life established one for Casterton.] * But she had a great horror of a system by which one school or college could buy promising pupils from others, and she held that it was hard on earnest students who were not naturally quick to see assistance given only to ability." ** Therefore her usual plan was to advance money, from her private purse, and see that it was returned "on the grounds that it might be of use to others." "There is a loan fund," she would say, when a girl who seriously wished to learn might have to leave on the score of expense. And one glance at Miss Beale's address to her staff in 1873, when the new building was opened, shows how fundamentally the woman headmaster differed from the man. "Let us ask for true wisdom [, for lowliness of heart, that we may esteem others better than ourselves. Let us ask, above all, for that most excellent gift of charity, without which all else is as sounding brass, or a tinkling cymbal. Something of this spirit of love for others does live among us, as we see by those who have come to join their prayers with ours today. I would ask them not to forget afterwards, but to remember us when they return to their homes; and I would fain hope that the College, though transplanted to a new place, will always be to you 'the old College.' "] † Hence a girl trained at Cheltenham, who had gone on,

* Marginal note: "175". The bracketed insertion is again from Raikes, p 175, and replaces Woolf's dots of elision. That she gave page numbers in the margin implies her intention to quote some or all of the elided material, here and in the other Raikes passages.

** Here Raikes continues: " 'I have refused,' she said at a later period, 'all scholarships except one, the chief condition of which is poverty. . . .' "

† In the text is written: "Let us ask for true wisdom . . ." with the Raikes page number, "159," in the margin; Woolf may not have intended to quote the entire passage supplied here.

as it was just becoming possible that she might have gone on to Somerville, would probably have erred as profoundly in describing the life of an undergraduate at Christ Church or King's in the year 1880 as a miner or a plate layer would have erred. The novels of Ouida give an extreme example of the ignorance of a very clever woman with regard to the other sex.

But though Eton and the Ladies' College differed profoundly in tradition, and in wealth, and in age, the masters and mistresses at both schools had to deal with boys and girls at a very impressionable and emotional age, and their problems were in some respects similar. [193] Miss Beale had "a horror of the unhealthy attachments which are often a source of danger in girls' schools." She would prevent herself from making friends with the girls from motives of "fastidious honesty." * And she would impress the same creed upon her teachers. The girls would certainly fall in love with their teachers. "The children should give you respect and esteem [and you can give them sympathy and affection too,]** and as they are children, they may have a helping hand; but make them give up, if possible, sentimental worship. They must not do right for love of you, but because it is right." † So far, presumably, Miss Beale was only saying what all headmasters were saying; even when she added: "What miserable, weak, sickly creatures many women are, who must always have a Pope." †† She was speaking rather as a woman than as a man.

* Marginal note: "256". This and the next passage quoted are from Raikes p 255–56, in a letter from Dorothea Beale to Clara Arnold, "afterwards Mrs Charles Robinson."

** Woolf may have elided this passage not from haste but for emphasis.

† The next paragraph in Raikes (p 256) reads in part: "I know there must be a certain amount of hero-worship in the young. They need help from parents and teacher, but we must train them out of dependence. . . . they waste time and strength in day-dreams about their idol. When a little older they are always fancying themselves in love, because they have got used to an excitement of feeling."

†† Raikes p 256.

Love, at any rate, was present in Edward's room that night, as certainly as money was present: but though in this respect his room at St Katharine's was not unlike the drawing room at 58 Abercorn Terrace, it is clear that the love which drove him first to look at Dr. Humphrey's portrait in order to conquer it, and then to write a poem to Persephone and then to lock the door against Ashton, and then to take out the photograph of Kitty Malone from between the pages of Byron differed very much from his sisters' emotions when they heard that Hugh Burke was home, and wished to meet him, or when they peeped behind the blind at the young man who was paying a call two doors down the street.

In the first place, his own feelings were much more familiar to him. Like Bobby, he had been free from a very early age to walk about London alone; and the knowledge that he acquired from the streets was soon supplemented by the boys at school. Then, of course, he learnt, as he grew older, [194] either from his housemaster or from older boys, the dangers of love; and the best method of exorcising love — he, himself, when he was a prefect, considered it to be one of his duties to exterminate the forms of love that were considered objectionable. And when, after drinking port and reading *The Antigone*, he felt sensations with which he had long been familiar, his mind automatically proceeded to combat them; and as the process was disagreeable, he felt, when he succeeded, not only a different and less disturbing emotion — a generalised idealisation of sex — but also some self-approval. He had conquered. This feeling, however, for the other sex, was not wholly wrong (when he thought of Kitty Malone, he was moved to write a poem to her), for even a prejudiced observer, like his sister Eleanor, would have admitted, if she had watched him writing a poem to Kitty, or looking at her photograph, that his face then took on a beauty and a sensibility which were quite absent from it when the thought of sex alone inspired it. Then he had looked flushed and uneasy — though there was nothing in his expression then that was more disagreeable or disgusting than the expression that Eleanor might have seen when she held out a piece of tea cake to the liver and white spaniel. The expression simply signified greed.

But the whole question of Edward's feelings, and of the true nature of love in his rooms in St Katharine's, in the summer of 1880, became much more complicated when he sat on the stool between Jack Gibbs and Tony Ashton. Then he felt a variety of emotions. For Gibbs he had a perfectly simple, if rather shallow, affection. For Tony, his feeling was much less simple and less shallow. For Tony not only loved him, but objected to his loving anybody else. Thus, without feeling anything that could be called love for Tony, he was [195] tempted to irritate Tony, by pretending that he was going to stay with Gibbs, not simply from malice, but because Tony's love for him conflicted with the peculiar passion which he had for Kitty Malone.

Even without reading the poem "To Persephone" which he had so carefully destroyed, it is plain that his feeling for his cousin was peculiar. It in no way resembled his feeling for Gibbs or for Tony, for one thing, because it was largely imaginary. She was his cousin, but the conventions which regulated the intercourse between undergraduates and their cousins, in the year 1880, were strict in the extreme. He had never seen her alone. He had only seen her half a dozen times in his life at dances and dinners and picnics. He saw Gibbs and Tony almost daily. They had discussed every subject — hunting, philosophy, Greek, sex — in common; they had eaten together and worked together. With Tony the intimacy had become so acute that it seriously threatened Edward's methodical habits of work. That, as he realised himself, was hopelessly bad. If he had written a poem to Tony or to Gibbs, it would have been quite different from his poem to Persephone. (And without too much license, one is justified in thinking that a poem written to a person whom the writer knows little, whom he idealises, whom he sentimentalises, is always a bad poem.) Nobody who has read much verse, or even prose, can fail to be aware that the worst literature is that which is inspired by a vague feeling of reverence, of ecstasy, of romance.

For though the feeling may be, as Edward's was, extremely strong, it contains [sentence unfinished]. It was not only, as he said, that he was not a poet; nor was it only that his ten years of reading Greek had so completely coloured his mind that when he wrote English, he wrote it in a Greek way — he imitated Sappho or Theocritus; not Herrick or Campion: he saw himself as a Greek shepherd, whereas he [196] was naturally far more an English youth, and, had he been a poet, would have gone instinctively to the English poets, had he wanted models; or better still, have gone to no model at all, but lingered outside the farm, when Gibbs was courting the girl there, and listened to the girls and old women singing as they hung up the washing, or rocked the cradle. It was not only that nature and education both made it difficult for him to express his genuine emotion in a genuine way; it was also that he was writing a poem to a girl whom he scarcely knew.* It contains elements of falsity. For when the writer idealises his subject he almost always sentimentalises himself. Without being like Mrs Pugh and piecing together the scraps of poetry on a sheet of newspaper, one may be sure that Edward's poem to Persephone was largely a poem to himself. In his ignorance of her, self-love and self-pity were sure to enter into it, however much the contortions of the metre might disguise them; because Edward approved of himself for having conquered himself; and, of course, the first condition of love poetry such as Sappho's and Theocritus's is "that the writer has eliminated herself or himself completely."

Edward's severe training at the hands of several learned men for ten years showed him at once that the poem was worthless. He tore it to fragments. But he by no means destroyed his own feelings. They remained difficult, conflicting, and very strong. The battle was only postponed, he remarked, when he went to bed and locked his door. And perhaps the best way to illustrate feelings which he himself

* "N (take in)". A memorandum to herself by Woolf. What was to be inserted here, from where?

could scarcely analyse would be to quote a scene in which the object of his adoration, Katharine Persephone Malone, revealed herself, and thus, incidentally, her relation to Edward.

[197] Kitty Malone was the daughter of Dr. Malone, the Master of St. Katharine's, and her mother had been a Rigby, and a cousin of Edward's mother who was also a Rigby; Edward and Kitty were cousins, though distantly. Kitty was an only child and at present about twenty-one.

[199] [FOURTH CHAPTER]

Nov. 24th [1932]

The clock, or rather the innumerable clocks, had only just struck eleven, but already the guests had gone, & Dr. & Mrs. Malone, the Howard Fripps & Kitty <Malo> were standing in the drawing room at the Lodge in the attitudes of people when a party is over, & it is scarcely worth while to sit down though one may stand about for a few minutes discussing the party before [*one*] going to bed. As Professor Howard Fripp (of Harvard) & his wife were staying at the Lodge, comment upon the party was [*less*] [*bound to be more*] restricted [*than*] on both sides, for the [*the*] Fripps were bound to say that the evening had been most delightful, it had been a great privilege to meet Professor [*Robinson*] [*Campermore, his wife was*] B <[*Bo*]> in the flesh; [*he*] Mrs. Dickson had [*been even*] [*lived up*] more than lived up to her reputation, & so on, while the Malones on their [*pa*] [*side*] <part> had to brush aside these compliments, <but> had to [*regret that*] assert that they had seldom known Mrs. Lardner* in better spirits — for that was a tribute to the charms of Mrs. Fripp — a handsome <& vivacious> American lady, whose dress [*had*] was far above the Oxford standard, though her accent — she was from the middle west — [*had*] & some of her expressions [*had struck upon*] [*carried some surprise*] <were so strange in Oxford circles that Mr Lardner & Mrs. Dickson & Professor Bonamy had all been secretly surprised>.

[*Fr*] On the other hand, nobody would have known that Professor Howard Fripp was an American. With his little goatee beard, his [*formal & courteous manners*] <fine distinguished face>, & [*his*] a pronunciation that [*was*] if it was not quite English was certainly

* "The Howard Fripps Miss Lardner" (note on facing page).

not anything else in particular, [*had he*] [*had*] he might have been a professor from any university; & a very distinguished professor too. ([*His*] He was probably the most cultivated person in the room.) Although his culture differed slightly from the culture of the other professors, it was just as great, in fact [*perhaps*] it was in some ways wider, & smoother, & more [*cosp*] cosmopolitan. His dress was perfect, & his manners courteous to the point of ceremony.

[I 100] [*He presented Kitty with a*] Kitty, a tall rather large boned [*youn*] girl, with the Rigby red hair & the red & white complexion that goes with it, <&> had dropped her handkerchief. [*Prof*] The Professor stooped & gave it her with a little bow. Old Chuffy Andrews, the historian, would never have done that even if he could have stooped, which [*a*] was becoming daily more impossible — [*for*] <since> his [*pas*] [*knowledge*] <love> of food was only second to his love of facts. Kitty took the handkerchief. She knew how to take handkerchiefs — [*one*] she bowed very slightly, & smiled [.] with a peculiar [*deferen*] <chary> deference to the distinguished man who had presented it

"Now ladies —" said Mrs. Malone <waving her hand> — in the cheerful & [*confid*] commanding tones of one who has spent so many years in taking the ladies into one room; leaving gentlemen in another — indeed she had been a hostess in Oxford for over thirty years — that [*there can be no doubt that*] the right moment has come. She was an extremely handsome woman still, though she was over sixty [. *She was dressed not quite in the height of the fashion, but very nearly; &*] <& she was dressed, if not quite in the height of the newest fashion, still in creditable imitation. [*There was nothing of the articles craze upon her*] She made no concession to the present craze for Liberty fabrics> her beautiful white hair was perfectly dressed, so as to frame a strong rosy face <in coils & whirls of white>; [*to which*] age was giving a<n> [*touch*] <air> of distinction — the distinction of character, rather than of intellect. Dr. Malone who was standing [*under*] <by> the Tudor fireplace, under the portrait of one of his predecessors, looked as if it would only need a few touches of the brush to hang above the fireplace himself — he was so dignified, so ruddy, so [*eighteen*] handsome in the Eighteenth Century style himself — [*took*] <He had> seconded his wife's remark, as he had [*always*] seconded such remarks for thirty years, [*& said*] by saying

[*Fr*] Well, [*Fripp &*] I will just [*smoke*] <give Fripp> one cigar in the study & then we will follow you."

Professor Howard Fripp then bent very low over Mrs. Malones hand; & not quite so low over Kittys hand; & then opened the door, for the ladies, [*to*] while Kitty kissed her father good night.

The ladies went slowly, carrying silver candlesticks, [I 101] up the broad old staircase with the carved banisters, to their bedrooms upstairs. Portraits of former masters of St Katharines looked down upon them as they went; & Kitty following behind her mother & Mrs. Fripp [*gave*] secretly blessed Mrs. Fripp for not stopping [*as they*] <as they went up> & asking to be told, just once more, who they all were. Mrs. Fripp, in Kitty's opinion, compared favourably with many Americans. Mrs. Fripp was rather fun. At least, they had got through the sights this morning in record time. She had never done the Bodleian quite so quick. Kitty felt a little guilty, [*that*] [*because of course*] perhaps she ought to have told Mrs. Fripp [*that they could have seen*] [<[*had*] *permission to*>] <they ought to see the> Spanish library — but [*when Mrs. Fripp*] as Mrs. Fripp [*did not know about the Spanish library*,] had yawned quite perceptibly after only two hours, & had said in her extraordinary nasal voice "Well my dear I guess you're a bit fed up with sights — what d'you say to an ice at that dear old bun shop [*in the*] with the bow window?" Kitty had concealed the fact that she [*had a note to*] had special permission to see — oh any number of things! She had only to mention her fathers name — if the curator, or the librarian, or the [*Dean*] porter, or the lodgekeeper, [*or the*] [*were so remiss*] did not know her by sight — but they always did — & then doors were unlocked, panels were rolled back; curtains were raised; charming men in gowns & [*surplices*] <caps> presented themselves, & [*so were*] the process of showing Americans the sights of Oxford [*became*] lasted not one morning but the better part of three days. So they had eaten ices instead of going to see the Reynolds windows. And Mrs. Fripp as she ate her ice [*th*] had talked on [*in*] in a way which had [*amused*] <made> Kitty laugh aloud, about [*in*] Oxford, & about Harvard, & about her own home in the Middle West. Kitty did not understand half [*what*] she said; [*her s*] [*she supposed that*] [*American slang was in the worst*] [*she knew that*] The Oxford Professors & their wives made fun of American voices, & American slang; [I 102] so that Kitty would never be allowed to use the words that Mrs Fripp was using; but she was very much amused, nevertheless, & really for a moment hoped that her parents would let her go [*out*] & stay with the [*F*] Fripps & see "what we're like at home my dear."

They had now reached the famous [*guest chamber wh*] <[*upper land*]> <room> in which distinguished guests [*were*] always [*lodged*] slept when they stayed at the Lodge. Mrs. Malone just [*looked in*] <opened the door>, to see that everything was all right; & to receive, for the thousandth time, her guests rapturous exclamation, as she saw the [*great bed,*] [*fourposter bed, the old cupboard, dressing tables*] [*the*] her own dressing gown & her husbands pyjamas laid out on the vast <fourposter> bed in which Queen Elizabeth had *not* slept (that was the [*little*] joke that Mrs. Malone [*had also made*] always made) & the silver candles, & the looking glasses & the dressing tables & the carved fireplace — & in short all the things that made staying at the Lodge "something one will remember all one's life, Mrs. Malone" — Yes, Mrs. Fripp said that too. But her night gown looked a little odd on the counterpane, Kitty thought: it was of brilliant green silk. And the dressing table was covered with [*jars & c*] little pots & jars. Could it possibly be that the wonderful complexion which had made all the Oxford ladies look a little pale [*or*] & lustreless owed its [*brilliance*] <wonder> to paint & powder? Mrs. Malone [*shut the door rather abruptly*] said good night with that additional courtesy which, Kitty knew, meant that she [*disapproved. Mrs. Fripp merely squeezed Kitty's arm.*] <did not altogether approve of the> wives of American professors. Kitty shook hands. To her surprise, Mrs Fripp kissed her. "Thanks [*a thousand times*] <ever so much> for showing me all these sights, Miss Malone" she said. For she had liked Kitty, & the curious look of resignation with which Kitty had said "Oh I'd like to awfully, Mrs Fripp" — Mrs Fripp had suggested taking a fly & driving out into the country "but I'm afraid I must be back for tea. <The> Undergraduates [*are*] [I 103] are coming, & Mama will want me to pour out tea" had touched her & puzzled her. Kitty obviously enjoyed her ice. Obviously she would have liked a drive. And just as obviously she did not in the least enjoy pouring out tea. Mrs Fripp had made some joke, in doubtful taste, about not wishing to deprive the undergraduates of Kitty. And Kitty had looked quite blank — Kitty [*had*] did not suppose undergraduates [*wanted her.*] cared about her: certainly she did not care about undergraduates. <Did she not enjoy this pouring out tea for undergraduates>

[*She*] <Kitty> said good night to her mother, & went on to her own room on the floor above. It was a warm night, but <as> the housemaid had shut the windows & drawn the curtains, Kittys first action was to thrust them open. Then she leant [*on her*] against the window frame & looked out. No, it had not been [*a very enjoyable*] <such a bad> day. •{ [*It might have been worse,*] but — [*Oh dear*] [*w*] <W>hat was the use of thinking the same thoughts every night? There was absolutely no way out of it — she knew that — over & over again? [*Wh*] After all, what [*did she want*] <was wrong>? She did not want anything in particular. Showing Mrs. Fripp the sights? }• Somebody had to show Mrs. Fripp the sights. Somebody had to pour out tea. And yet, Kitty [*had come to feel*] felt tonight again that unless she could escape, somehow somewhere. — [*She looked round the room. It was a lovely old room. She would*] — she paused. How could she possibly escape? Where to? [*What did she want?*] To what? After all, it always came back to that when she argued the question with her mother. She was not a girl any longer. She was 'out': she was grown up. And she had every advantage — if she had not enough to do at home, she could help Mrs. Dickson in her district. Or, if she wanted to keep up her music, she could have lessons. She could take up a subject if she liked & work in the Bodleian. <Some girls did do that.> At the same time Mrs. Malone always said, there was plenty for [*an*] <the> only daughter [*to do at home. After all, "your fathers position, Miss Malone, of the Master of St Katharines to do merely*] of a man 'in your fathers position' to do at home. There were the [1 104] undergraduates. Mrs. Malone made a point of asking every undergraduate [*either*] to some meal at least once a term. [*She was* [*at h*] *'at Home' on Tuesdays — today was a Tuesday — & then they*] She considered it part of her duty as the Master's wife. Thus few days passed without having an undergraduate to lunch or tea; &, as today was a Tuesday, & Tuesday was her at Home day, there had been more undergraduates than usual. Oh how they bored her <she hated under[graduates]>! To Kitty an undergraduate was not a young man; he was an uncouth, tongue tied, rather pink, very awkward, [*rather*] [*generally*] youth who <was discovered standing alone in the drawing room [*— they would cause her such*]> flopped down in a chair, sprang up to hand bread & butter, flopped down again, <took a [*pi*] cup> had [*huge*] red hands, answered in monosyllables, but only if you asked him the right question; — She knew by this time what questions <to ask> the rowing men, the reading men, the [*p*] Eton men, the Winchester men, the Rugby men, [*answered,* [*& which*] *& then lapsed into dreadful silences. But*] & yet one which they did not answer; but lapsed into dreadful silences <[*wh. were so*] or only with yes or no> She had known a<n> [*young*] undergraduate sit silent for twenty minutes. And all the time somebody had to go on talking. Her mother could talk almost incessantly. Her father [*was*] had a series of remarks which he made according to circumstances & then disappeared. [*It was all very well for him*]

— he had [*Chapel*] work, in Chapel, or somebody to see in the study. But she had to sit there listening to her mother asking Mr. Philborough [*what he*] about the college boat, or the college cricket, or the beagles, or the football, or the lecture, or the concert, according to the time of year. And sometimes [*the undergraduat*] all these topics were exhausted, & still the undergraduate sat on; even Mrs. Malone could think of nothing <truly> to say. <She had reason to use [*m*] <She asked him to> Still the undergraduate sat on. Mrs. Malone gave him every help. She was an expert in helping undergraduates to go. But still the undergraduate sat on, <at last the dressing bell rang> An undergraduate had been known to stay in the same chair, without [*opening his mouth*] speaking from half past four to a quarter to eight. And yet Mrs Malone [*always*] [*said that it was*] had argued, "Poor boy, he comes from Repton."

The Eton boys & the Harrow boys could at any [I 105] rate be trusted to go. Some of them were apparently at their ease. [*But*] And there were others like Edward Pargiter [*&*] <or> Anthony Ashley who [*emerged for*] were not just 'undergraduates' <& so they came to lunch>. Edward was a cousin; & Mr. Ashley was the son of [*an*] old friends. And of course Lord Lammermuir was what her father called 'a very able young fellow —" He would go very far — [*He was*] Paragraphs about his speeches at the Union <already> appeared in the London papers. St Katharines had produced several prime ministers, several ambassadors, several viceroys & several permanent heads of colonial, [*the great dip*] offices. Indeed, [*no*] when Kitty had done pouring out tea for the undergraduates she would change into evening dress, & help her father & mother to receive [*these same undergraduates, whom she could <just> remember, when she was a child*] [*as undergraduates, & they had now become*] cabinet ministers, generals, explorers, [*men*] diplomats, who had been undergraduates when she was crawling about the floor after a coloured ball. "[*You ha*] Most girls would give their eyes to be in your position" her mother would conclude — for these arguments between mother & daughter were fairly frequent; & then Kitty would wander off to her own room, & stand [*ju*] as she was standing tonight, & wonder what on earth she could do to escape.

[*The bells began ringing again:*]

The bells of Oxford were striking eleven. Kitty began to undress. With some difficulty she unhooked her white satin frock; & <then> unfastened her necklace of small but genuine pearls, & then she stopped again & looked out of the window. How she hated Oxford! It was all very well for people like the Fripps, who came for a night or two & then went away; or for her father & mother — they loved being Master & Mistress; & presumably it was all right for the undergraduates — at least Kitty, standing at the window, could hear a roar of laughter now & then, [*& a cr*] which seemed to prove that when they were [I 106] alone in their own rooms [*they had plenty to say to each other,*] <the undergraduates> enjoyed themselves; but for her, [*Oxford wa*] who had been born in Oxford & lived in Oxford all her life, [*& Oxford was*] & was the daughter of the master of an Oxford college — Oxford was [*well, all she could say was that*] the dullest place in the whole world. She knew it all by heart, to begin with. [*She felt that*] She had stood at that window & heard those bells ever since she could remember. — [*the room had been her nursery.*] She had poured out tea [*almost*] ever since she could remember. She knew all her father's stories <about Oxford> — such of them at least as were told in the presence of ladies. And it was her own fault if she did not know [*which college was which, &*] the history of Oxford by heart, too, since [*she had gone*] [*shown visitors round Oxford for many years now; &*] her father was one of the greatest authorities upon Oxford [*li*] alive< . > [*& was engaged in writing a monumental history of St Katharines in which he would have been*]

As for [*St*] Katharines <itself>, [*was she not*] <she was> called [*after*] of course, [*that*] <the> great lady who had endowed the college, some five hundred years ago[*? And*] < , > & she could have known, had she chosen, more about the history of Katharines than any woman in the world, for her father was writing a monumental work upon Katharines, & would have been only too glad, as Kitty knew, [*if she*] of her help. [*She had once helped him,*] There he used to sit, of an evening, with all his documents round him — And he would have liked nothing better than that she should sit too, deciphering, transcribing; & helping him in those minute researches which were the delight of his life into the [*life*] careers of every man who had ever been at Katharines in the course of five hundred years. But [*then,*] she had upset the inkpot once — she could never forget the sight of that black stream flowing imperturbably over a genealogical tree — & she [*had made*] had made some awful [I 107] mistakes too — "You [*are not*] share the inability of your sex, my dear, to grasp the importance of historical [*truth*] facts" her father had said with ironical courtesy once when she had hopelessly muddled up [*the*] two different [*branches*] men with the same name. But her father had been very patient. He would willingly have taught her palaeography. And when she made [*excuses*] excuses, & gradually stopped coming to his study after tea, he had accepted the fact that his daughter was not an historian, with a [*gentle*] resignation that had made her ashamed of herself. [*The*]

"Thats the worst of it" Kitty said to herself, as she unfastened her necklace, "Theyre both so awfully [*nice*] <good> to me — Both her father & her mother only wanted her to do what she wanted to do — within the limits that were imposed by her being so young, & so nice looking, &, after all, the daughter of one of the best known men in Oxford. Kitty took her brush & comb & began brushing her hair in front of the looking glass. Her hair [*w*] wanted an immense amount of brushing — it was the thick red hair that had been the bane of so many little Rigby girls, for it took about twice as long to brush as other little girls hair, & [*then*] stood up "like a fuzz bush"; at the slightest provocation. Kitty as [she] brushed vigorously [*peeped at her own*] saw her own face in the glass, with the pursed expression natural to one who is brushing vigorously. <But even

when she was not pursing her lips> She was not [*particularly beautiful.*] really pretty at all. She felt like a cart horse beside Mrs. Fripp — in fact she felt like a cart horse beside most girls of her own age — her cheek bones were too prominent, & her eyes were too wide apart, & her mouth was too big. Her [*great*] beauty was her <clear> skin — that was beautifully white & red & soft — indeed it was covered with the finest down; & her teeth were white & strong & regular; [*& she held herself very well,*] & her body though too big & [*strongly made*] tall was [*well*] <'flat between the shoulders' She knew her points> She was [*ab*] five foot nine — was well proportioned & she held herself very [I 108] well, though she did not hold the perfect erectness of her mother's carriage. <But then her mother used to sit for 3 hours a day with a quill pen tied upright under her chin> The action of brushing her hair & seeing herself from time to time in the glass naturally made her [*think*] wonder whether she had been looking nice at dinner — [*had*] <what had> Mrs. Fripp thought [*her ni*] of her? Mrs. Fripp had looked perfectly lovely, Kitty thought, especially in her evening dress.

[*And Mrs. Fripp had kissed her — the thought*] Kitty [*looked*] suddenly remembered that with [*pleasure*] a start of pleasure <Mrs. Fripp had kissed her> What fun it would be to go to America, Kitty thought — though she supposed that Harvard would <only> be Oxford <over> again [*only*] <rather> smaller. Still, they might make expeditions into the country — she & Mrs. Fripp together, while Papa & Mama were [*going to the usual*] being shown round Harvard.

But Kitty was not <largely> endowed with [*that <any> inconvenient faculty of*] the true day dreamers [*power*] <power> of inventing scenes — her reason told her that nothing was less likely than <that> she should go to America. And so, still brushing her hair, she thought again of the dinner party; & how very dowdy Mrs Dickson had looked beside Mrs Fripp; & how old Chuffy had [*given his*] spilt the soup <as usual> into his beard; & how Mrs. Lathom had glared <as usual>

— & then she went back to the tea party — Thank heaven that was over for another week — & [*from the*] then [*she thought about*] & then thinking of the [*horror of*] horror of pouring out tea for fifteen undergraduates, she remembered, as [*she had not*] one remembers afterwards what one has not time to think about while it is actually happening, how different [*Tony*] Mr. Ashton was from the others — Why had he come, again?

[*Kittys knowledge of undergraduates was necessarily limited in the extreme.*] [I 109] This was the third time that Tony Ashton had come to the Lodge this term.

When undergraduates took to coming to the Lodge of their own accord, — & they sometimes did — only one construction could be put upon their conduct — [*&*] at least by Dr & Mrs Malone; & they put it, when they were alone together, [*rather in the*] [*after*] something after this fashion. "That young Hammond was here again — Mrs Malone would say. "I dont know that I [*think*] want him for a son in law." Let me see, let me see, which is Hammond?" the doctor would reflect. "[*Quite an able youth; but —*] Ah yes — Quite an able youth — but . . ." [*& then*] or Mrs. Malone would say, [*I rather suspect*] "Lord Lammermuir [*obviously*] couldnt take his eyes off Kitty ⟨all the evening⟩" — an announcement that Dr. Malone, without being really worldly, took more seriously; for Lord Lammermuir [*would be a*] had a very important career before him — he was the son of the foreign secretary — & though Dr Malone was perfectly content with his own position, as Master of Katharines, he [*had a distinct*] [*appreciated*] was rather ahead of his time in wishing to bring Oxford into touch with the [*wider life*] ⟨larger world⟩ of London, & a [*daughter*] son in law who was in the very inner circle of [*Whig*] Tory politicians would have helped to bring about a union which [*was desirable* [*for*] *on both sides*] ⟨had much to be said for it⟩. But, of course, [*the matter must be decid*] [*left entirely to Kitty herself. Neither Dr. or Mrs Malone*] This was a matter for Kitty to decide for herself — neither Dr or Mrs. Malone would ever have brought pressure upon their daughter — they only wanted her to marry the man who would make her happy. <And on principle they set their faces very steadily against any attachment whatever between their daughter & any undergraduate>

Thus when Tony Ashton called at the Lodge for the third time in one term Kitty supposed for a moment that he was attracted by her. And yet — as she took off [*her brooch, &*] poured out [I 110] a tumbler of water & began to brush her teeth she recalled [*Tony*] the strange apparition of Tony Ashton among all the other undergraduates & her instinct told her that whatever the reason was that led Mr Ashton to come, it was not the same reason that had once led Mr Hammond to come, or <that had led> Lord Lammermuir to look at her. No, Tony Ashton did not [*like her*] look at her in that way at all. He looked at her quite differently. He did not like her <she guessed. She was not sure> She did not think that she liked him. Yet he was much easier to talk to than most of the undergraduates. [*He was*] Had he been at Eton? She thought not. Anyhow he was much more at <his> ease than most of the undergraduates — & he had beautiful hands, she remembered. And they had talked about Edward Pargiter. [*Of course*] That was natural, because Edward was her cousin, & Edward [*&*] <was> Tony Ashton<'s> [*were*] great<est> friend[*s*] — they were in the same set.

Kittys knowledge of undergraduate life was extremely limited. She sometimes went to tea [*with their*] [*when*] with her mother; [*or with their mothers*] — <but> She had never been alone in the room with an undergraduate in her life. But she knew of course that they had [*societies & debating*] societies of all kinds among themselves, & that [*they*] there were different sets — [*the b*] the rowing set, the reading set, the Eton set, the Winchester set, & so on. Tony Ashton was in the reading set. Edward was more or less in the reading set too. Edward had an enormous admiration for Tony Ashton — he had told her so. And Edward, Kitty was beginning to suspect, was falling in love with her.

Heavens, she thought, brushing her teeth as vigorously as she had brushed her hair, what a bore that will be" — she meant that it would be a bore having that particular scene all over again with Edward. [*Of course, she*] <It> had been rather fun the first time — with Edgar Hammond. [*But for some reason,*] [I 111] [*Edward Pargiter, with his beautiful Greek nose, & his little crest of hair, & his general*] & she had minded very much, refusing Alan Hammond — he had gone so white & then so red, & [*had*] the tears had actually come into his eyes & he had clenched his fists when he asked her to marry him <she refused him> at the Balliol Ball last year — She had sobbed herself to sleep that night — though by now he was in India & had probably forgotten all about her. But Edward, with his beautiful Greek nose & his little crest of hair & his [*general*] reputation for being good at everything somehow irritated her. She felt that he would be very persistent [*. It would be impossible to make him understand*] <& [he] would never believe that she did not want to marry him. She feared his tears.> . . . So, in the intervals of pouring out tea, she had run down Edward to Tony Ashton, so that Tony might give Edward a hint. No, she did not like Tony Ashton. [*He was like a snake.*] There was something cold & clammy about him. <He was like a snake.> [*He was physically disagreeable to her. She did not like*] <she reflected thus on the look wh> It was his complexion partly — he was so pale: & he looked so sickly; but of course he had beautiful hands, & a <smooth> face that was rather like a womans. But why on earth Tony Ashton came to tea, she could not imagine — unless it were to find out something about her & Edward. It was quite obvious that he was the sort of undergraduate who [*loathed tea parties.*] hated tea parties — And yet he was much easier to talk to than the other undergraduates.

The bells were beginning all over again. It must be half past eleven. She finished undressing & put on the long white nightgown that was laid on the counterpane. Then she went to the window; & blew out two of the candles on the dressing table — the third she would place on the table by her bed — But she must not stand [*at the window*] at an open window in her nightgown, even with only one candle — anybody might see in — & if somebody saw in — she had [*been*] got into [I 112] dreadful hot water with her mother already for doing that — Her mother had said that [*with all those*] she must be even more careful, with all those young men about, than most girls of her age. So, as the night was very warm, she [*no*] removed the candle to her bedside, & because nobody could 'see in' if she lay in bed with a candle beside her.

And yet though the last bell — which was it? — She ought to have known every bell in Oxford by its sound ⟨as her father did⟩ — was still [*saying*] striking half past eleven, & half past eleven was considered late, she was not at all sleepy. She would read a little before she put out her light. What she ought to do, she reflected, sitting on her bed, with naked feet, was to finish the seventh chapter of Stubbs vol 3. Stubbs vol. 3 was staring her in the face [*on*] ⟨in⟩ her little book case. A bookmarker was stuck about [*the*] a third of the way through. If she read [*ten*] twenty pages of Stubbs daily, she had calculated that she would have finished vol. 3 by the end of May: that left — how many vols. did it leave? [*Only*] Four more. [*And in the long vacation she would have more time, & might read*] But she had not read twenty pages of Stubbs daily — no, she had missed two days this week completely, partly owing to the Frippses, & there had also been [*a*] the [*New*] Christ Church Ball. So that really she ought to read sixty pages of Stubbs vol. 3. if she were [*going to*] tonight.

The task seemed to her impossible; but she had a dogged strain [*he*] in her, — her grandmothers had [*not*] been the wives of Yorkshire squires for generations — & [*so she did not like*] & after all, [*she had*] Gibbon was longer than Stubbs. She had read every word of Gibbon — cutting the notes. Notes did not count. And often a days reading of Stubbs was mercifully curtailed by the fact the actual reading matter was only [I 113] two inches at the top of the page.

She opened the book in order to see whether her luck was in tonight. She pulled herself together & took the book from the book case. Her collection of books was small; [*but rather queer.*] There were the books she had read as a child — like the Fairchild family; [*& there*] & a prayer book & a bible; & there were also two copies of Sesame & Lilies — indeed she had a third but as that was presented by the author, Mrs. Malone kept it for her in the book case downstairs. And then there were three more bound volumes ⟨[*historys of Oxford*]⟩ ⟨on Law & Duty⟩, also presented by distinguished men, friends of pupils of her fathers. [*But she was no great reader;*] (the only book [*she would*] that tempted her was the Fairchild) [*Mrs Malone only allowed her to*] [⟨*&*⟩ *so many books like Jane Eyre,* ⟨*&*⟩ *were forbidden; that so*] ⟨But as⟩ most of English literature was forbidden, [*so that*] it was a happy chance that she had no particular wish to read it, & [*only*] [*what*] [*such immoral works as Jane Eyre, bored her ra*] when she did get hold of such immoral works as Jane Eyre, they bored her so much that she was glad to accept her mother's ruling that [*she was too young to read them*] they were not [*nice*] ⟨fit⟩ reading for a girl. [*As a matter of fact,*] The only subject for which she had any real liking [*was history;*] in spite of her misadventure with the ink pot, was history. She [*approached it*] came to it by way [*of*] ⟨of⟩ her passion for Yorkshire, [*& as her*] [*because*] ⟨[*by way of*]⟩ ⟨[*because*]⟩ ⟨in wh. county⟩ her mothers family, the Rigbys had been settled [*in Yorkshire* ⟨*since*⟩] since ⟨the village of⟩ Rigby [*was called Rigby,*] had been called Rigby [*or they*] after them, or they had been called Rigby after it — ⟨which was⟩ a long time before the conquest. •{This seed, falling upon a mind which was active & [*vigorous in some ways*] practical & liked to enquire into the}•

She would have liked to know all about Yorkshire; & so something about the lives of English people all through those centuries during which the Rigbys [*had*] [I 114] had been farming, fighting, preaching, lawmaking, marrying, bearing children & dying: so that when her father had [*giv*] asked her [*what subject she would*] which of her lessons interested her most she always said history; & [*it was*] <thus,> when he pronounced against Cheltenham, <for one reason> & <against> Somerville Hall for another, he had made enquiries & found that there was an admirable lady called Miss Craddock who [*was p*] lived in Oxford & taught [*the daughters of the Oxford*] young ladies who had left school.

When Kitty thought of Stubbs, she always thought of Miss Craddock too. She loved Miss Craddock — perhaps she loved her better than anybody in the whole world. (At any rate, the two hours she spent weekly reading history with) And yet it was a very strange kind of love. Miss Craddock was over fifty & her natural plainness [*she had a l*] she was very small & had a great forehead & very bright little blue eyes & <a hooked nose like a birds beak> [*mouth that always seemed pursed up to say something sarcastic,*] — was exaggerated by the fact that she strained her hair tight back off her forehead, & dressed with a [*plainness*] <severity> that was only [*more*] [*tolerable than*] [*painful than her*] <[*chas*] tolerable> <by comparison with> [her] finery; [*when, on great occasions she thought it necessary to put on a*] [*for her bonnets & mantle turned the*] for when she appeared on great occasions in bonnet & mantle she [*was*] looked like a parrot [*that had been*] caught & dishevelled [*by*] <in> a gale — her bonnet [*was*] always crooked & her mantle was tufted with bows sewn on by Miss Craddock herself in deference to [*the*] <a> frivolity that she vaguely felt to be expected at garden parties [*even of old women like herself.*] if one belonged to the female sex. She was extremely poor. She lived in lodgings, & the room in which she received her pupils was in reality her bedroom; which explained the presence of a sofa. But sitting [*at*] <on> a [*high*] <hard> chair at a table covered with oil cloth she taught Kitty all that Kitty was ever destined to know of English history; & such was her enthusiasm for [II 13]* history in general & Bishop Stubbs in

* Manuscript volume I ends with the date "Nov 28th 1932" on page 114; volume II

particular that Kitty used to feel that she must read Stubbs if only not to disappoint Miss Craddock.

Of course she always did disappoint her, she thought as she opened Stubbs vol. 3.; because she never worked hard enough.

"I see. Dancing again" Miss Craddock used to say as Kitty stumbled out her excuses. But what was the use of complaining? Miss Craddock knew by this time that none of her pupils could be expected to work in Oxford in the summer term — certainly not if they were the daughters of [*the*] Masters & 'had' to [*help Mama.*] <do this & that & the other.> "<I had to> We had people staying in the house" Kitty would explain. [*Or Mama wanted me all the morning. Or Papa was*] [*Mama*] [*Papa has been in bed with a chill.*] But Kitty hated [*say*] offering these excuses, though they were true, because Miss Craddock had a way of brushing her hand across her mouth, when she was disappointed. She also had a way of looking over her spectacles <& beaming> when Kitty [*wou*] said something intelligent. And though she had torn up several of Kittys essays because they were not worthy of a lower girl at Cheltenham — Miss Craddock had been at Cheltenham — there was one that Miss Craddock [*had praised.*] <had kept.> "[*You*] D'you know Kitty, if you'd only give your [*mind to it, you would do very well*] [*self a chance*] <give more time to your work,>" she said, "you've got a [*remarkable grasp of"*] very <quite an> original mind[."] <if you'd give yourself>

"Quite an original mind" — Kitty repeated the words over & over again to herself in secret. She used them now to spur herself on to read her [*sixty pages before*] ration of Stubbs. And for some time she applied herself to her task, reading page after page by the light of one candle. And then her mind wandered — just as her cousin Edward, over the way, had felt his mind wander, when he read the Anti-

---

bears the title "2 / The Pargiters / Continued / Nov. 28th 1932" on page II 12 — preceding which are 19 stubs of leaves that had been cut away. (Of these stubs, 11 sides contain remnants of writing, not identified but bearing dates of "5th Sept. 1932" (on p 1) and "Sept 17th" (on p 9); they have been paginated by the librarian.)

gone, so hers wandered; for though she had certainly not [II 14] tired herself by reading hard for eight hours a day, she had tired herself almost equally by showing Mrs. Fripp the sights, by pouring out tea, by sitting [*nex*] between old Chuffy Andrews & Mr Lathom at dinner. Only her tiredness showed itself [*rather*] in the annoying way in which scraps of talk, [*what she had said & he had said,*] came back to her; & [*then she began wondering what Mrs. Fripp had thought, what*] little scenes. She could not fix her mind on Stubbs — her original mind.

So she would have to go to Miss Craddock tomorrow with the usual excuse. "I'm so sorry Miss Craddock; I've not had time . . ." But somehow she felt that the little plain old woman [*was*] understood — She was a Yorkshire woman too. She came from the country of wide moors & great distances that Kitty loved from the depths of her heart. Her father had been <[*a*]> a doctor in a village [*near*] near Settle. And sometimes, after the lesson, Miss Craddock wd invite Kitty to stay to tea, & they would talk about Yorkshire & how years ago when Miss C. was young she had [*n*] driven with her father for miles & miles over these moors. [*She had*] There were so many of them at home that her mother was glad to be rid of one of them. She had wandered all over the moors, before she [*went to*] went to school. She had gone to classes at Queens College London — & then Miss Beale had asked her to teach at Cheltenham, & [*she had written*] a little book on the Angevin Kings; & she made Kitty feel that ●{ [*The passion*] She loved learning — any scrap of knowledge — [*as*] as she loved the Yorkshire moors,* with their heather roots & [*their*] the little flowers that spring their — she would have a saucer, of these little flowers on her mantelpiece, sometimes; & it was wonderful how long they lasted if you kept wet moss at their roots.}● [II 15] that learning was a wonderful thing: or was it that Miss Craddock was a wonderful woman; or was it both together?

* A marginal note here, "Kitty told her how she hated Oxford", is not used until the next paragraph.

Fourth Chapter

For a week or so, Kitty [*herself*] had [*dreamt*] cherished a dream of becoming a learned woman, an historian herself. But then she remembered her fathers irony — [*how no woman*] [*about having*] about [*the*] 'sharing the inability of your sex to grasp historical truth' & the ambition, which was not of undue strength, had faded away. (She [*knew*] <guessed> [*quite well*] that Lucy Craddock was not learned at all in her father's sense of the word. He had dismissed Miss Craddocks little book on the Angevin Kings with a kindly smile. [*She was a very*] <saying that she was a very> worthy woman [*he had said; &*] [*but*] & [*had deserved*] had worked very hard. But the book on the Angevin Kings was [*quite*] quite unreadable — Kitty herself felt that. When Miss Craddock wrote, she was as dull as ditchwater. But then she [*was always so*] <would> quot[*ing*] <e> [*Bishop Stubbs*] <Dr Freeman>. [*She was always*] Dr Freeman was her god.) And she remembered her mother's little shrug of impatience <sarcastic comm> when Miss Craddock came to the Lodge "Oh these learned women!" she had said. <For> Mrs. Malone was [*one of the opponents of the*] not at all in favour of the women's colleges that were just coming into existence.

And yet Kitty loved Miss Craddock, & had come indeed to tell her things that she never told anyone else — how she hated Oxford for instance. The climate was certainly relaxing. Miss Craddock agreed.

But it isnt only the climate, Miss Craddock" Kitty [*went on.*] began.

Miss Craddock checked her. She had some scruple about receiving confidences from her pupils — that was not what Dr Malone paid her for, she felt. And she felt, having had experience in such matters, that Kitty loved her, as so many girls love older women who teach them, & [II 16] that this emotion, touching as it was, especially to a woman without husband or children, was apt to lead a girl [*to confide*] [*confide*] to say things about her parents that she ought not to say; & altogether to indulge in what Miss Beale called "unhealthy attachments." So she observed drily that [*Kitty had better*] [*had made another gro*] the state of the Oxford climate had nothing to do with the Angevin Kings: upon which Kitty blushed & felt herself rebuked. Only, when she was buttoning up her macintosh to go, — [*it was a*] the summer of 1880 was very wet — [*she did*] Miss Craddock repented for a moment of her severity & drew the girls attention to a saucer full of [*small yellow flowers*] <sprigs of red heather> on the mantelpiece.

"My sister [*sent them*] picked [*them*] <it> on the moors" she said. And then Kitty<'s> [*had in*] face had changed completely. And she had [*touched the little yellow*] looked at the heather that had been picked by Maria Craddock on the moors above Settle as if the whole of Oxford with its domes & towers & bells & the professors, its masters, its undergraduates, its tea parties, & [*ei*] balls, its Eights week <picnic> were nothing but a mist through which she saw [*a*] the purple of a Yorkshire moor.

That was what she saw now, as she closed Bishop Stubbs vol 3. [*And she saw a*] She always thought about the moors as she was dropping off to sleep. For not only was she descended, on her mothers side, from generations of Yorkshire Squires, [*in*] but whenever she had had the measles or the whooping cough as a child she had [*been*] <always been> packed [*off to recover to*] [*at*] to Carters, a farmhouse near Settle; [*which was*] [*Mrs Carter had been*] <because Mrs Carter the farmers wife> was Mrs. Rigbys old nurse, Snap. Kitty called her 'Snap' too; indeed she was now known as 'old Snap' because she was going on for eighty. [*But*] And [ii 17] at Carters Kitty had [*gr*] spent far & away the happiest days of her life. She had been allowed to run wild all over the moors. — for the farm was only reached by a track — it stood alone, on the moors. And she had milked the cows & found the eggs, & seen a [*pig killed*] <calf born> & learnt how to make real bread, the kind of bread Miss Craddock also made; & she had eaten huge meals, sitting [*beti*] beside <old> Snap on a high chair [*at*] in the great kitchen, with the hams swinging from the rafters; & [*the*] she had heard the Yorkshire farmhands talking as they also ate huge meals; & once — but this was later, when she was about sixteen, [*Georgie ha*] the [*boy*] farmers son, a <splendid young> man of twenty six, had rolled her over in the hay & kissed her & kissed her. That was one of her worst scrapes, as it turned out, for [*old Snap had*] Carter, the father, had suddenly loomed up, leading a bull by a ring through its nose: & George had slunk off, merely at the sight of his father: & Old Snap [*had given Kitty such a scolding*] <[*had been*] [*Snap was so*]> had told Kitty that if ever she caught her at such games again she would tell the Mistress: & then Kitty would never be allowed to come <to Carters> again.

The thought of that kiss [*in the h*] behind the haystack was also one of the thoughts that would come back, when she ought to have been reading Stubbs vol three. [*Once more*] Kitty thought of that kiss <again tonight>. <How she had enjoyed it — Compare Tony Ashley with George Carter — She suddenly thought. or Lord L. either. He cd knock them both —> George had a farm of his own now, & was married, & had three squalling babies. And so Kitty [*came to her usual*] shutting Stubbs [*with*] <after> only ten pages had been dispatched, out of her allowance of sixty, sank back in her pillows, & thought how one of these days she would buy a farm herself near Carters, — she knew [*exact*] the very place; with some land, but not too much land. Why should [II 18] she not become a farmer? That was her dream. She would have to marry, she supposed, in order to become a farmer — & her parents wd. never let her marry a farmer.

But no force on earth [*she thought*] would make her marry Nigs: & settle down, & live in Oxford — Stubbs fell with a thud on the floor. And, as the bells of Oxford began ringing all over again, she blew out the candle, & lay, hearing the rain, [*falling*] but in her dreams it became the wind, roaring over the Yorkshire moors.

Nov 29th

[II 19] [FIFTH ESSAY]

Nov 30th [1932]

Love and money are again present in the Master's Lodge, though much less obviously than in Edward Pargiter's rooms, or in the Pargiter's drawing room at 58 Abercorn Terrace. The Lodge itself owed a good deal to money that had been given to the College by the Church before the Reformation, or taken from the Church after the Reformation. Then, of course, the Lady Katharine and her husband had given money to endow the Chapel; and these early benefactors had been succeeded by others in the course of the six hundred years of its existence, who had given money for prizes, for lectureships, for statues, for windows, for the salary of the Master who should preside worthily over a house of learning to which not only the first nobles of the land could send their sons, but to which the "poor scholars" would come, as they had come, since the middle of the Thirteenth Century to lodgings and teaching and "at least two meals a day and as much meat and beer as they needed" at a rate which suited their meagre purses and fed their eager brains.

Thus Dr. Malone himself would be in receipt of a substantial income, though one by no means in excess of the demands that his position made upon it. The scale of pay was not high. Only "a very few privileged Professors," Mrs Humphry Ward says, "possessed as much as a thousand a year. The average income of the new race of married tutors was not much more than half that sum." [II 20] Thus, though the visitors like the Howard Fripps must have felt the wealth, the size, the power, and the importance of the ancient city whose sights were enough to require three days to see them in; and even then, as Dr. Malone could have told them, they had only seen a very few things and in a very superficial way. [But] the wives even of the Heads of houses themselves had anxious moments over their weekly books. There must be no ostentation, of course, but also there must be no cheese paring. The beauty of the old house must be preserved and handed on as it had always been preserved and handed on. Curtains must be cleaned, chairs mended, and carpets renewed before certain bald patches became unpleasantly visible. Then the Lodge was the centre of hospitality. The cups of tea that Kitty poured out, and the slices of bread and butter that the undergraduates consumed cost very little; but the dinner that was set before the Fripps at Oxford had to compare not unfavourably with the dinner that would be set before the Malones at Harvard. Besides, there were always distinguished visitors. It was the Master's duty not only to entertain his own pupils, now grown distinguished men, but also to invite guests, of equal distinction, from London, Paris, Harvard, and to invite his more distinguished pupils to meet them — for nothing helped a young man more than to meet men of the greater world. Why, even Oxford men themselves, living as they did in little communities of their own, profited by meeting men from the outside world.

Thus Mrs. Malone was speaking no [II 21] less than the truth when she said that there was plenty for Kitty to do at home. Mrs. Malone herself only got through the day's work by being very punctual, and very methodical, and by the fact [that] her mother had taught her a good deal about housekeeping before she married. Even as it was, there were constant difficulties with servants. The Lodge was badly planned, like so many beautiful old houses, for modern life. The servants' quarters were decidedly dark. They had a great many stairs to climb, a great many rods to polish, a great many cans to carry. Mrs. Malone was on the whole what is called "lucky" in her maids — that is to say, she knew enough about housework to know what is possible and what impossible; she could teach a girl the right way of doing almost every household duty; and thus, though the wages were extremely small in those days — a wage of £16 was considered high for a lady's maid in 1860 — not enough to allow of many outings or pleasures, her maids stayed with her, partly because they respected her, and partly because to be trained by Mrs. Stubbs ("Mrs." was a courtesy title), who had been trained by Mrs. Malone and was now her great standby, was considered by the mothers of little Oxford servant girls an admirable start in life. Still, as Mrs. Stubbs was autocratic, there would be scenes, and Mrs. Malone was faced several times a year by the sight of a pale trembling girl, who gave notice, and yet could not explain when Mrs. Malone asked the reason, why it was she merely stood there sobbing. "Ah, these Oxford girls; they don't know what work is," Mrs. Stubbs would say. And another tin box was packed and another furtive, foolish, illiterate girl [II 22] stepped behind her box out of the Master's Lodge to find another place elsewhere.

But Mrs. Malone always appeared punctual to the minute, well-dressed, good-tempered, in her drawing room, to receive her guests; the Master himself, sharply though he looked into the year's expenses as a whole, never knew that Ellen or Dolly or Lizzy had given notice; for Mrs. Malone would have thought it a crime on her part to worry him with such matters, just as she would never have forgiven herself if any guest had complained of the quality of the food, of the cleanness of the linen, or the coldness of the shaving water. To see to the house was as much her duty as the Master's wife, as to be able to say the right thing to undergraduates, and to keep the peace between old Chuffy and Mr Lathom at dinner. But undoubtedly the strain was considerable, and sometimes affected her temper. She could be very sharp with her daughter. Thus, although Mrs. Malone herself, of course, never received a penny from the College directly — she dressed both herself and Kitty on the small income which she had inherited from her father — the Lodge was based on money, running subterraneously, out of sight.

Love was also present, though that suffered many restrictions, and was concealed under many disguises. Kitty — and the analyst would naturally examine her first, since it is commonly supposed that love is strongest in the young — felt a very different kind of emotion [II 23] from that which Edward, who was her contemporary, felt for her. It was not merely that the portrait of Edward suggested only a rather priggish youth, with eyes set too near together, who would settle down in Oxford; but she was so much restrained by the conventions of the society in which she lived that her response, even if Edward had attracted her physically and ideally, as she attracted him, would have been instantly checked by the knowledge that she must conceal it. From her earliest childhood, ever since she was allowed to come down into the drawing room in a starched white frock, she had been taught a very strict moral code, which in childhood prevented her from kicking up her legs in the presence of the other sex; and as she grew older, prevented her from being alone in the room with them, from standing at an open window in her nightgown, from saying anything or doing anything which could suggest even remotely that she felt physically or ideally attracted by them. So that when, at the age of sixteen, George Carter had kissed her behind the haystack, the pleasure was great, but she knew that she was committing an appalling crime; and when, at the age of twenty, Alan Hammond had proposed to her, and Lord Lammermuir had admired her, she felt much less, physically, than they did — for the physical side of love had been so repressed not only in her, but in her mothers and grandmothers, that [II 24] it was much weaker, even in a girl of perfect physique like Kitty, than in a young man like Tony Ashton who was physically less perfect, but sexually much better developed, since no restrictions had been placed either on him or on his fathers or grandfathers that were comparable in severity with those that had surrounded Kitty almost since birth.

How far the passion of the man is naturally stronger than the passion of the woman it is extremely difficult to say: and good judges differ. Montaigne, for example, held that the passion of a woman was by nature stronger than that of a man; but was repressed, very painfully, by the rigours of convention. Tennyson, on the other hand, if "Locksley Hall" can be taken to represent his own opinion, held that women's passions were intrinsically weaker than those of his own sex. But then, as Montaigne wrote about 1400* and Tennyson about 1880, the rigours of convention which Montaigne had noted had been on for almost five hundred years — almost as long as the Oxford Colleges had been in existence, and may have produced its effect. Kitty, who was 21 in 1880, therefore inherited the effects of an education which, if we attribute any importance to education, was bound not merely to teach her a certain code of behaviour, but also to modify the passion itself.

That it survived even, as strongly as it did — and Kitty undoubtedly felt very considerable emotion when she was kissed by George Carter — seems to corroborate Montaigne's opinion, rather than Lord Tennyson's. But Tennyson [II 25] was certainly right in his judgment of the young women of his own time. The student of mid-Victorian poetry and fiction can hardly deny that the young girl there described has hardly any passion left. Either it has been extinguished by the process of education, or, as happened with Kitty, passion still existed, but was so much restricted, both because, as Delia Pargiter had observed, the economic position of women did not admit of their bearing illegitimate children, or because the common opinion disapproved, that it was a furtive, ill-grown, secret, subterranean vice, to be concealed in shame, until by some fortunate chance, a man gave the girl a chance, by putting a wedding ring on her finger, to canalise all her passion, for the rest of their married lives, solely upon him. The chance of marriage was, moreover, precarious. For as Lady Lovelace has pointed out, there was in the eighties a "shortage of the unattached male. It was already felt, but to a less degree in Jane Austen's day; for she constantly bears witness to the value set upon a sufficiency of 'beaux.' This shortage

* Actually Montaigne's dates were 1533–1592, only three hundred years before Tennyson. (In the margin, Virginia Woolf subtracted "1400" from "1880.")

is the price that we pay for our splendid Empire, and the price is paid mainly by women." But the price of the Empire fell much more heavily upon some women than upon others. Kitty, in common with many girls whose fathers were of good social standing, would receive five or six [II 26] proposals before [she] married. Others, though perhaps prettier, and perhaps better educated and of higher intellectual standing, like Delia Pargiter, would receive not a single proposal in the course of their lives. And since sexual intercourse was then in their class impossible, their contribution to the British Empire was a very high one.

But Kitty, either because she was assured of much more than her share of proposals of marriage, or because she cherished a secret passion for becoming a farmer, which led her to underrate the advantages of the male society of Oxford, was at present very little concerned with the other sex. Her emotions were roused rather by Miss Craddock than by Lord Lammermuir. Had she been to school, no doubt this feeling would have shown itself, long before, in friendships with girls of her own age. But when her parents enquired into conditions at Cheltenham and discovered that a music teacher "gave a lesson to four pupils at once, the same piece being performed simultaneously on the treble and bass of two pianos" because the Ladies' College was so poor, and the expense of providing the requisite number of teachers and pianos for so many pupils was so heavy, they concluded that Kitty could be taught better at home. Kitty then had never mixed with girls of her own age in any number. She knew the daughters of her parents' friends at Oxford, of course; but save for Dorothy Hughes, the daughter of the Professor of Mathematics, she had a rather superficial acquaintance with these girls; since [II 27] their meetings were purely social, they were unable to come to grips in the arguments and rivalries and intimacies of school life.

The love she offered Lucy Craddock was thus singularly unimpaired, and yet since Miss Craddock was over fifty, and very plain, Kitty undoubtedly mixed up with her love for Miss Craddock many other loves. She did not see the Miss Craddock whom her father and mother saw — the worthy, plain, industrious old maid: she saw a woman who had fought her way, as Kitty would like to fight her way, through obstacles; who had read her book while she waited in the gig; who had mastered mathematics while she baked the bread; who had gone short of firing and clothing and food in order to attend classes at Queens College; who had at last, after years of labour, written a little book that Dr. Malone tossed aside — indeed it was very dull — and finally had won the right to live in a bed-sitting room, in an Oxford lodging, with a saucer of heather on the mantelpiece; this was the woman that Kitty saw; and in her eyes, Miss Craddock was not beautiful — no: but Kitty counted the days between one lesson and another. She treasured every word of praise that Miss Craddock gave her; she invested all Miss Craddock's relations with glamour; kept every note she had from her; and left a pot of white azaleas at her lodgings once when she was ill. This idealisation of the woman teacher was by no means uncommon in the eighties. Mrs. Humphry Ward says that what she learnt at school — between 1858 and 1867 — was worthless "as far as intellectual [training was concerned.]"* [II 28] But she adds, "What I learnt during those years was learnt from personalities. . . ." And she continues to pay a tribute to the woman teacher of later days, the women who teach women, as Miss Craddock taught Kitty.

Kitty, therefore, when she fell in love with Miss Craddock was falling in love with something which seemed to her wonderful, new, exciting — the disinterested passion for things in themselves; so that however much she scamped her history, she knew that history to Miss Craddock was a thing to starve oneself for; to drudge after; to love for itself: so that she could never pass the commonplace red brick villa in which Miss Craddock had lived in after years

* Mary A. Ward *A Writer's Recollections* (London 1918) p 96. The next passage quoted occurs on p 97 and is followed by grateful allusions to three teachers, one "an ardent Evangelical, with whom . . . at the age of fourteen or fifteen, I fell headlong in love, as was the manner of schoolgirls . . . ."

without feeling her pulses quicken, though Miss Craddock was dead, [and] her poor little book on the Angevin Kings deservedly forgotten.

Miss Craddock's love for Kitty was, of course, influenced by the fact that she considered it her duty to repress it, in Kitty's own interests, and in the interests of that learning which she was paid five shillings an hour by Dr. Malone to impart. But when the lesson was over, and Kitty stood up fastening her mackintosh if it were wet, or putting on her little flowered hat if it were fine, Miss Craddock could not help feeling stirred by the sight of youth and health; and to her, though Kitty was commonly thought to be too tall, and not pretty, because of her red hair and her big cheekbones — though it [II 29] was commonly allowed that her complexion was perfect — to Miss Craddock Kitty was the most beautiful girl she had ever seen. When Kitty stroked the heather with her finger, the tears came to Miss Craddock's eyes. She repressed them instantly; but for a moment she felt — for her feeling was much mixed with foreign elements — "What can I teach her?" For a moment, a shadow crossed Stubbs himself. What was "history" after all? What did it matter if Kitty never "knew" it, when — and here Miss Craddock was undoubtedly influenced by some long suppressed, almost extinct, sexual instinct — "when she knows, because she is young and beautiful and has learnt, from her childhood, how to walk through the streets of Oxford without attracting attention, and to pour out tea in her father's house, more about life and its difficulties than I, who always a plain little brat with my nose buried in a book, ever guessed, or could ever possibly know? It is for Kitty to teach me," Miss Craddock felt for a second, as she piled up her books; by which she meant also that she knew quite well how very difficult it was for a girl like Kitty who "had to help Mama," to read her twenty pages of Froude every day with attention; how impossible it was to go straight from entertaining distinguished guests to an impersonal survey of the constitutional law in England; how impossible, therefore, it was even with an original mind — that she had — and a love of history — that she had too — for Kitty ever to reach even half the standard of historical learning which the young men at College seemed to reach without any difficulty at all. But then, Miss Craddock thought, as she put away the books, and shook hands with her pupil, "You know a great many things [II 30] that those clever young men will never know," in which remark — curious as it was on the lips of one to whom the mere sight of Mr. Froude or Mr. Freeman or Bishop Stubbs, as they sauntered down the High, roused feelings comparable with those that devout believers cherish for the persons of their saints — may be found the influence of love again. Kitty was so considerate to Miss Craddock; she was so sorry to be late; so kind in bringing her a flower when she was ill. And Miss Craddock had not drunk tea at the Lodge without observing — even while she trembled to think how foolish Dr Malone thought her, and how dowdy Mrs. Malone thought her clothes — that Kitty bore herself to both parents and to their friends with an unselfishness which showed how completely she had learnt to subdue her own wishes, to put herself at their service so that to call Kitty "uneducated" was, in Miss Craddock's view, a most curious misuse of terms. She had discouraged Kitty's confidence, but she guessed that Kitty hated Oxford: that she loved Yorkshire: yet here she was, in her lovely lawns and laces — Miss Craddock had almost a male ignorance of what a dress was really made of — smiling, silent, attentive, pouring out tea.

It was partly this difference in the education that each received that led Kitty to think, perhaps with undue harshness, of the undergraduates. Why were they so awkward, so silent, so uncouth? she asked herself. Why must one talk to the rowing man about rowing, [II 31] and to the reading man about reading? Why could they never talk about things that interested her? That was true; but it was also true, of course, that she could not talk about the things that interested them. Her little stock of book learning was soon exhausted with the reading men; and though she knew the right questions to ask about the college eight, sport bored her, as it tends to bore people who have never played a game themselves; and the knowledge which can be picked up by "looking on" at games is so superficial that it seldom deceives a young man who spends a great part of his life in active pursuit of it. Thus there were silences; and while she did her best to conceal those silences, as her mother did, Kitty secretly considered that young men were so much less developed than she was, that she could only feel at ease with men who were old enough to be her father. She made an exception, however, in favour of Tony Ashton. With him she could talk quite easily. Indeed, sometimes the usual position was reversed. She found him, actually, taking an interest in her. He asked her if she had enjoyed her ice; and then, as if he read her thoughts, whether she had not admired Mrs. Fripp, and then whether she would not like to go to America? Such sympathy with her, from an undergraduate, was so unusual that Kitty was at first inclined to confide in this strange young man who did not seem to belong to any of the usual classes. And then she was repulsed. What was queer about him? Why was he "snaky"? Why did she like Edward better, and Lord Lammermuir better, and Alan Hammond better, and — to confess the truth which she had never told a soul — George, the farm hand, best of all?

Such subtleties of liking and disliking played a very large part in Kitty's secret life, however ignorant she was of literature [II 32] and philosophy, and Greek and Latin, and mathematics and history. For, severely trained as she was from early childhood to observe the rules of conduct; and early impressed by nurses, governesses, and parents and dressmakers with the qualities of her body, she knew her "points" by heart. She had stood in front of looking glasses for hours being fitted and being turned this way and that under the scrutiny of trained eyes. She was naturally, she was inevitably, highly sensitive to the impressions of her body. Her body would be signalling to her, even while she poured out tea, "That man has red hands." "That man has big ears." "That man [has] a horrible way with his knife and fork." And at the same time she was receiving their impressions of her body. Thus, after a dance, she could have given, with extraordinary accuracy, a full account of what each of her partners had felt for her. Long before Alan Hammond proposed to her, she knew, from the way he took his tea cup from her, that he was about to fall in love with her. She was in no doubt that Lord L[ammermuir] was physically attracted but had, at the same time, to consider the duties of his post, and she knew without being told that Edward cherished an absurd photograph of her, holding a sword, representing the Lady Katharine. Knowledge of this kind poured in upon her all day long without her seeking it or valuing it.

Now, therefore, when she encountered Tony Ashton's eyes — his steady searching intelligent eyes — she knew that he did not look at her as other men did; and that knowledge led her to a curious division of feeling. It was agreeable to her to be looked at dispassionately: she was at her ease. At the same time, there was a coldness in his glance which led her to call him "snaky" — meaning by that, that her body and his body had so little natural attraction for each other that they were singularly at ease. And yet, some stimulus was so lacking, that talking to Tony, in spite of her sympathy, left her cold. She would never be intimate with him, never wholly at her ease: she would never lose herself, as she had lost herself with the farmer's son, never feel the flood of excitement and power that she had felt then.

[II 33] This knowledge, because it was largely traditional, and had been acquired, consciously, from childhood upwards, had become to Kitty a great deal more instinctive and probably more complete than Edward Pargiter's knowledge of Greek. Without being specially subtle, she was aware of a variety and complexity of human relationships of which he was ignorant; just as, when Edward took up *The Antigone*, the Greek conveyed to him a thousand meanings and suggestions which Kitty, who could only read Greek in translations, missed completely.

But Miss Craddock had been right when she said once after reading a paper of Kitty's on the character of Henry the Eighth that Kitty had "quite an original mind." What she meant was that, for once in a way, having taken time with her work, Kitty had expressed, in very awkward English it is true, her own opinion of Henry, and not merely repeated, as girls mostly did, what she had read in Froude or what she thought would please Miss Craddock herself. Naturally, it was not an opinion of any value. But now and again Kitty used the same gift to interpret for herself the swarm of impressions which her body was always giving and receiving in daily life. It was thus that she had come to the conclusion that for her, at any rate, the life of a farmer was infinitely preferable to the life of a don's wife at Oxford. She felt, as Miss Craddock had guessed, that talking to undergraduates about their [II 34] interests and pursuits was not so amusing — her analysis was carried out in the simplest terms — as living in the country and running a farm for oneself. In coming to this decision, she was helped partly by what is called an "original" mind — that is, she had by nature certain convictions (she was half a Rigby); and she was further helped to express them by the fact that her mother was an extremely competent housekeeper, so that Kitty had no regular housework to perform, and so could enjoy not entire liberty of time or of opinion but more than her mother had had. She concealed most of her desires and opinions, and was perpetually interrupted even in her history — but still, in the summer of 1880, Kitty Malone enjoyed a freedom from household work and a freedom of opinion which were unknown to her mother, at the age of 21, in the year 1848.* Mrs. Malone had been born in the year 1827: her upbringing in the heart of Yorkshire had been primitive in the extreme. When she married

* Virginia Woolf's faulty arithmetic is jotted in the margin: 63 in 1880
63
———
1827
21
———
1848

in 1850, she was an expert housekeeper — but little else. And indeed one of her chief reasons for marrying the shy Oxford youth, Paul Malone, who spent one summer reading with her uncle, the clergyman at Malham, was that if she married him and became the wife of a learned man, she might leave her native Yorkshire with its long winters, its solitude, its perpetual talk of hunting and sport; and live — as they had lived — in London; in Oxford: where the opportunities for seeing cultivated people, and hearing music, were so wonderful; and then the work of running a house was a thousand times less arduous than in a Yorkshire village, where [II 35] one might be snowed up for weeks at a time.

Kitty thus had much more spare time than her mother at her age; many more opportunities of seeing cultivated people; and instead, therefore, of accepting implicitly, as Mrs. Malone had done and still did, the absolute rightness of Dr. Malone's occupation, the absolute necessity of her own, the undeniable though naturally unquestionable greatness of Dr. Chuffy Andrews and Professor Lathom — Mrs. Malone never read their books, but she had them all, with inscriptions from the authors, under glass in the drawing room — Kitty sometimes asked herself questions.

"Tuesday again!" she would sigh, waking to the chirp of thrushes in the garden on that particular day. "That means I've got to sit in the drawing room from four till seven pouring out tea. And why should I? When I want to go off for a walk by myself in the country? And why can't I walk by myself in the country? And why mayn't I stand at the window in my nightgown? And why mayn't I play football if I want to? And why must I sit next old Chuffy at dinner?" Chuffy's habit of spilling soup into his beard was extremely disgusing. She disliked his grunts and gobblings also. Once she had had, what she called "a shot at Chuff's books" and they had bored her horribly. And why had she to keep the peace between him and Professor Lathom? Why couldn't they settle their silly quarrels? "They're as vain as two peacocks," she used to think. "It's like feeding two quarrelsome, dilapidated, mouldy old birds, keeping the peace between these sharp-tongued old fogies" — to her they seemed incredibly old — [II 36] "about some ridiculous row they've had about a book or an appointment" — she could not remember which it was — "centuries before I was born." However, there was nothing for it. One had to sit and simper between them. And then they gave one *Sesame and Lilies.* Professor Lathom did, at least; she preferred old Chuffy because he was at least downright rude and told her not to talk nonsense when she made some silly remark — off her own bat, heaven knows what possessed her — about Henry the Eighth. Such thoughts had never occurred to Mrs. Malone, whose heart swelled with pride when she could introduce the Howard Fripps not only to Chuffy himself, but to Professor Lathom, who never dined out, and finally to Sir Hugh Charters who was Secretary of State for — whatever it was: knowledge of that particular kind she left to her husband.

Such questions, however, did occur to Kitty; and undoubtedly had their share in making her conclude that she, at least, intended to be a farmer. And then she went on, prompted here by her sentimental idealisation of Miss Craddock, to ask why Miss Craddock was so poor. "Why didn't they give her a professorship or something — a fellowship anyhow?" Five hundred a year would make all the difference in the world to Miss Craddock; then she could spend her entire life grubbing in the Bodleian, which was what Miss Craddock liked, though the taste seemed to Kitty a strange one. Of course, that was impossible because Miss Craddock was a woman; and Miss Craddock had said once that it would be years and years before women were allowed to take degrees "if indeed it happens in my life time —" she had added. Kitty herself [II 37] had not the least wish for a degree; her facilities for grubbing in the Bodleian were already beyond her powers of use. But still, Kitty would ask herself, as the undergraduates stumbled in and out, and the Professors and the Dons and the Masters drank their port and smoked their cigars and lapped their old stories, and fingered the lovely college silver, under the old portraits of dead Masters, and spoke with reverence of the great men who had been at Katharines, and of Katharine herself, who had endowed the Chapel — "Why on earth," Kitty asked herself, "if these old buffers have had such a good time at College and are always buttering each other up and saying how important learning is, and history and mathematics and philosophy — Why don't they give Lucy Craddock whatever it is that Lucy Craddock wants?"

For her own part, Kitty would willingly have bestowed the Lodge, the Chapel, the College, and the *History* of Katharine's itself upon Lucy Craddock and her friends — the ugly, spectacled, learned women — if they wanted them. Of course, the learned women were very ugly; but then they were very poor. She would like to feed Chuffy for a term on Lucy's rations and see what he said then about Henry the Eighth. As for Professor Lathom, with his Greek tie pin and his cameo on his little finger, and his smooth voice, and his dreamy eyes — she thought he would know a great deal more about Greek art — only perhaps it was Latin art that he knew more about than anybody in the whole world — if he scrubbed out his bed-sitting room as Lucy Craddock did.

And there the old humbugs were, floating into Chapel behind a mace and a sceptre and all the rest of it, [II 38] to celebrate somebody or other — perhaps the Lady Katharine whose money they had enjoyed — looking for all the world like a flight of rooks. And then there would be the College Sunday dinner, and they would eat such vast masses of food, that though Kitty as her father's daughter had the privilege of watching them as they dined, from a little gallery in the hall, she felt that to see Chuffy eat his ordinary meal was enough for her: to see Chuffy and all the other old gentlemen eat what they ate on great occasions would be more than she could bear. So she sat in the garden with her mother, and wound the silk for her mother's embroidery; and listened to the Grace, which floated musically down to them through the trees; and then to the murmur of speech-making;

and then to the cheers; and then, when her mother, gathering her things together, for it was getting chilly, hoped that it had been a great success, Kitty, stooping to pick up rugs and fold up chairs, asked herself, "Why do men enjoy such things?" But the question was not spoken aloud. She had no freedom of expression.

"Now go to bed, Kitty," Mrs. Malone said when they got into the drawing room. "You look tired, my dear," said Mrs. Malone, when they got into the lamp light in the drawing room. "Go to bed. It's been a long day."

"But you, Mama. Aren't you coming?" asked Kitty.

"No. I shall wait for Papa," said Mrs. Malone.

"But you've been on your feet all day, Mama, "[II 39] said Kitty, noticing as her mother sank into a chair that she looked suddenly very old and lined, though her hair was as beautifully curled and waved as ever. "Surely Papa and Sir Hugh can go to bed by themselves." But Mrs. Malone only smiled and adjusted her eye glasses at the mockery of her daughter.

"Papa will want to tell me all about it when he comes in," she remarked.

"But Papa will be very angry if you're tired tomorrow," said Kitty. "And there's the luncheon party, remember."

"I shall not be tired tomorrow, " said Mrs. Malone, looking up at her daughter, as much as to say, "You, too, will know all about this when you're married." She had her duties as the wife of the Master. And so, since argument was useless — Mama always would sit up, and Kitty always knew precisely why she would sit up until Papa came in — Kitty left her.

Indeed, though Kitty had a sufficiently original mind and sense to ask questions of herself (though the difficulty of reporting intelligently the questions that people ask themselves may well lead the reporter to an exaggerated use of slang), she was by no means free to express them. The feeling between mother and daughter was so strong about marriage and motherhood, that they seldom troubled to express it in words.

She concealed all her opinions about standing at windows in nightgowns, Tuesday "at Homes," Chuffy's beard, old peacocks dull as ditchwater, *Sesame and Lilies*, &c. &c. from her parents; and indeed from everybody in the whole world, with the solitary exception of Alice Hughes, the [II 40] daughter of the Professor of Mathematics. To her she would let fly sometimes; but Alice, who was determined to become a doctor, would counter her arguments. But there was nobody else to whom she could express her opinions; and as Alice had now gone to live in London, Kitty's opinions circulated in the privacy of her own mind, and took on from that concealment a certain degree of exaggeration. Many people would have felt it a great honour to sit between Dr. Andrews and Professor Lathom; and to dismiss their works — which were even then of great repute and are now collected in those many volumes which make part of all respectable libraries — as Kitty dismissed them, was frivolous in the extreme. To have sat between them at dinner and even to be allowed to offer remarks of one's own would have been felt by many people a very great honour.

It is true that Kitty's own remarks were not taken very seriously; but then, Dr. Andrews probably found himself much in the same predicament that Mark Pattison found himself in when he sat next to young ladies in the eighties. He felt, Mr Tollemache says, that "in arguing with women (always excepting the very best) it is hard for men to maintain the same perfect frankness, or rather directness, which they maintain in arguing with each other."* He also felt that "When I, an old man of seventy, am talking on intellectual subjects to a young girl of seventeen, she and I are on quite different planes of thought." ** Therefore, he would either flatter her: "I always agree"; or, if she persisted in talking nonsense, [II 41] he embarrassed

* Marginal note at the head of the next page: "Toll. 21". The quotation is from Lionel A. Tollemache *Recollections of Pattison* (London 1885) p 21.

** Quoting Tollemache p 20.

her by the blunt remark: "Your conversational utterances are feeble."* Who can blame him? After all, the difference in learning was immeasurable; and besides, there lay between them, among other obstacles, Mark Pattison's belief that "in arguing with. . . ." ** The difficulty was further increased by the opinion which was certainly Mark Pattison's and was probably [that of] many other learned men of his time: "Pattison" to quote Mr. Tollemache again "stood in special need of that [restful sympathy which women know how to give, which good women will give when they feel that it is valued, but which men can neither give nor take away. Yet he learnt by experience that even this rose is not thornless. In particular, he found that the art of instructing and correcting women without affronting them is not easily acquired. . . .]" † And he went on to define the art of pleasing: "The art of pleasing [," I heard him say, "] consists in entire self-effacement."

When Kitty made her unfortunate remark about Henry the Eighth, she was not really consoled or instructed by feeling Dr. Andrews' hand upon her knee. Thus, the social intercourse between learned men and girls with original minds in the eighties was full of difficulties and misconceptions on both sides. Nor could Kitty be expected to understand why the "vain old peacocks" needed so much sympathy:

* *Ibid* p 21.

** To repeat the quotation above.

† Marginal note: "17." This and the next supplied passage are from Tollemache p 17. The subject is introduced on p 16:

" 'Like all good men,' says Mr. Leslie Stephen, '[Samuel] Johnson loved good women, and liked to have on hand a flirtation or two, as warm as might be within the bounds of due decorum.' It is undeniable that this somewhat exclusive test of goodness would not exclude Pattison, who at times seemed to agree with the hero of *Amours de Voyage* [Clough's poem] that *Vir sum, nihil foeminei a me alienum puto*. To speak more seriously, he sought and obtained what has been called the one compensation of growing old. The praise which Wordsworth bestowed on Nature, may more truly be applied to a good woman — she never yet betrayed the heart that loved her; and Pattison stood in special need. . . ." On p 20, Tollemache says of Pattison: "Indeed, his love of paradox led him to speak as if he imagined *Ens rationale* to be the definition, not of *Homo*, but of *Vir*."

What did their "silly old quarrels about a book or an appointment" matter to her? What she saw was simply an ugly, ill-mannered man who pinched her knee and spilt the soup into his beard. Dr. Andrews was justifiably annoyed, and subconsciously perhaps hardened in his determination to oppose the admission of women to the University. It would be no exaggeration to say that Dr. Andrews, [II 42] like Pattison, "had rather strong views as to the intellectual inferiority of the average woman to the average man." When the door shut upon Kitty and her mother, and Dr. Andrews was free to speak with perfect frankness and directness to his own sex, his views upon women — and their charms, and the absolute necessity of keeping them out of the University at all costs — were by no means concealed. But as women, in 1880, always left the men to smoke and drink for at least half an hour after dinner, these views did not reach Kitty or her mother in the very expressive language which Dr. Andrews used in their absence. Perhaps if Kitty had been admitted to those sittings when the men talked frankly, she would have revised her opinion that learned men are the "dullest old bores in creation." As it was, why Miss Craddock envied her the privilege of sitting next to distinguished men, she could not imagine.

But though the low estimate in which Dr. Andrews and Professor Lathom held the intellectual powers of her sex did not reach Kitty directly in the vivid and racy language which they used over the port and cigars, she would need to have been a great deal simpler and more insensitive than she was not to perceive it. The emphasis that was laid upon her personal charms, the demands that were made upon her sympathy, served daily and hourly to remind her that intellectually she, and all other women, had no claims whatever upon the attention of men. She had seen for herself, often enough, that if a woman was ugly, poor, badly dressed, like Lucy Craddock, [II 43] she had no value for men whatsoever. Poor Lucy's little book on the Angevin Kings was treated as the scribbling of an industrious child. It was true that George Eliot had been seen walking in the grounds of

Balliol on the arm of Dr. Jowett. But George Eliot was, after all, only a novelist. Chuffy himself might have conceded that women had a certain faculty for the very inferior art of making pretty little pictures of daily life. After a hard day's work, no man was to be blamed for relaxing over a novel: Jane Austen was really gifted in that very lady-like occupation. But when it came to history! to mathematics! to philosophy! to anything that required real intellect and real knowledge, (these notes of exclamation are the fullest indication of the scorn which could be detected, even through the dining room door when the subject of women's intellect was discussed) women were, had always been, and would always remain — the word that Dr. Andrews used to sum up the women's intellects is still too forcible to be committed to print.

But without hearing that word, Kitty observed it effects. Women were making efforts to establish some kind of College for themselves in Oxford in 1880; Somerville and Lady Margaret's were actually founded in 1879. But the contempt which these efforts roused in the ordinary don and undergraduate, the opposition [with] which all requests for money to build, or for the right to attend lectures or share in the educational advantages of men were received [II 44] could scarcely fail to impress the mind of an intelligent girl of twenty-one. Kitty herself took no part in the discussion either way. Her mother tacitly assumed that women who asked for such privileges were very foolish; the prospect of their ever succeeding appeared remote in the extreme, to one who lived in the Lodge of an Oxford Master; and not a term passed without some incident which proved to Kitty, who sat silent in her "ribbons and laces," listening, smiling, pouring out tea, the complete negligibility of her sex intellectually; and the proper way in which any attempt to assert equality with men would be chastised if any woman were so rash [*as to desert her proper sphere*] and make it. For example, there was that incident when one of the new women's colleges aped the men's colleges and gave a "gaudy." "It was a brilliant affair, and almost every Oxfordian of note," whatever he may have felt secretly about women's colleges, was present. Walter Pater, whose views upon women were too well-known, one would have thought, to accept an invitation from such a source, was present. And in the course of the evening, the lady Head of the house dropped her white kid glove in front of Pater; and Pater, at least, thought that she did it on purpose. Therefore, he "instead of gallantly picking it up, walked on and trod on it."

Did[n't you see *that?* whispered a friend who stood near.

"Didn't you see how I rewarded the action?" followed Pater. "If I had not remembered how, in spite of the honours heaped upon him by Queen Elizabeth, Sir Walter Raleigh was in the end led out to execution, perhaps I, too, might have made a fool of myself. Believe me, my dear sir, it was an insinuation of the devil that caused this woman to drop her glove."] *

Kitty, as she listened to the story, asked herself why then did he go to their party? For surely, if you held Mr. Pater's views on women, it would have been easy to stay at home.

[II 45] (These inconsistencies and complexities of social life in Oxford naturally gave Kitty, who had no particular love of intellectual pursuits, food for thought; or perhaps it would be more accurate to call it an instinctive preference for the life of a farmer, in Yorkshire.) But there was also, Kitty was dimly aware, chiefly through her friend Alice, the embryo medical student, another school of thought in Oxford; although it could scarcely be said to be well-represented in authoritative quarters. Alice mixed in quite a different set from Kitty. Her father was merely a coach: a self-taught, worn-looking, elderly man, who had come to Oxford from a grammar school, and whose father had been a working man. His opinion of

* Marginal note: "131". Woolf is here quoting Thomas Wright *The Life of Walter Pater* (London 1907) II 130–31. The space left blank after "Did" (the beginning of the first word on page 131) has been filled from the 1969 facsimile reprint (New York: Haskell). The rest of the page goes beyond the episode of the glove, to compare Pater's low opinion of women's wit with Swift's and to quote Pater on women's perversity as the reason for his disapproval of marriage.

women was as high as Dr. Andrews' was low. He owed everything in life, he would tell Kitty, when she came to tea, to his own mother — a common working woman, he called her. [*She was not a Yorkshire woman, as Kitty had hoped, but she was Scotch, which was the next best thing.*] And he would tell them how his mother had saved for his schooling; and how she had taught herself to read when she was over forty; and how she had a better brain than any professor in the place; and how when she came to Oxford, she had remarked of All Souls that it would make an admirable Co-operative hall. His attitude to Kitty was the opposite of Dr. Andrews' and Professor Lathom's. He was not polite. He did not pick up her handkerchief, or tread upon it. He never pinched her knee. He talked to her as frankly as he talked to a man — at least [II 46] Kitty never felt that the talk completely changed its character when she and Alice shut the door upon the jams and cakes and slices of cold beef that made their high tea, and the rather thick smoke that came from their shag tobacco. Once Mr. Gabbit asked her if she wouldn't try a pipe herself — Kitty. And then she would hear talk of the women's movement; but it was not in the least like what she heard at the Lodge. Very little importance was attached to degrees. It was felt in that yellow brick villa that it was important for women to earn their livings. "It was time they did," Mr. [Gabbit] said. "And you women are a great deal more important in the future, than we men." But this unfortunately for Kitty meant that her friend Alice had to work as hard as a man, and go to London; for in her secret heart, she despised Oxford. All the future lay in London, not down here. And somehow Kitty, as she buttoned on her mackintosh, felt that she [Alice] took a slightly sarcastic amusement in her frills and flounces. She was sure of a respect and an admiration from the wizened little man himself and from his sons, which made her ask [herself] another question: Was it true that some men really admired women? not as old Chuffy and old Lathom admired them; that they did not tread on their handkerchiefs or pick them up? that one could therefore respect a man? and find him interesting to talk to? — though nobody could compete with Lucy Craddock. Still Kitty loved, in a sense, that wizened little mathematical coach: he would have taught her mathematics, she really believed. She had the oddest feeling, as she went home to the Lodge, that men were not bores: [II 47] one need not always be "self-effacing" and pleasing with some men: not with working men whose mothers had brought up twelve children on — how much was it a week; for though Kitty would never hope to be a woman like that, she dimly felt, when she was with the [Gabbits] that there was something in her, something adventurous and strong and truthful — just as there had been in old Mr [Gabbit] — [and] that she too was a human being and not merely the Master's daughter. But Alice had gone to London. And Kitty, as it turned out, never had an opportunity of meeting Dr. Joseph Wright.*

Even from so rapid a sketch as this, it may be concluded that the difficulties, inconsistencies, and complexities of life in Oxford in the eighties for a girl like Kitty were numerous; and puzzling enough to perplex a mind that was original enough to ask them, though not original enough to ask them openly. The only question that Kitty could put openly, and was determined to put to her parents on the 1st of September 1880 — the day was marked with a cross on her calendar — was, "May I leave Oxford and become a farmer in Yorkshire?" But however tactfully she phrased it, she knew the question was [II 48] so wrapped up with all those other questions — about pouring out tea, and standing at the window in a nightgown, and not going for walks alone, and always calling undergraduates "Mr", and never meeting them except with her mother, and talking to rowing men about rowing and reading men about reading; it was so involved also with the

* The manuscript continues, with an elision for matter to be inserted: "And though Dr. Joseph Wright, was of opinion that. . . . The opinion of Kitty's world was much more that of another cultivated man, Walter Bagehot." Actual quotations from Dr Wright begin further on (see II 54 ff). Bagehot's opinion is quoted above, I 42 n. Here Woolf may have meant to juxtapose their contrasting views.

opinions of great men like Gladstone who thought that women must be chaste, and of Walter Bagehot who thought that they could be labourers but not capitalists, of Mark Pattison who thought that [he] [*stood*] in special need of "the restful sympathy which women knew how to give", of Walter Pater who thought that "it was an insinuation of the Devil that caused this woman to drop her glove", of Oscar Browning who thought that the lowest man is intellectually the superior of the cleverest woman; it was so complicated, further, by the fact that there was no way in which a woman could earn her living; and therefore no way in which she could be independent of such opinions; and therefore no way in which she could bear a child without being married. And finally, it was so profoundly affected by the fact that Kitty's body had been trained to send out and to receive a multitude of impressions about her body and other people's bodies for generations — as she stood trying on clothes before looking glasses, and sat pouring out tea, and kept the peace between Chuffy and Professor Lathom at dinner. The whole question that she was going to put to her parents on the 1st of September 1880 was so profoundly and subtly and obscurely affected by all these opinions and customs and [II 49] laws and conventions that for a novelist to record them all, or for Kitty herself to analyse them all, would require more volumes than Mr. Proust has devoted to *la Recherche du Temps Perdu*. Moreover, in the above list, no mention has been made of the Hughes family; and as any attempt to write about Kitty in 1880 would be grotesquely incomplete without some brief mention of them, a scene from their life must be attempted.

Nelly Hughes was undoubtedly Lucy Craddock's favourite pupil. She was perhaps the only girl Lucy taught who took her work seriously; but then she was the daughter of a poor man, and was going to earn her living as a doctor. She had none of Kitty's charm, to Miss Craddock; she was short and round and wore spectacles; but she worked like a nigger; [and] it was a great pleasure to teach her. Not only had Kitty heard, very enviously, the praises of Nelly, but once or twice she had met Nelly at Miss Craddock's; the two girls had talked; Kitty had invited Nelly to tea at the Lodge: Nelly had invited Kitty to tea at her father's house — in Pinbright Road, which is, of course, not one of the fashionable quarters of Oxford. But Sam Hughes was one of those self-taught men, of working-class origin who, in the eighties, by means of scholarships had succeeded in finding employment at Oxford in some rather nondescript capacity. To go to tea in Pinbright Road was for Kitty a great adventure.

[II 50] [FIFTH CHAPTER]

Dec. 9th [1932]

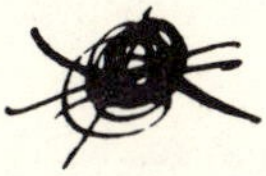

It was embarrassing, [*to*] Kitty felt, as she stood in the little front room at ⟨11⟩ Pinbright Road, [*to g*] waiting for the maid to fetch Miss Nelly, to feel so very tall. [*She felt that her head touched the ceiling, &*] Not only was the room small, but it was so crowded with small bamboo tables & [*hanging*] [*shades lamps &*] [*& hanging lamps & everything was*] [*the mantelpiece was so crowded with vases & candlesticks, &*] & the tables were so crowded with photographs, & the mantelpiece was so crowded with vases & [*clocks st*] bronzes, & the walls were so crowded with [*what appeared to be*] family groups & what appeared to be [*framed*] certificates also in frames that Kitty felt herself even larger than usual; &, what was stranger, excessively well dressed. She had only time to read a certificate testifying that Samuel Hughes had passed an examination at South Kensington when Nelly came in: & all Kittys fears were confirmed — she was much too well dressed. [*And yet*] It was only the dress she always wore to go out to tea in. But Nelly was wearing [*only*] a pinafore — which covered her entirely as if she had been doing housework. The room in which they had tea* was at the back overlooking the garden. And Kitty was introduced to Mrs Hughes, & then to [*Merton Hu*] Dickie & to Meg. As Dickie & Meg were only eight & seven, they merely stared; but Mrs. Hughes who was well on in the forties, stood up to shake hands; & again Kitty [*ashamed*] felt not only much too tall — Mrs Hughes was very short & stout — but again horribly well dressed: Mrs Hughes was dressed exactly like Biggs, the Cook at the Lodge; in plain black, with a cameo

* See II 58 for a different draft of the following passage.

fastening her dress at [II 51] the neck. And she wore steel rimmed spectacles, just as Biggs did; & her hair was ⟨parted⟩ brushed absolutely smoothly on either side, again just as Biggs brushed her hair. But Mrs Hughes had large steel grey eyes, which looked straight at Kitty [*as*] with a searching &, as Kitty felt, severe expression [*w*] which was quite unlike the [*jolly*] ⟨respectful if familiar⟩ expression with which Biggs received Kitty when Kitty was sent to give an order in the kitchen. Mrs Hughes was in the habit of giving orders — not of taking them — Kitty felt that at once, as she sat down, & disembarrassed herself of her gloves under the shelter of the table cloth. Then Mr. Hughes came in — & he was just as short as the rest of his family, Kitty [*felt;*] ⟨observed;⟩ [*on a very small, but very &*] she noticed how stubby his fingers were; & how very hard he gripped her hand; & then she noticed — that both Dad & Mum (so Nelly called them) talked [*Yorkshire*] — was it Yorkshire? They talked with an accent that reminded her of the Carters — but it was not quite the same. Anyhow it was beautiful, in Kitty's ears; & their manners, — Mr. Hughes was much more friendly than Mrs Hughes, [*w*] but interested Kitty so much that she almost forgot to think about her ridiculous clothes. She had never met people like them before. Dad, Mrs Hughes called him dad, was an Oxford don — or something of the kind — at any rate he lectured & taught undergraduates: & yet [*he had come in from*] his hair stood up all over his head; & he [*behaved*] sat at the head of the table; [*he*] he talked broad Yorkshire; he called his wife "Mum"; he ate like a working man; he was a working man; he had no manners at all; he was far the nicest man she had ever met. He chaffed his daughter. He said that [*Mum had*] Kitty must have another slice of Mum's bread. And Mum then had made the bread, had she? And was that why she would not come to tea at the Lodge? And what a great lady she was — [II 52] by which Kitty meant that just as her own mother would get up & shake hands with the Duchess of Newhaven, whose son was at Katharines, & [*they*] think no more about her being a duchess because after all Mrs Malone was a Rigby, so Mrs. Hughes having noted at one glance that Kitty was far richer & better dressed than her own daughter, thought no more about it, because Mrs. Hughes was — [*what was she?*] <Mrs Hughes.> And what was Sam Hughes? And how did [*people like that, who*] they come to live in Oxford, & where had they lived before, & did Mrs Hughes do the cooking, & did Sam < the mathemati> mend the boots & why were they not in the least ashamed, or proud, or uneasy, or in any way curious that this huge [*splendid*] tea, with its jams & its [*cak*] home made cakes (it was their dinner) was not what the Masters daughter was used to: [*& why*] nor was Sam in the least like Professor Lathom. [*How extr*] What an adventure for Kitty that tea party was! — partly because they talked Yorkshire; & then, [*after tea,*] half way through tea in came the elder brother, Jo[*seph*], & that too was so different from anything Kitty had ever known. He waited on himself; & he gave himself no airs whatever, Kitty reflected, comparing him with the Pargiters, the Ashtons, [*the Hamm*] & the Lammermuirs. As for 'admiring' her, that from Jo, whose hair like his fathers was rough, but he had been doing something to the shed — there was a little shaving stuck in it — as for looking at Kitty as those young men looked at her, she felt physically convinced that if Jo Hughes liked her, he would [*kiss her;*] <tell her so in plain English;> just as she felt convinced that if Sam Hughes asked her about her history — as he did — he would listen to what she had to say about Henry the Eighth [*without*] just as seriously as he listened to what [II 53] his daughter Nelly was telling Mum about her chemistry <lesson:> as for pressing Kittys knee under the table, like Chuffy, Kitty could have sworn, & Kittys oath on such a matter was worth having, before tea was over, that [*such a demand for sympathy*] any man making that demand for sympathy upon a girl at 10 Pinbright Road would have been kicked out of the house by the master. This Kitty knew, beyond all possibility of doubt, merely by the way in which Mr & Mrs Hughes chaffed each other. She knew before tea was over that

Mr & Mrs Hughes [*had a very great respect for each other — so had her own parents; but then things were so different for them. Mr & Mrs. Hughes, Kitty felt, were*] had been of course lovers: that was taken for granted; years ago; very poor — obviously; & Sam had got his chance — gone to London; yes; taken his degree — yes: leaving [*Ann*] [*Jane*] <Jenny> (Jenny he called her, once, during tea) leaving Jenny in Yorkshire: & the children: & his job — well, how much wd. it be likely that Sam could send her, from London <to Yorkshire> — her job, cooking, washing, feeding & [*taking in charing*] doing charing too, to make both ends meet, her job, Kitty divined from the way they chaffed each other, was every bit as important to Sam as Sams was to Jenny. [*Only*] True, she was more openly proud — it was her doing, framing his certificates & hanging them in the front room, together with the [*tea*] salver presented by [*Sa*] Sam's grateful pupils when he left Yorkshire — to become a great man in London: but what a different way of treating women Sam's was from Chuffy & Professor Lathom! And how Kitty envied Nelly! Why, [*they were*] her father was proud of her work. He was much prouder of her than he was of Jo. Mrs Hughes was prouder of Jo; but before the tea was over, Kitty [*had*] knew perfectly well that Mrs Hughes was absolutely set upon Nell's passing her exams. & becoming a doctor. And [II 54] Mrs Hughes set no store by Oxford ladies, whatsoever. They might never have heard of Eights week & Common: as for a college Gaudy, no doubt Mrs Hughes would have said something very sharp about all that waste of good food; though she saw to it that her Sam had the best food in England — their [*Yorkshire*] Sunday dinner with Yorkshire pudding cooked by Nell under her mother's eye as Yorkshire pudding should be cooked [, *followed by*] <outdid in succulence all the dishes of all the [*Lodges*] Colleges at least in Sams opinion> cooked by Mrs Hughes herself because no Oxford girl could learn the right way of it — though she was teaching little Maud — their only servant — in short, Kitty felt when she left the Hughes family in P. Road that if she had had

Sam for her father & Jenny for her mother [*& Jo for her brother*] she would have [*enjoyed life*] been forced to become a farmer: she would have been trained for some job. Mrs. Hughes though unduly scornful of the Oxford ladies, [*she*] might have said like another Yorkshire woman "Why, to tell you the honest truth, they are stuck-up, conceited things, with nothing much about them; they are all outside" * — & rather narrow minded as to the advantages of reading in the Bodleian & writing books, was, nevertheless, [*one*] even more advanced in her views of women's rights than the [*Committee*] Aclands & the Arnolds, the Sidgwicks, & the [blank space] She insisted, Kitty learnt, that her Nell was to earn her own living; because, Mrs Hughes said, no daughter of hers should marry a working man, & live in a one roomed cottage & bring ten children into the world, as her own mother had done.

[II 55] Kitty scarcely opened her lips except to say yes & no & thank you; [*in the*] She was terribly shy. She was terribly afraid lest she should say the wrong thing; [*on*] moreover, the [*usual topics of*] topics that she was accustomed to discuss & to hear discussed at the Lodge were of no interest here. Dances? dinners? commemorations, picnics — the Brooks had never been to them. Jo, with the flake of wood in his hair, was clearly not a rowing man or a reading man; he was not Eton or Harrow or Rugby or Winchester. And Mrs Brook had never, Kitty felt, [*paid a call upon any Oxford lady;*] been to an At Home, or paid a call in her life. Sam of course had heard of Dr. Malone; but for the first time in her experience, Kitty had the odd sensation that she was nobody's daughter in particular. [*And*] Accustomed as she was merely [*to have to*] <for the bare> mention [of] her name, [*for*] to [*excite*] [*produce in those she*] to

* Marginal note: "Wright 21". Woolf is quoting here from Elizabeth Mary Wright *The Life of Joseph Wright* (2 vols London: Oxford University Press 1932) I 20–21. It is a remark of Wright's mother and is given in Yorkshire phonetics in his *English Dialect Dictionary*. The photograph of Joseph Wright's mother reproduced on an adjacent page of the *Life* corresponds to the photograph which Kitty is shown in the Hugheses' (or Brooks') parlor, in II 68.

make those who heard it say "The daughter of Dr. Malone?" — for her appearance in any college to cause doors to be unlocked & curtains to be drawn asunder, it was extremely queer to feel that here, in Oxford, she was having tea with people to whom the name Malone stood for nothing whatever. Kitty was Nell's friend — that was all. Thus, while Kitty [*racked*] hunted for something to say that would not seem silly to the Brooks, she was aware that there were a great many things that she could say here, & nowhere else.

"You're reading history with Lucy Craddock?" Sam Brook asked her. And [*it suddenly occurred to Kitty that*] the way he spoke, simple & direct as it was, made Kitty feel that she could discuss the character of Henry the Eighth with Sam: as she could never discuss it with her father even. [*Yet*] Of course, with Nell [II 56] there — Nell who really put her back into her work — Kitty would have felt shy [*; but*] of talking about history; but [*that*] the sort of shyness that Nell & Sam made her feel — as if they were eager terriers hungrily waiting to pounce on what she said because they pounced on all facts like that — [*they were t*] was quite different from the condescending interest of Professor Lathom, the rudeness of Dr Andrews, or the ironical manner which for some reason her father always used, both to men & to women. ⟨when he talked about serious things.⟩

"I like history" Kitty said. "But I dont get much time — I'm awfully lazy" she added.

Mrs. Brook looked at her with her searching severe eyes. The apparition of a frilled & flounced young lady at her tea table was by no means to Mrs. Brook's taste. The narrowness of her own education & the hardness of her own life [*had*] naturally made her censorious. She could say, to their faces, extremely cutting things to the wives of Dons who invited her to join their organisations, to come to their parties. But her judgment, though very narrow, was shrewd. Although Kittys dress, shoes, gloves, had caused Mrs. Brook to think meanly of Kitty when she came in, there was something in her height, & strength, in her broad cheekbones & honest [*tho*] eyes, set too far apart as they were, that [*pleased*] <gave> Mrs. Brook [pleasure]. <She was thinking that if Kitty had been her own daughter, she could have made something of her> "Thats the moor, at the back of our house" she remarked, seeing that Kittys eyes were fixed upon a very highly coloured watercolour that hung over the mantelpiece. It was an impossible daub — the Brooks taste in art was [*feeble*] conventional in the extreme —; [*but*] but Kitty, [*while knowing that it was*] who knew enough about painting to know that, knew enough about Mrs Brook to know that she was firmly persuaded that there was only one [II 57] county in England that mattered; only one people; only one way of life; only one sort of cooking, of [*house*] keeping a house, of bringing up children, of educating them, [*of*] — & there was in Mrs. Brooks case, in her bearing such a queer charm for Kitty — like the old Duchess of Newhaven, she was such a personage — that Kitty felt just as she did with the Duchess, that she would give anything for Mrs. Brook to think well of her.

So, blushing rather, in case she might be saying the sort of thing that Mrs Brook would think silly, Kitty told her how her mother's family came from up there. She carefully concealed the fact that their name was Rigby, lest Mrs. Moor might think her well born. But when Mrs. Brook asked straight [*t*] out, [*who her*] what her mother's name might have been, & Kitty said "Rigby", greatly to her delight Mrs. Moore approved. that is to say she had been in service with an old Miss Rigby before she married. Here Sam chimed in. He was a little perhaps self-consciously proud of the fact that his wife had been a cook. Perhaps for a moment he wished Kitty to understand that *that* was the sort of people they were; for of course, being a man of wider experience than his wife, & attached to the University in some nondescript way, he knew that, socially, the daughter of the Master of Katharines was condescending in coming to tea with them: sometimes, for a second, [*the*] Sam liked, as his wife liked, to rub in the fact of their humble birth, [*& sin*] when the memory of all that they had gone through before they could afford a house in Pinbright Road & furniture & pictures & a maid [*to*] sleeping in the house made him speak Yorkshire with a broader accent than was ⟨now⟩ natural to him. But when he had asserted the fact that his wife had been a cook, he was far too well bred, to refer to it again. [II 58] He had already come to the same conclusion as his wife that here was a [*nice*] very nice girl, whose parents were doing their best to ruin her by the way they brought her up.

[*with*] the room in which they had tea* was at the back overlooking the garden, & [*with her*] as her powers of observation were sharpened by the unfamiliarity of her surroundings, Kitty [*observ*] noticed that there was a shed & hen coops in the back garden at the same time that she saw two small children [*sitting at a table*] & an elderly woman sitting at a round table spread with a [*variety of*] great many [*dishes*] cakes. Dickie & Peg, Nell's small brother & sister, merely stared: Mrs. Brook[*e*] stood up. Either, Kitty thought once more, she was remarkably tall, or the Brook family were remarkably small. Mrs. Brook[*e*] was very short, but [*very*] very broad. And again felt that she was absurdly overdressed.

(take in) *200* **

[*However she had no time*] ⟨[*But*]⟩ Kitty was terribly shy. The children looked at her. Mrs Brook looked at her. Then, rather peremptorily Mrs Brook told the children to get on with their tea; & the bread & butter which they had momentarily suspended was slowly raised once more to their mouths. Then Mr. Brook himself came in; & [*not only w*] he too was remarkably short & very broad. Kitty noticed his alpaca jacket; [*his rough*] & how [*his*] hair[*s*]⟨y⟩ [*stood up on end*] ⟨his face was⟩ & how stubby his fingers were, & how hard he gripped her hand, when he said, very heartily, with [II 59]

* This is a new draft of the passage begun on II 50.

** No explanation has been found for this or the similar note on II 61, "(take in 208)". Presumably Woolf is directing herself to insert matter from some other manuscript, or possibly some book.

a curious accent, Pleased to see you": what the accent was, Kitty did not know. It was not Oxford anyhow. In fact, she had a queer feeling that she [*had*] was [*no longer*] <not> in Oxford. [*She was completely at a loss*] — any longer. She [*felt certain*] [*could not place*] [*this tea party*] [*The Brook family*] — She had eaten [*tea wi*] meals with farmers, & with Dons, & with a Duchess or a Marchioness now & then; but never in her life had she sat down to a meal with the Brook family. <For the Brooks were not farmers: & they were not Dons> She was terribly shy: she [*was terribly*] scarcely opened her lips except to say yes & no & thank you. [*For the sort of*] Clearly, the sort of talk she made & heard at the Lodge — about dances & dinners & commems. & Eights weeks & picnics — was meaningless here. She had only to look at Mrs. Brook to see that she had never paid a call in her life. And yet Mr. Brooke was a sort of lecturer too — The Brooks talked; that is to say Mr Brook chaffed his daughter; & Nell chaffed her father: [*but*] & the little boy volunteered as children will a story [*about a*] <about a goose> that was unintelligible to everyone except his mother; & Kitty eating her bread in servile imitation of the way in which they ate their bread — spreading the butter thick — felt gradually more at her ease, because, though she did not take the point of [*Sams*] <Dad's> [*(Mrs. Brook*] remarks ([*Mr & Mrs Brooke were called Dad & Mum, just as*] for all their names were abbreviated — <Dad, Mum> Dick, Peg, Nell — [*to suit*] perhaps to suit their own shortness of body) & Nells chaff she felt that they had not altered their style of conversation to suit her: they talked like this always. [*Soon too*] she had the odd sensation that she was nobodies daughter [II 60] in particular. Accustomed as she was, at the first mention of her name to be asked "The daughter of Dr. Malone? And how is your father?", just as she was accustomed on presenting herself with Mrs. Howard Fripp [*to ha*] at a College to have doors unlocked & private treasures shown, it was extremely queer to be having tea, here in Oxford, with people to whom the name of Malone meant, apparently, nothing. [*Dad, of*] Sam [of] course — his wife called him Sam <or Dad>: he called her [*Mum or*] Liz or Mum — must have heard of Dr. Malone, since he was in some nondescript way attached to the University: but he never asked her "How is your father?" And thus, [*though*] Kitty still felt extremely shy, particularly of Mrs. Brook who looked at her severely now & then, but said nothing — indeed she was busy with the children — Kitty began to be aware that there were a great many things [*sh*] that she could say here, to Sam & Nell, once she found her tongue.

"You're reading history with Lucy Craddock?" Sam Brook asked her. Kitty liked Sam at once for the way he said Lucy Craddock', — as if her dear Lucy were not a dowdy old bluestocking, but a human being: [*rather an admirable human be*] [*someone*] <a woman> Sam [*w*] liked. You're fond of history?" he asked her, cutting himself a huge hunk of cake (Kitty began to suspect that tea meant dinner) Yes I am" she said, feeling that she might be able to discuss the character of Henry the Eighth one of these days with Sam without being snubbed. Yet he was some kind of lecturer. [II 61] Anyhow, Kitty much preferred Sams way of talking to Chuffy's; or to Professor Lathoms — great men though they were. (But had the Brooks ever heard of them?) Chuffy was so gruff; Professor Lathom was so condescending. Even her own father, whom Kitty loved, always used a specially ironical manner when he talked about serious things, both to men & to women. It was as if he were afraid of being taken seriously. But the difficulty with Mr. Brooke, Kitty felt, would be that he took things too seriously. Nell, Kitty knew, worked like a nigger. If one were Sam Brook's daughter one would work like a nigger too.

She stumbled therefore. "I like history. But I dont get much time — I'm frightfully lazy". Now Mrs. Brook looked at her with her searching, severe eyes.

(take in 208)*

* See preceding note.

one had only to be perfectly frank & Mrs Brook wd like one.

But Kitty had now identified the Brook accent — now that Mrs. Brook had spoken a whole sentence to a grown up person. She must be from Yorkshire. That exceedingly [*sentim*] melodramatic sunset must be taking place over her own Yorkshire moors. So, blushing [*s*] rather in case she might be saying the sort of thing that Mrs. Brook would think silly, Kitty told her that her mother's family came from up there. She carefully concealed the fact that their name was Rigby lest Mrs. Brook should think her [II 62] well born. But when Mrs Brook asked her straight out what her mother's name might have been, & Kitty said Rigby, greatly to her delight Mrs. Brook approved. She said she had "wurrrked" [*with*] <for> an old Miss Rigby before she married. Here Sam joined in. "My wife was a cook Miss Malone," he said. "We used to do our courting in the scullery —" that was what Kitty understood him to say; but either the memory of those days, or some subconscious desire to impress Miss Malone with the fact that he was a working class man, & very proud of being one, made him exaggerate his dialect to such an extent that Kitty could hardly understand him. Being a man of much wider education & experience than his wife, he knew that the daughter of the Master of Katharine's was condescending when she had tea with them. For a moment doubtless, he wished to avenge himself for all the hardships he & Liz had gone through before they were in a position to rent a house in Pinbright Road, & fill it with the furniture that Kitty <brought up in eighteenth century furniture> thought so ugly, & have a maid sleeping in. So he lapsed into a dialect that had long become unnatural to him; & his children scarcely spoke. But he [*had*] <was> much less class conscious with women than with men; & already, he had come to the same conclusion as his wife — they often came to the same conclusions — that Kitty Malone was a very nice girl whose parents were going the right way to ruin her by the way they brought her up. [*So he*] When he had asserted that his wife had been a cook, & [*they*] that they had [*be*] done their courting in the scullery while Kitty's remote cousin sat in the drawing room [II 63] doing whatever that somewhat mythical figure did do in her drawing room — Kitty prayed fervently that she [*had*] <had done something sensible &> treated her cook well — he spoke the English with which he had begun tea. & told Nell to tell Jo that [*he was to*] they weren't [*keeping*] sparing the cake. Nell departed on an errand that seemed to be addressed to yet another Brook somewhere in the background. But Mrs. Brook had evidently been roused, by the mention of Rigbys & Yorkshire, by the memory of early days & sculleries, to a more friendly feeling towards Kitty. The children were eating peacefully. This girl was not just an Oxford lady; [*in*] Mrs Brook despised Oxford ladies; she had good stuff in her. [*For the first time*] And Kitty on her side [*felt that*] forgot about her gloves & her [*fr*] flounces. [*Of*] Mrs. Brook, [*was*] reminded her, oddly enough, of the old Duchess of Newhaven. They were both alarming at first; & [*but they had both the same as*] They were both small & broad; & they both sat very upright; & then they both made one feel anxious not to say the wrong thing: being both of them very dignified, very [*simply*] downright, <apt to bite one's head off> & rather intolerant of humbug. The Duchess of course would be sitting in an armchair in Grosvenor Square, [*surrounded by*] where one room opened out of another, & there were a great many stools miniatures, & two footmen, & a Reynolds <picture> over the fireplace. But the old Duchess [*was*] dressed very much as Mrs. Brook dressed. And she had the same parted hair — only she wore a lace cap; & a diamond brooch instead of a cameo: [*but she too spoke with an accent, & she too*] Yes, Mrs. Brook reminded Kitty strongly of the Duchess. [*So*] She felt the same comfortable — [II 64] comfortable after the first shyness wore off — feeling that [*one could be quite*] one had only to be quite straightforward with either of them — And then, Mrs. Brook could talk about Yorkshire.

Mrs. Brook was very ready to oblige. It was two years since she had been home; the children made the journey too expensive to go often And yet though Oxford was her home now, Oxford, [*& its*] & [*its*] Oxford shops & streets & trades people, & the rich [*Oxford country,*] fields & woods, [*& the*] round Oxford, & the grand people & the grand homes & the great colleges — were all daily compared with Mackley (the village where she was born) & [*the moors &*] the Cooperative Stores & the moors & the [*cobbled*] Yorkshire girls much to the disadvantage of Oxford. Thus she & Kitty had a great deal in common. Though [*they lived*] Carters farm was twenty five miles from Mackley, Mrs. Brook had once been within a few miles of it, [*on a*] in a char a banc. As that [*had*] outing had been a great occasion in her life, she remembered every thing, she had seen; & by piecing together their memories, Kitty & she arrived at the exciting conclusion that they <[*had*] even> both had tea at [*a certain*] the same Inn; & [*both*] <when> Kitty could supply the name of the Innkeeper, which had for the moment slipped Mrs. Brook's memory, Mrs. Brook [*was*] positively beamed[.] on her.

And then the door opened & Jo came in. [*In the*] At the back of her mind Kitty <had> connected [*his appearance*] <him> with [*the*] a persistent sound of hammering which had been going on in the back garden: Certainly the hammering stopped. And there was a [*flake of*] shaving of wood in Jo's hair. And, she realised with surprise, having altered [II 65] her focus to meet the short men of the Brook family, Jo was a tall young man — [*alm*] about her own height. [*And he helped himself. He went into the kitchen & brought back a kettle & filled the tea pot.*] The presence of a young man of her own age immediately changed the perspective [*in which Kitty was seeing things, owing to the*] <of the> highly trained condition of her senses. Her body began to send out impressions & to receive back impressions [*just*] as it did at the Lodge or at the Balliol hall: the same question — does he like me? do I like him? occurred to her; & she had instinctively applied the usual curb, — [*to*] so that the result [*of*] of these investigations might be secret; & had therefore assumed [*all*] the manner of a well bred young lady[*; when sh*] [*sitting very* *upright; though &*] conscious of her appearance; which had been forgotten; [*when she felt that once more she was*] <but here at the Brooks this was> so completely wrong — <she felt> out of touch, out of tune, out of harmony — she did not know how to express it — but [*anyhow*] somehow she was once more an alien & [*a*] almost an enemy in the Brook family — just as she had been getting on so well, too[.] But Mrs Brook, having opened the tea pot, [*told her son*] [*& gazed in*] told her son that [*if*] he [*want*] must fetch the "kittle" — which he did. And the fact that Jo waited on himself somehow helped Kitty to retain that queer sense — of being on a spree, [*alone,*] on her own, which reminded her of the rare occasions when she had given her nurse the slip at Oxford; or when, up at Carters, she had been free to wander off by herself on the moors.

Jo paid her no particular attention. [*He was hungry.*] He had been mending a rotten hen coop it appeared. He was not altogether on the [II 66] best of terms with his father, Kitty felt: [*his fa*] Sam was much prouder of his daughter. Mrs Brook, however, admired her son enormously Kitty felt: for the first time she rested, leaning back in her chair, with her hand resting on her tea cup, from which she took a sip now & then, in the manner of one — to whom strong tea [*is*] has been the comfort, or <at least the> companion of many [*years*] hours of hard work. And she looked at her son.

Kitty [*'s attitude to Jo, was m— she*] < [*attit*] > began to feel <either> that no 'attitude' <to Jo> was needed, or one so different from the attitude that was needed [*by*] <to> rowing men, reading men, sporting men, Eton Winchester & Harrow men. — [*J*] one glance was enough to assure her that Jo [*fell into*] <came under> none of those headings — that she could not adopt it off hand [*or was*] she sat & listened. [*Jo had*] Sam's attitude to Jo was not [*at all*] entirely benevolent. Sam was a hard task master to his children, Kitty guessed. In Sams opinion mending a hen coop was not a job that need take the whole afternoon. [*The fact was that Sams standards were*] And Sams memories of what he had done when he was Jo's age [*now seemed to be*] [—] even now that he was a lecturer he always mended the family boots on Sunday — seemed, — or so Kitty felt, [*as she listened to Sams sarcasm & Jo's surly* [*si*] *replies*] — to be responsible for the sarcastic way in which Sam insisted [*that mending a hen coop*] [*he could mend a hen coop in half the time it took his son*] upon the ⟨most⟩ time needed to mend a hen coop: Sam himself, Kitty concluded, had plenty of time to mend hen coops — as a matter of fact Sam mended the family boots — [*as usu*] without neglecting his books.

[*Instead therefore of*] Kitty found herself being rather sorry for Jo. Jo was supposed to mend the hen coop & to work, she gathered: He too was reading for some examination or other — [II 67] [*he was*] engineering, she thought it was. [*But if*] And then there was her friend Nell. She looked at Nell, in her overall, small, round, spectacled; & she guessed that Nell would help wash up. But would they let her help to wash up? Did she know how to help wash up? Next time she came she would come in her old serge frock. Next time — & then she [*fo*] she was asked to pass the jam, & as she passed it, Jo looked at her: [*&*] no, it was not in the least the look that the Pargiters, the Ashtons & the Lammermuirs gave her. [*As for*] It was the sulky respectful honest look: as if by no means implying that he did not admire her; but at the same time Kitty felt that if Jo did admire her he would seize her in his arms & kiss her. [*If*] but not here: not in his fathers home. As for pressing her knee under the table, like Chuffy, Kitty [*wa*] could have sworn — & Kittys oath on such a matter was worth having, that any man making such a demand for sympathy under the table cloth at 10 Pinbright Road would have been kicked out of the house by the master [*How*] [*The*] Kittys senses had divined by the time tea was over that [*Mr & Mrs. Brook were*] the relations between Mr. & Mrs Brook [*were*] differed [*in some way*] from those [*of the*] ⟨of [*other*] the⟩ husbands & wives, she knew — [*so that*] [*in a w*] & [*that this difference was the*] that was [*why*] one of the reasons why [*everything was* *different*] [*she would not*] everything was different; why Jo [*was*] looked at her differently.

But what the difference was she could not say, until, tea being done, [*Nell*] <&> [*she*] Nell [*hanging*] disappearing for a moment, perhaps into the [II 68] kitchen, she found herself majestically ushered by Mrs. Brook into the little front room; & then Sam followed; & then Kitty was shown, just as her mother would show the pictures at the Lodge, the certificates [*the salver*] & the [*family portraits enlarged*] <life sized> photographs & the silver salver. Mrs. Brook showed the certificates — they were her husband's: [*he had passed examination after examination:*] they showed what examination he had passed; & the salver had been given him by his old pupils: but when they came to the photograph[s], Mr Brook who had been fidgeting with his watch chain, humourously tolerating his wifes narrative, stepped forward & [*said &*] asked Kitty what she thought of that old woman? That old woman was obviously got up in all her finery & a row of little buttons ran down the front of her dress: her hand rested stiffly upon the photographers table. She was an old working woman in her best dress. But Kitty [*standing between the Brooks*] understood her; [*Mrs Brook was*] she was [*an old*] Sams mother; she had [*worked in a mill; she had*] [*her husband had left her;*] her husband had drunk; & she had brought them all up; & though Sam never said a word to that effect, [*Kitty*] [*the*] Kittys senses again told her, [*in*] undeniably, that he [*was*] respected & admired that old woman, [*(hence his attitude to Lucy Craddock; to his wife; to his daughter; to Kitty herself)*] & thought her [*worth all*] <more than> the Masters & Mistresses in Oxford <(hence his attitude to Lucy Craddock; to his wife; to his daughter; to Kitty herself)>. [*She was dead now; but she had lived to see her son*] — That was why Jo looked at her so differently from the other young men. That was why Mr & Mrs Brook seemed so [*different*] — That old working woman [*ha*] whose husband had drunk who had gone out charing who had saved her pence to give her sons an education, [*who had*] & had lived to see her Sam a [*gen*] great man was at the back of [*the*] it all — Kitty meant, [II 69] Sam doesnt despise women; he doesn't sneer at them, or tread on their gloves or press their knees under the table. Oh no — [*Mr & Mrs Brook were married in a way that none of* [*her*] *parents friends were married*] so that she could feel quite free with Sam. And that old woman, [*with her*] Kittys senses told her, was the reason why Nell worked like a nigger; [*for*] why indeed, though she might clear away the tea things ⟨as she was doing now⟩, she never [*did*] helped in the kitchen ⟨but was driven up to her books;⟩ •{for if [*there was one conclusion that Mr & Mrs. Brook*] thought [*held*] if [*Mr & Mrs Brook were generally of a mind,*] there [*was*] no [*be*] [*conviction*] ⟨[*decision*]⟩ that [*they held more firmly*] [*Mr & Mrs Brook had*] }• One thing that Mr & Mrs. Brook had made up their minds about, it was that no daughter of theirs should marry a working man & bear him ten children in a ⟨single room⟩ workman cottage in Yorkshire — like that old woman. Nell [*was to earn*] ⟨was to be educated & to earn⟩ her living, ⟨[*as*]⟩ even if they had to keep two servants [*in*] sleeping in instead of one. ⟨(Mrs. Brook felt that as much as Kitty. Compare her parents. Buy a farm.)⟩*

Even if they had to keep two servants instead of one sleeping in, Nell was to pass her examinations & earn her own living. Nell was not to live the life her grandmother had lived before her. [*of*] ⟨About⟩ that Mrs Brook was even more determined than her husband. Her son might [*ta*] take things easily, if he chose; ⟨waste his time at his own risk;⟩ but not her daughter. Grimly though Mrs Brook regarded the Oxford ladies & their efforts [*organisations*] for the higher education of women, [*sarcastic*] ⟨indifferent⟩ though she might be [*as*] to the architectural beauties of Oxford, & sarcastic though she certainly was as to the amount of food & drink that was consumed by [*Dr. An*] Chuffy Andrews & his like at College feasts

* This insertion was made in pencil.

& Gaudies — but as she cooked her Sam the most succulent Yorkshire pies, cakes, & was famous for her Yorkshire salad her [II 70] sarcasm [*was*] <in this respect was> to some extent justified, — notwithstanding these narrownesses & acerbities, there was no woman in England in 1880 who was more determined that her daughter was to [*earn her own living &*] be an educated woman & earn her own living than Mrs. Brook, [*the miners*] whose [*father had been a*] mother had been a milk hand & borne seven children to a husband who was a miner.

[*With the egotis*] Kitty turned away from the life size photograph of Mrs Brook the elder with a pang of envy at her heart. How easy it would have been, she thought, had she been their daughter, to say to Mr & Mrs. Brook "Let me leave Oxford & become a farmer". [*They*] She envied her friend Nell. [*Nell had*] Everything was quite easy for Nell. Nell hadn't got to pour out tea. Nell hadn't got to dine at Balliol. She remembered with a start that that was precisely what she had to do — this very night — to dine at Balliol in a [*white*] pink [*sat*] satin frock & sit next Chuffy again no doubt; or next Lord Lammermuir; or next her cousin [*Ni*] Nigs. Oh to be the daughter of a working man, she sighed — silently — as she shook hands with the Brooks. Oh to be free; to be herself; on her own; to earn her living; to be a farmer; to dig & cook & bake with her own hands; to wash up the tea things in an old serge dress; & then to — the thought did strike her, [*whether*] though probably it was a [*th*] very wrong & immodest thought — & then to fall in love with Jo, & be [*a farm*] the wife of a man with a shaving in his hair who mended hen coops, while she [*bred*] bred pigs in Yorkshire!

[II 71] Such were the thoughts that came to her as she walked down Pinbright Road that summer evening. Soon she found herself in the High & the undergraduates came strolling past in their gowns with their books under their arms; [*or*] [*& they*] & she hated them all. And she passed this college & then that college; & the Bodleian & the Sheldonian; [*& this that*] & she hated them all. For [*after the*] [*after Pinbright Road*] they had never seemed to her so silly, so pointless, so heartless, so extravagant, so uninteresting, so frivolous, so worldly, so insincere, so set upon things that didn't matter one scrap, as they did after tea with the Brooks in Pinbright Road <as if the proportions of [*ev*] things [*had*] had been changed>. The same queer sense of changed proportions came upon her even more strongly when she reached the Master's Lodge. [*There it all was, going on just as usual.*] She peeped into the drawing room. It looked very large, very stately, very still. [*after the crowded little room in Pinbright Road.*] It looked very dull, very solemn, very pretentious [*& she echoed*] <But it was not only the house that looked different.> She echoed the words that her cousin Eleanor Pargiter had used when she came back to 58 Abercorn Terrace from having tea with Mrs. Levy in Lisson Grove. "How they enjoy life — the poor" The Brooks were not poor, as the Levys were poor: but how they enjoy life! Kitty thought, as she went up the broad staircase to [*change*] <dress> for dinner. And that night before she went to bed she drew another circle round September the First in her calendar; as if to [*emphasise*] the fact that whatever happened, she would force herself to find a way of becoming a farmer & leaving Oxford.

[II 72]

[SIXTH ESSAY]

Dec. 16th [1932]

This change of perspective — this comparison between Ten Pinbright Road and the High, between the Brooks and the Masters and Dons — added another question, of course, to those that Kitty was already in the habit of asking herself. If it was so easy for Nell to ask her parents to let her become a farmer, why was it so hard for Kitty? Why was the Brooks' attitude to life so different from the Malones'? Standing in front of the enlarged photograph, Kitty had felt that the profound difference lay somewhere there — Mr. Brook had an enormous respect for his old mother. His old mother had been a working woman. Hence the curious and invigorating feeling she had in Pinbright Road. She need not provide that "restful sympathy which women knew how to give." It did not look as if old Mrs. Brook had been an adept in the art of pleasing which "consists in entire self-effacement." * Yet, undoubtedly, Mr. and Mrs. Brook were on the best of terms with each other. And they were not farm labourers. Mr Brook was a kind of lecturer — "a very remarkable fellow" Dr. Malone had called him once. [II 73] Kitty was puzzled. She loved her father and mother. She believed implicitly that the relation between Dr and Mrs Malone was the best that can be between husband and wife. And she never doubted that her own life — if it had not been for her own fault — was far better than other people's lives. Now she was puzzled.

There was perhaps some excuse for Kitty's bewilderment. She was practical by nature. She had only dipped, under great restrictions too, into the poetry and fiction of her day. Thus she had very little general knowledge of human nature and human life besides that

* Here Woolf is quoting Mark Pattison, as above, II 41.

which she had gained from her own experience. She knew nothing of all those grades of society that lie between the working class and the upper class. Of the working class she only knew the Carters: of the upper class, only her own class, in the persons of some dons and professors, and the aristocracy, in the persons, for a time, of earls and a duke or two. This narrowness was not supplemented by such theoretical knowledge as may be won from books. [*She knew something about the feudal system and the Wars of the Spanish Succession; but what human nature*] She held vague general ideas of conduct, of love, of the natures of men and the natures of women — though at the Balliol Ball, for example, her perception of the particular situation was, in some respects, acute in the extreme. Hence, Kitty had always supposed, until she had tea in Pinbright Road, that [II 74] the proportions of life as a whole were more or less settled; that right and wrong had been decided many years ago by universal consent; that the standards and ideals of the year 1880 would continue more or less for ever.

Her history reading had taught her that there had been some difficulties and some doubts in earlier ages; but she felt that these had been solved. The activities of Mr Gladstone were to her only something that her father discussed with other old gentlemen while her mother knitted; and though there was talk of electric light, Kitty never thought that any illuminant could displace the admirable oil lamps in the drawing room. But whatever changes might come in oil lamps, Kitty took it for granted that the laws of conduct were fixed. A woman behaved in one way and a man in another. Ever since she could remember, she had been trained as a woman. And the *Concise Oxford Dictionary*, though published in 1929 — more than fifty years later* — still preserves in its definition of woman-

* Woolf does the arithmetic in the margin:

1880
1929
51

liness, in a compact form, [*the ideal*] which governed Kitty's life in 1880: "Womanly . . . having or showing the qualities befitting a woman . . . modesty, compassion, tact, &c." Nor did Kitty question the same authorities' verdict that manliness consists in "having a man's virtues, courage, frankness, &c."

And in 1880, even Kitty, who was no great reader of poetry or fiction, was still aware that the poets expanded this dictionary dryness in a way that was flattering in the extreme. [11 75] She had once, as a little girl, heard an old gentleman make a speech at some kind of meeting; at the end of which he had turned with a little bow to Mrs. Malone (who was holding a bouquet) and had quoted:

> A perfect woman, nobly planned
> To warn, to comfort, and command
> And yet a spirit still and bright
> With something of an angel light — *

whereby Mrs Malone [*burying her face in the lilies of the valley*] had buried her face in her bouquet. And somehow, the quotation, cut from a local newspaper, had found its way to the nursery and, being pinned by Nurse, under a picture of Red Riding Hood, served to emphasise the fact — for it was a fact that had to be emphasised rather often — that Kitty would never have that said of her if she refused to stand still and have her hair brushed. Nor could Kitty forget the little catch in her father's pleasant eighteenth-century voice when he read aloud Tennyson to Lord and Lady Kerseymere — and reached some lines about a perfect mother. And there was also something about a perfect wife in Mr. Browning. And there was also something about woman's beauty being like genius. And there was Mr. Ruskin in *Sesame and Lilies* — "A princess, a washerwoman. . . ."

* The phrase reads "of angelic light" in the final line of Wordsworth's "She was a Phantom of Delight."

Thus, whatever Kitty's ignorance in other respects, she was aware that there was an ideal to which she ought to attain. She admired it very much. Though her mother was severe with her, she profoundly admired her, largely because she alone knew how much trouble her mother took to warn, to comfort and command, and yet to appear — as the Master's wife had to appear — urbane, self-possessed and full of small talk from one end of term to another. But the difficulty of reaching the standard set by the poets and aimed at by women like her mother and the graceful and beautiful Lady Kerseymere was very great; and one of Kitty's earliest impressions was [*that she herself*] by nature had [been] disqualified for the high and noble calling. And if one was disqualified, it was a very serious matter; for, as Kitty had frequent opportunities for observing, if a woman failed to reach that standard set by the poets, she was of no account whatever. [*The argument that was the most frequently used in Oxford against the higher education of women was that it would unfit them to be women.*] According to the code in use in the Master's Lodge, every honour and compliment would be paid women, so long as they behaved like Mrs Malone; but once let them withdraw their knees, or let them publish little books on the Angevin Kings, or let them ask for money to build Colleges, or let them ask to share in the privileges of the University, and they met, [II 77] as Kitty had innumerable chances of observing, with rudeness, with derision, with rebuffs.

And then at Pinbright Road, all was changed. Mr Brook was actually proud of his daughter's brain. Mr and Mrs. Brook were determined that she should earn her living. Was there another "ideal" then of womanhood? Could it possibly be that there were men who — Kitty once more saw the life-size portrait of the old working woman — who respected women, not as spirits, exactly: Kitty recalled the shrewd stout old woman in her tight clothes: respected them, honoured them, just as if they were men! No, not as if they were men. As if they were — here Kitty referred to her curious physical sensations in the presence of Mr Brook and his son Jo — as if they were better than men: well, not better, in the way in which they were "better" at the Lodge, for that was Lady Kerseymere's way — the way of angelic sweetness and unselfishness: but better in — this way; a man felt — Mr. Brook felt — "You've done all the hard work: you've got nothing for it; and there's nothing nothing nothing I can give you" — (she felt certain that this was in Mr Brook's mind) — "I can't give you anything to make up for it. But by Heaven" (or whatever Mr Brook's private oath might be) "I'll see that Nell has a good time." And the radiance of his belief somehow oozed out of him, as he wrung Kitty's hand, and made her feel, "That's the man to go to, if one wants a friend. Sam's my friend if I want one."

It was not altogether [II 78] Kitty's fault if the impression made on her by one tea party at Pinbright Road was so violent, for her experience, even of Oxford, was narrow. Had it been wider, she might, even in 1880, have known that there were other points of view even in Oxford. Already, working-class men, like Mr. Brook, were coming to Oxford; and a few years later, she might herself have come to know Joseph Wright, the great dialect scholar [*whose earliest recollections were of life in a work house, in 1888 was living in Oxford and came to Oxford to teach under the auspices of the Association for the Education of Women*] Whether it was that Joseph Wright had never had a day's schooling himself, a fact that seemed to him no disadvantage, for "Unknowingly I developed an individuality which is unique in its kind";* he certainly held a view of life which might have puzzled Kitty, accustomed as she was to the views held by men who had had every advantage that education can bestow — men like Mark Pattison, Walter Pater, Oscar Browning, and Walter Bagehot. [II 79] "In the first place," Joseph Wright remarked, "the world may talk [of the 'weaker sex' as much as it likes, the whole idea is based upon the body and not upon the mind, soul, and heart. I have always held woman far higher than man in] God's

* Marginal note: "W 266". The remark is in *The Life of Joseph Wright* I 266.

creation." * But that was no new idea. The poets had often said that. What was new, was that here was a man who actually put his ideas into practise. (If women were far higher than men in God's creation, had they not a right to a share in some of the fruits of the earth?) He went on to say, "If it were otherwise, I should never have been so intensely interested in the general welfare of womankind." And he was "intensely interested in the general welfare of womankind." He had the temerity to blame St. Paul. "St. Paul [and the likes of him have much to answer for, and it is ever my most pious wish that they will reap their due reward. It is due to them, and them *alone*, that woman has been such a downtrodden creature in the past. It is only the present generation of women that is beginning to realize the abject state of woman] in the past." ** Therefore [*when he married he not only used the language of a lover* [but] *actually put before his wife an ideal of marriage.*] his conception of marriage was revolutionary. His wife was not to darn his socks; she was not to do housework. "It is my greatest ambition that you shall *live*, not merely exist; and live too in a way that not many women have lived before[, if unlimited devotion and self-sacrifice on my part can do anything towards attaining that end. . . .]" †

But the force at the back of such opinions was not merely that Joseph Wright himself had received no schooling: he was not the product of Eton or Harrow, and King's and Christ Church: and therefore had no interest in them comparable to the interest of men like Bagehot, Pater, Pattison, and Oscar Browning who [II 80] [had] all the best of reasons for appreciating the advantages of public school and university education. He was much more profoundly in-

* Marginal note: "W 1.315". The matter is supplied from *Wright* I 315.

** Woolf's lacuna is filled from Wright I 315. Joseph Wright wrote this on September 5 1896 in a letter to Elizabeth Mary Lea, who was to become *Mrs* Joseph Wright approximately one month later.

† Marginal note: "W 1.311". The matter supplied, where Woolf left space, is from *Wright* I 311.

fluenced by his mother. "It was she who sowed the seed, and we shall reap the harvest." The union between Joseph Wright and his mother was extraordinarily close. After all, when they left the workhouse in which the fourth child had been born, it was to live in a one-roomed cottage. His father died when he was eleven,* but Dufton Wright "never was a worker."** Sometimes his wife had only empty gunpowder barrels to sit on after his death, being left with four sons. She went out charing at three halfpence an hour. "She also took in washing, and often had to stay up all night to wash for herself and other people."† At six, Joseph helped his mother "by driving a donkey cart from seven in the morning till five in the evening." Neither mother nor son could read or write. But his mother was ambitious for him. She made him leave the donkeys and go into a mill. (Just as later she made him spend his savings on a term at Gottingen University. Meanwhile Mrs Wright went on charing.) She made him leave the mill and become apprenticed to wool-sorting. It was a better opening, though the pay was lower. But because she was an ambitious woman, she "did extra washing and charing and made up the two shillings" the change cost them. Indeed, once Mr Wright told a friend that "there was one occasion when she thought she ought to have had her photograph taken, and that was once when she fell asleep with her hands in the tub in which she was washing her boys' clothes." ††

And [II 81] so at last Joseph Wright came to Oxford, to teach women German and Old English; and his house, when at last he had a house, was full of cushion covers and mats worked by his mother. And the tops of his stockings were her knitting too. And

* Marginal arithmetic: 1855
1866
——

** Marginal note: "1.26".

† Marginal note: "28".

†† Marginal note: "W 1.51". The passage is from *Wright* I 51.

when, in her last years, she used to come to Oxford, she thought very poorly of the southern ladies. "Why, to tell you the honest truth, they are nothing but stuck-up, conceited things, with nothing much about them; they are all outside." * And she threw Shakespeare's plays out [*of the window*] into the street; and she cooked first-rate Scotch collops and broth, and made the best bread in the world — with a dash of milk and a trifle of lard in it; "and her Yorkshire pudding, eaten before the meat, served with good gravy, and eaten with three-pronged steel forks, was food for the Gods"; at forty-five, she taught herself to read; and when she grew old, her son Tom, a lame man owing to insufficient food, gave up his work at the mill in order to live with his mother; and sold clothing on a weekly instalment system, walking from house to house. He did all the rough work of the house for her, and waited on her when she was ill. She had no daughter. When she died in 1903, Tom could not bear the presence of another woman in the house, so he lived on alone, and baked and washed and starched his own collars, and amassed a fund of various information by talking to people in the streets and in trams and trains; so that he was the finest company in the world; and could talk with equal readiness to a king or a pauper. And he was severe upon humbug and hypocrisy; and hated the poor to ask for relief: and used to [II 82] quote a Psalm to the effect that "I have been young, and now am old: and yet saw I never the righteous forsaken, nor his seed begging their bread." It was a great comfort to Joseph also to help his mother. And when he met his wife he said, "I am sure you will not mind my having *some* love for my dear old Mother. So to say, I have been father, husband, son, and companion to her for more than *thirty years*. . . . And my dear Mother and I did struggle hard for the sake of my two brothers. . . . We were determined that their lot should not be so hard as ours**. . . . It was she who sowed

* Marginal note: "20". From *Wright* I 20.

** Marginal note: "265". *Wright* I 265.

the seed, and we shall reap the harvest. It was just our great devotion to each other that instilled into me the profound respect I have always had, since I grew up, for womankind." *

Attitude to his wife and marriage

Such a training led to opinions which were rather singular perhaps in Oxford in the eighties. "Among people who have been well (!) brought up, there is a great tendency to mistake ignorance for stupidity and dulness of intellect. I know lots of people who are learned, but at the same time positively stupid and utterly incapable of giving birth to a new idea." ** He had just had a letter from his mother who "can't write" but "every word is like a page." † It was his training that led him to hold opinions of marriage that in the eighties were highly original. "There will never be a 'lord and master' in our home. . . . We shall be *one* in all our ways and deeds. . . . I should lead a most unhappy, and I will say, a most [II 83] miserable life . . . if you could, under any possible circumstances, ever become a mere Hausfrau. . . . It is my greatest ambition that you shall *live*, not merely exist; and live too in a way that not many women have lived before, if unlimited devotion and self-sacrifice on my part can do anything towards attaining that end. . . ." ††

But Kitty Malone never had the honour of knowing Joseph Wright or of hearing his views on education, society, and the proper conduct of life. All she could divine from her tea party at Pinbright Road was that proportions are not the same in different places. Much depends upon training and circumstances. What is right at Pinbright Road is not necessarily right in the Master's Lodge. The Bodleian looks different to different people. Learning may be ignorance and

* Marginal note: "334". *Wright* I 334.

** Marginal note: "275". *Wright* I 275.

† Marginal note: "274". *Wright* I 274.

†† Marginal note: "1.311". The first two sentences of the quotations are from *Wright* I 318, and the remainder from I 311.

ignorance knowledge. Scotch collops and Yorkshire pudding may be as good as oysters and champagne, according to where you have had tea. A shaving in the hair does not necessarily disqualify a man from marriage. Sympathy does not necessarily mean self-effacement. Money is not everything. Love . . . . but by the time she reached this word, Kitty, who, it must be remembered, though she had been having tea at Pinbright Road had been dining at Balliol, thought so many thoughts about Lord Lammermuir and Nigs and Jo and Chuffy and standing at the window in a nightgown and the moist hands of great professors; and her mind was such a whirl of questions and doubts [II 84] and difficulties; she felt so young, so excited, so strong, so adventurous; so fettered, so impeded; so indignant; so flattered: so full of excitement and envy, and hope and fear; so conscious that Nigs' eyes were too close together; and that Lord Lammermuir's hands were beautiful; but he must marry an heiress as the estates were mortgaged: she felt so many things — among them that she had not knocked off Stubbs Vol. 3. — "but Oh, how exciting to see Lucy Craddock tomorrow!" — ("Dancing again, my dear?" "No, Miss Craddock. Dinner at Balliol — "). All these thoughts and ideas and sensations beat such a tattoo in her brain — but none of this could by any possibility be spoken to anybody — that there was nothing for it but to take her pen, dip it in red ink, and draw another circle, very firmly, round September the 1st. Partridge shooting begins.

The rain fell still in the garden over the syringas; the bells chimed out the hour: and Kitty fell asleep. This was in June 1880. Mr. Gladstone was in power; Mr. Bradlaugh had declined to take the oath; and at the head of the Irish party was a new leader, Charles Stewart Parnell.

Dec. 19th 1932 *

* The next page (II 85) is dated January 31st 1933 and is headed "The Pargiters (additions to Chapter One)." In the rest of Volume II and in all of Volume III Virginia Woolf begins recasting the preceding matter, dropping the Essays ("interchapters") and revising these five pseudo "Chapters" into a single "Chapter One," a unit that finally became the "1880" section of *The Years*.

APPENDIX

SPEECH

[Manuscript Notes]*

21st January 1931

Your secretary, when I was asked to come here, suggested that I might speak about "my professional experiences", since your society is concerned with Employment for Women. Well, I am a woman, and I have an employment; but I doubt that I have much to tell you about my professional experiences.

My profession is that of a writer. That is much less a profession than any other. One shilling is all the outlay needed: ink 3d. paper 9d. pen and nib 3. There you are — set up.

And again, Dame Ethel Smyth has been telling us her difficulties — how she had to smash and bribe and wheedle. I had none of that to deal with. Women have been writers for some time now — they have broken down most of the barriers, long ago. And so when I came to write, there was little to prevent me. I doubt whether I ever suffered much obstacle. A few. I began simply as a reviewer: Novels were sent to me. I was paid a guinea a thousand words. I think I made 50 guineas my first year, and without much trouble, went on reviewing novels, making guineas.

What an easy and unheroic lot, compared with Dame Ethel's! I suppose of all ways to earn a living, this is the easiest. But wait. I think there were barriers. Let me put it in this way. Editors used to send me lives of Dickens, and Jane Austen, and books about [sentence unfinished]. I do not know if you are engaged in the same pursuit. But before I began my review, I always knew what I was expected to say. I felt some pressure on me to say what was agreeable. Dear old Henry James — he must be praised. One must not attack the crass stupidity of Carlyle.

* Berg Collection, Virginia Woolf Manuscripts: Articles, Essays, Fiction, and Reviews IV 1930–31. Insignificant deletions and revisions are not transcribed.

A set of values was ready-made. And these values were almost always half an inch to the right or left of my own. To say what one thought — that was my little problem — against the prodigious Current; to find a sentence that could hold its own against the male flood.

Now, I believe that you won't find it difficult to make money by journalism. But I think you will find it extremely difficult to say what you think — and make money. For instance, about the war. If I were reviewing books now, I would say this was a stupid and violent and hateful and idiotic and trifling and ignoble and mean display. I would say I am bored to death by war books. I detest the masculine point of view. I am bored by his heroism, virtue, and honour. I think the best these men can do is not to talk about themselves anymore.

Of course, none of this would be printed. Then I would say about literature, I suspect that half the books now written on Shakespeare are footling. I suspect the view which is palmed off for insincerity and humbug. Now, this is where I think, as a writer, your excruciating difficulty lies: to stand up for your own point of view.

When we come to imaginative literature, there again, I think the difficulty is [in being] women. Take Mr Joyce or Proust. One of the achievements of their books is their honesty, their openness, their determination to say everything. For women, the prudery of men is a terrible bugbear. Dr. Johnson said, "We were shocked to see a woman cross her legs". So until the year 1850 (I daresay), women never crossed their legs. Now men are shocked if a woman said what she felt (as Joyce does). Yet literature which is always pulling down blinds is not literature. All that we have ought to be expressed — mind and body — a process of incredible difficulty and danger.

A certain attitude is required — what I call the pouring-out-tea attitude — the clubwoman, Sunday afternoon attitude. I don't know. I think that the angle is almost as important as the thing. What I value is the naked contact of a mind. Often one cannot say anything valuable about a writer — except what one thinks. Now I found my angle incessantly obscured, quite unconsciously no doubt, by the desire of the editor and of the public that a woman should see things from the chary feminine angle. My article, written from that oblique point of view, always went down.

[Here begins a heavily corrected revision of the early part of the Speech:]

When your secretary invited me to come here, and I rashly agreed, she said that your society is concerned with the Employment of Women, and suggested that perhaps I might tell you something about my own professional experiences. Well, of course, I am employed, and I am a woman. But I wonder what professional experiences I have had?

None, at any rate, to compare with those of Dame Ethel Smyth. After what Dame Ethel has told us — and much that she has not told us — I feel as a little sailing boat might feel, which follows in the wake of an ironclad. She is of the race of the pioneers: She is among the ice-breakers, the window-smashers, the indomitable and irresistible armoured tanks who climbed the rough ground; went first; drew the enemy's fire; and left a pathway for those who came after her. I never knew whether to be angry that such heroic pertinacity was called for, or glad that it had the chance of showing itself.

In my own profession — literature — path cutting had to be done. There were pioneers. I suppose when the history of women's lives comes to be written — it is not written yet — we shall be amazed to find how much time and energy were needed before a woman could publish a book. This is part of the unwritten history which perhaps some of you will write. I am not concerned with it now.

When I came to write, there were no obstacles in my way like those that stood in Ethel Smyth's way. Writing was a reputable occupation: the family peace was not broken by the scratching of a pen. Nor was it an occupation that drew upon the family resources: no piano, no teaching; no studio with a north light; no paints, models, and brushes were needed. For ten and six, one could buy enough pens and paper to write a whole book. And undoubtedly, the cheapness of writing material must have contributed to the fact that women wrote before they painted or composed music. So you see, when I came to write, it was not difficult. An editor sent me a book to review: I reviewed it: I received one pound, ten and six in the course of a few weeks; and with that one pound, ten and six, I went out — this will show you how little I can tell you about women's employment — I went out and bought a cat — a very fine Persian cat. Undoubtedly, I think that this reviewing is the quickest and easiest way in which a woman can make money.

[The paragraphs that follow are drafts of unconnected passages in the typescript.]

O you old humbugs — I should have begun. O you who enjoyed all these centuries of comfort and prosperity. O you who profess devotion to the Lady of Clare, and [*love of the sentiment of*] colleges. Would it not be better to spend your 6000 pounds — not upon a book clothed in the finest dress of paper and black buckram — but upon a girl, who, as you can see for yourselves if you turn to the very next page in the *Nation*, has only one room to live in, and that faces North and is over-run with mice. A College, I entirely agree with Mr Keynes, is a gracious sight; but difficult of imitation. If the members of Clare handed over their 6000 pounds to [*Newnham*] Girton, some of the difficulties of imitation would be removed. I am sure that the Lady of Clare would say, "Gentlemen, you have done me honour".

That is more or less how I should write that review; but it would not be printed.

You feel that you are very heavy and important. Also, you know that you own a home and servants. That, roughly speaking, must be what it feels like to be a man. And now, you women who have your professions have put the man into a very awkward position. Let us try to imagine what it feels like to be him.

But things were not allowed to remain like that. Women like Ethel Smyth were being born; women like Ethel Smyth don't allow things to stand still. So they take matters into their own hands. They go off to Germany and get educated. So one day, the man came home to find that his servants had gone — they had set up for themselves and there they were, playing the piano, becoming doctors, barristers, chemists, accountants, civil servants, dentists, architects, veterinary surgeons, probation officers, factory inspectors, journalists, scientists, meteorologists, librarians, publishers, artists, metallurgical chemists, publicity managers, solicitors, dealers in antiques, bankers, dancers, actuaries, demonstrators in plant pathology, managers in house property, court dressmakers, aero-engineers, correspondents at Drases Limited, history instructors, directors of H. P. Truefelt Ltd., biochemical research workers, voluntary workers, organizers of Women's Peace Crusades, Great House proprietors, craft workers, newspaper representatives, Income Tax consultants, technical officers in Royal Airship works, officers in charge of [the] London section first aid nursing yeomanry, proprietors of book shops, advertising agents, teachers of speech training, estate managers, house decorators, lecturers in law, radiologists, surgeons, factory inspectors, foreign correspondents — as well as being married women.

Books by Virginia Woolf
available in paperback editions
from Harcourt Brace Jovanovich, Inc.

The Voyage Out
Night and Day
Jacob's Room *and* The Waves
The Common Reader: First Series
Mrs. Dalloway
To the Lighthouse
Orlando
A Room of One's Own
The Second Common Reader
Flush
The Years
Three Guineas
Roger Fry: A Biography
Between the Acts
The Death of the Moth and Other Essays
A Haunted House and Other Short Stories
The Moment and Other Essays
The Captain's Death Bed and Other Essays
A Writer's Diary
Granite and Rainbow
Contemporary Writers
Mrs. Dalloway's Party
The Letters of Virginia Woolf. Vol. I: 1888–1912
The Pargiters: The Novel-Essay Portion of *The Years*